AFTERSHOCKS

MARK PARRAGH

Aftershocks
by Mark Parragh

A Waterhaven Media Publication
First Print Edition – May 2020

Copyright © 2019 by Waterhaven Media, LLC. All rights reserved.
ISBN: 978-1-7339756-3-6

Cover Design by Kerry Jesberger, Aero Gallerie
Editing and Production Coordination by Nina Sullivan

This book is a work of fiction. Names, characters, places, and incidents are the product of the author's imagination or are used fictitiously, and any resemblance to actual persons, living or dead, or to events or locales is entirely coincidental. No part of this book may be reproduced in any form or by any electronic or mechanical means, including information storage and retrieval systems, without written permission from the author, except for the use of brief quotations in a book review.

CONTENTS

PART I
PENDULUMS

Chapter 1	3
Chapter 2	6
Chapter 3	11
Chapter 4	17
Chapter 5	20
Chapter 6	26

PART II
SNEAKERNET

Chapter 7	37
Chapter 8	40
Chapter 9	45
Chapter 10	51
Chapter 11	55
Chapter 12	59
Chapter 13	64
Chapter 14	69
Chapter 15	73
Chapter 16	77
Chapter 17	82
Chapter 18	86
Chapter 19	91
Chapter 20	95
Chapter 21	100
Chapter 22	105
Chapter 23	109
Chapter 24	114
Chapter 25	118
Chapter 26	124
Chapter 27	128
Chapter 28	132

Chapter 29	138
Chapter 30	141
Chapter 31	146
Chapter 32	151
Chapter 33	156
Chapter 34	162
Chapter 35	168

PART III
SOMETHING SMART

Chapter 36	173
Chapter 37	180
Chapter 38	187
Chapter 39	192
Chapter 40	199
Chapter 41	204
Chapter 42	208
Chapter 43	214
Chapter 44	221
Chapter 45	227
Chapter 46	233
Chapter 47	240
Chapter 48	246
Chapter 49	251
Chapter 50	257
Chapter 51	264
Chapter 52	268
Chapter 53	275
Chapter 54	282
Chapter 55	288

John Crane will return...	293
Want even more?	295
Also by Mark Parragh	297
Contact Mark Parragh	299

PART I
PENDULUMS

CHAPTER 1

Yaoundé, Cameroon

The battered van carried six men through the crowded, dusty streets of the capital. There was the driver, a spotter in the passenger seat, and four men sitting on the floor in the back wearing bandanas around their necks and holding machetes. They'd been cruising the streets for three hours in the afternoon heat, and tempers were short.

The driver honked his horn and yelled in French as he swerved around a bright yellow taxi. This threw the men in the back to one side and provoked a half-hearted round of curses.

"Find one already," one of the men snapped. "Shit, just someone who looks like one of them."

The spotter ignored him. He held a scarred Kalashnikov in his lap and three photographs. The photos were of a middle-aged woman, a teenage girl, and a young man in a suit and tie. The spotter had studied the faces until he knew he could pick them out of a crowd. Now he searched for them among the pedestrians on the crumbling sidewalks and on the motor scooters weaving through traffic.

"Let's try the market again," he said to the driver. "Then back to Mimboman."

The driver shrugged and took a right at the next intersection. They made their way to a makeshift neighborhood market spread out across a large roundabout. The streets here were even more clogged with carts, hawkers, and customers. They went once around slowly and saw nothing, then headed back up the hill toward the residential district of Mimboman. They wove around parked cars and passed houses surrounded by small, walled yards and the occasional tree.

"There!" the spotter said suddenly. "On the right. That's her. The wife!"

This stirred up some movement among the sweating, lethargic men in the back.

"Are you sure?" said the driver.

The spotter pointed out a woman walking up the hill. She carried a pair of bright green plastic grocery bags stuffed with produce. "Of course I'm sure. It's her!"

"All right," said the driver, "all right." He scanned the street. It was wide enough for a three-point turn in the van, but there was a steady line of traffic coming at them and a panel truck rumbling behind them.

"Get ready," said the driver, and the men in the rear pulled their bandanas up over their faces. "Don't forget behind us," the driver said to the spotter.

The men in the back were keyed up now, ready to go. The driver slammed on the brakes, and the van's side door flew open. The four men tumbled out, shouting and waving their machetes.

The spotter leapt out with his Kalashnikov and fired a long burst into the engine of an oncoming Renault sedan. It stopped short, steam erupted from the radiator, and the car behind it rear-ended it with a solid crunch.

The spotter ran around the van. He glimpsed machetes held high, gleaming in the sun. He heard screams. Behind the van, the truck driver was desperately trying to back away, to turn around and get out of there. He'd block the street the way he was going. The spotter emptied his clip into the cab, shattering the windshield and blowing out tires. Traffic was locked down in both directions now, and they had a clear path out.

"Let's go!" the driver shouted, and they all piled back into the van. Even before the side door was closed, the van lurched backwards in a tight turn. It slammed into the front of the crippled Renault and pushed it out of the way. Then the driver shifted gears, and the van sped away down the hill, back toward the commercial district. It had been stopped for less than thirty seconds. It left behind wreckage, terrified bystanders, and a bloody heap lying half in the street.

CHAPTER 2

"For God's sake, Georges, stop fretting!" Professor Bona straightened Georges's lapels and smiled. "Trust me, they'll be impressed!"

Georges nodded and stared down the long hallway of the École Nationale Polytechnique, at the double doors that opened onto the campus green. He didn't seem to know what to do with his limbs. No matter how he held them, the suit jacket felt awkward. He kept shifting his weight and repositioning his arms, but it was never quite right.

"I'll do my best, sir," he said. He knew this was a big deal for Professor Bona and for the college. So he let his teacher assume he was simply nervous about the presentation. He didn't know how to tell this man, who had done so much to bring him to this day, that the panel of dignitaries waiting inside wasn't what worried him.

He shouldn't have come here, he thought. With his father away, his place was at home, watching over his mother and sister. But his mother had insisted this opportunity was too important to miss. "This is where your future begins!" she had said that morning. "No one takes this from us. You go and make us proud!"

In the end, she shooed him out the door and watched him walk stiffly in his new suit all the way to the corner where the mini-buses picked up passengers headed downtown. He looked back once, and she stepped out onto the porch and waved, her face glowing with pride.

"It's time," said Professor Bona. "I'll introduce you. Just tell them what you've done. And smile, Georges! Confidence!"

Then Georges was alone in the hall. His thoughts raced in all directions. It seemed only a few seconds before he heard Professor Bona saying, "...young man we're very proud of, and I think he will make all Cameroon proud. Allow me to introduce third year student, Georges Benly Akema!"

Then his hand was on the doorknob. He was entering the room. It was as if he was watching it happen. There they were; a half dozen men in suits and a pair of women at the end. Georges had seen the list. They represented the Education and Trade Ministries, the Cameroon Development Bank, a couple of NGOs. He recognized the youngest of them as the CEO of Yaoundé's biggest Internet startup.

All here to see him. It was incredible.

Georges stumbled through his introduction, but he began to feel more comfortable as he got past that and into the nature of his project.

"A supercomputing analysis architecture, based on the work of Joshua Sulenski," he said. "You may know that, in America, Sulenski built a tool that captured the data outputs of the New York Stock Exchange. Every trade, every change in price. It looked for patterns in the numbers and projected trends into the future. Eventually, he was able to predict the movement of the overall market several seconds in advance."

Some of them knew what Sulenski had done. Others knew

him only as another rich, young American on television. But that got their attention.

"Are you saying you can do this, too?" one of them said, leaning forward.

"I'm afraid not, sir," Georges said with a wan smile. "Eventually, my system might be able to do what his did, but that would be very expensive. Also, his techniques are now in use across the developed world. They'll always have more computing power than we have here in Cameroon. Even if we could look ahead, they will look still further."

The man nodded and sat back in his chair.

He went on to explain how he'd built a less sophisticated version of Sulenski's computer out of leftover PCs and open source software. And then he'd created a much simpler system for his computers to study: a dozen pendulums of different weights and lengths. He gave his system cameras to track the position of the pendulums and sensors that detected the forces applied to them. When it was ready, Georges had set his pendulums swinging, and the computers watched them. For days they recorded the state of the system many times a second, and churned through the mountain of information.

"Eventually, they figured out how a pendulum works," Georges said. "They were able to derive Newton's laws of motion independently, just by observing the behavior of the pendulums."

He could see that some of them were impressed, mostly the business people who understood the computing implications. One of the older men waved a hand for his attention.

"What applications do you see for this, if not in finance?" he asked.

"Oh, there are financial applications, sir," Georges replied, "on a smaller scale. But the general principles could apply to many fields. Anywhere there are large volumes of data to mine for patterns. For example, medical research, for isolating and measuring the effects of a virus or a new drug in a large study population. Or geological applications, like interpreting seismic data to make oil exploration quicker and reduce the risk of test wells."

They were starting to get it. One of the ministers was furiously scribbling on a notepad.

"Of course, Sulenski's system was a general-purpose architecture, while I designed mine around the specific problem I wanted it to study," he said. "But the principles are easily adapted. A similar design could be created for any of the examples I mentioned, or many other applications." He grinned. "And of course this is much cheaper than the American system."

That got a laugh, and then they started talking among themselves. He heard a woman say, "Just 20 years old." Two of the technical people were talking about analyzing Internet traffic. In the back of the room, Professor Bona smiled and gave him a quick thumbs-up. He had gotten through to them. He had done it.

Then the door opened, and a grim-faced policeman entered. The conversation suddenly ceased.

"Georges Benly Akema?" the policeman asked.

The whole room looked to Georges. He felt the ground falling away beneath his feet.

"Please come with me, sir," the policeman said. He paused, then added, "There's been an incident involving your mother. I'm to take you to the hospital."

Georges had spent hours watching pendulums, just as his computers had. They swung upward, upward, as if they would keep going forever. But they always reached a point where they could go no higher. They stopped, hung there for an instant, but then all that remained for them was to fall down again, back to the very bottom of their arc.

The policeman took a tentative step toward Georges. "We should go," he said softly.

Without a word, Georges followed him out of the room and down the long, empty hallway. His future receded behind him with each echoing footstep.

CHAPTER 3

As they drove through the packed streets, the officer didn't want to tell Georges what had happened. Finally, he admitted that his mother had been attacked in the street on her way home from the market. They knew nothing yet. The investigation was still ongoing.

"She's going to make it," the officer said to Georges as he sat in shocked silence in the back seat.

At the hospital, they took Georges through a crowded waiting room loud with misery, back to a small alcove. Men and women in scrubs hurried past as a nurse filled in forms and asked Georges questions: his mother's full name, age, address, questions about her medical history that he had no way of answering.

"I want to see her," he snapped finally. "Take me to my mother now!"

The nurse led him down a hall to where a doctor stood outside a closed door. He was a young man, and handsome. He could have been a model, Georges thought. That seemed wrong to him. Doctors should be old, compassionate, and wise. Nothing here was as it should be.

"The son," the nurse said to the doctor, and left him there.

"She's lucky," the doctor said, incongruously. Georges was having trouble connecting one thing to another. What was lucky about this? "It could have been much worse. There was no saving the right hand. But we were able to save all but one finger on the left. We reattached the scalp flap, saved both eyes, I think. We'll know more when she wakes up. But there will be significant scarring. And we don't know yet about long-term damage. There have to be some severed nerves. I'm sorry."

Georges let the words wash over him. He could only take in the briefest flashes. All of it at once was too much for him.

"I want to see her," he said.

"She's unconscious," the doctor said. "We'll need to keep her that way for a few days."

"I want to see her."

The doctor shrugged. He opened the door and stood aside. Georges stepped into the doorway but found he could go no further. A shape lay in the bed, completely swathed in bandages, faint red stains already starting to seep through. He saw nothing of his mother. It could have been anyone. For a moment he was seized by the fantasy that this was someone else entirely. There'd been some ghastly mistake, and his mother was still safe at home wondering how his presentation had gone, how many companies wanted to hire him straight away, what government minister would take him under his wing.

But he knew none of that mattered now. The figure began to tremble. Then it let out an inhuman wail, punctuated by sharp, gasping cries.

The doctor pulled him aside, strode into the room, and closed the door behind him. After a few moments the noise ceased, and Georges took a deep breath.

The police officer appeared and led Georges back to the

waiting room. Near the door, a man in a wheelchair moaned in pain, and Georges started as if pricked by a pin.

"Come," the officer said gently. "Sit here. Sit down. You're going to be okay."

Georges sat, and the officer took the seat opposite him. Georges looked straight ahead, into the man's uniform shirt with its neat creases and polished badge that said his last name was Makoun.

"Can you think of anyone who would want to do this?" Officer Makoun asked.

Georges looked up at his face. It was not unkind, but he was a man with work to do. Georges considered the question. He knew what had caused this, but he didn't know enough to tell the officer anything useful.

"Where is your father?"

"He's in America, at an academic conference. He works at University."

"Can you reach him there?"

"Men came to our house," Georges said. "About a month ago. It was late. My sister was in bed already, but I was up. My father sent my mother and me upstairs. I knew something was wrong." He recalled the look on his father's face. It had unsettled him even then.

"I couldn't hear much, but I understood they wanted my father to do something for them, and that he refused. I remember he raised his voice. He said it was wrong, what they asked of him, and he wouldn't do it."

"But you didn't hear what they wanted?"

"No. Something to do with his job; it had to be. I don't know what such men would want from an Academic Department Administrator. But there's nothing else to him. Just his job and his family."

Officer Makoun made some quick notes on a pad.

"After that, there were threats," said Georges. "People watching the house. An envelope left on the door. My father kept it from us; I don't know what it said. I knew my parents were nervous. But when I asked what I could do, they said it was nothing. We thought when my father went to America, it would stop. We thought we were safe. At least while he was there."

Georges looked around the room, at the rows of people suffering with their personal, individual pains. He felt himself growing ashamed, then angry. It welled up from within him, and he could feel it washing over him, changing him.

"Who did this?" he asked Officer Makoun. "How do I find these men?"

"What do you mean to do?"

"I'm going to make them pay," he said, trembling uncontrollably.

"That's my job, you know. You should let me do it."

"No!" Georges snapped. "It's my fault. I wasn't there. I should have stayed with her."

The officer put his notepad away and carefully snapped the flap of his shirt pocket closed. Then he leaned forward and looked into Georges's eyes.

"Twelve years in this job," he said. "I've seen a lot. Let me tell you what I've learned. If you'd been there, your mother would still be in that room. And you'd be in the room next door. Or dead more likely."

"But I did nothing!" Georges said. "I didn't protect her. I was boasting how clever I am!"

"Listen!" Officer Makoun snapped. "If you want to be useful, listen to me!"

Georges glared for a moment, then let out a breath and nodded.

"I don't know who these men are," Makoun said, "but I've seen a thousand like them. They're strong and cruel, and you're not. That's their power. Don't try to fight your enemy on his ground, with his weapons."

Makoun's expression softened. "At the school," he said gently, "they told me that you're smart. Very smart. The kind of smart government men come to see. That's your power. If you want to help your mother, do something smart."

Georges sat back in the cracked vinyl chair. He didn't know what to think. He sensed the officer was trying to help him, but what could he do?

Then an orderly appeared. "Mr. Akema," he said, "please come to the telephone. We have your father, from America."

He rose and stood motionless for a long moment. He met Officer Makoun's eyes, and his voice was faint when he spoke, as if it was all he could do to force out words.

"Thank you," Georges said.

Then he followed the orderly back to the receiving counter. They handed him a telephone, and through the static of the connection he heard his father's voice. It was an older voice than he remembered. Something had gone out of it. But then something had gone out of him, too.

"Are you all right?" his father asked.

"I wasn't there," he said.

"I need you to do something for me," his father said. "It's important."

Georges paused. The phone sounded like a seashell held to his ear. "All right," he finally said into the line noise.

"I'm not coming home," his father said. "I'm going to stay here. There are people here at the conference who can help. They speak good English. They will help me with the paperwork. They can put me up until we get settled, and they'll help me find work."

For a moment, Georges thought his father was abandoning them. It was insane, but nothing made sense anymore.

"I need you to go home," his father said, "and get your sister. Pack whatever the two of you can carry on an airplane. I'll arrange tickets and travel documents. Stay inside until you hear from me. Then you'll come here."

"What? What about mother?"

"She'll join us when she's well enough to travel." Then his father turned to speak to someone there at the other end. "I understand," his father said in English. "Yes, please apologize for me. A family emergency."

"I need you to do this," his father said to him after a moment, and Georges heard his voice nearly crack. "I need to know you and your sister are safe. Can you do this?"

"I can," Georges said.

"Good, good." They both listened to the sound of their breathing over the wobbly connection. Georges didn't know what to say and apparently neither did his father.

"Your mother," his father said at last. "Is she...?"

Georges thought of Officer Makoun. He had seemed to be a decent man, and he had more experience of these things. What was it he had said in the car?

"She's going to make it," Georges said.

CHAPTER 4

Palo Alto, California – One Year Later

Jaipur Masala closed at 10:00, but a large table stayed late, ordering drinks and samosas and making noise. Georges gathered their startup had attracted new financing. It was nearly midnight by the time he got off work.

Georges walked through dark and silent streets to the bus stop, waited for the night bus to East Palo Alto, and rode quietly back to his neighborhood. Outside, the condos of Silicon Valley's wealthy slid by. It was a surprisingly short ride from there to East Palo Alto, where those who didn't rule the world eked out their unimportant lives.

Georges was startled as they passed a street corner. A girl stood waiting for the light, and for a moment Georges thought she was his sister, Romy. But Romy wasn't here anymore. As soon as she turned 18, she'd announced that her parents had no more right to tell her what to do. She'd gone off with a man, and Georges hadn't seen her since. Her last email claimed she was in Utah, working at a convenience store. She claimed everything was fine. That had been months ago. He could only wonder where she was now and hope she was happy.

The bus let him off on Bay Road, and Georges walked down a side street past crumbling apartment buildings, a mural with slogans in Spanish, and a construction site behind a high fence that promised workspace lofts with fiber connections. Even here, it was just a matter of time before the tech workers squeezed them out.

The apartment was quiet as Georges let himself in, but he could tell something had happened. Light and shadows fell strangely across the living room. A lamp had been overturned. His father sat on the sofa with a bottle of gin, staring into the wood grain of the coffee table. Georges saw the remains of a shattered plate on the floor.

His mother had had another episode.

Georges closed the door and locked the deadbolts.

"Was it bad this time?" he asked his father softly.

"She doesn't mean it," his father replied in slurred French. His English was still terrible, which was a big part of why he couldn't find work. "She gets frustrated. People stare at her. It's hard to do what she used to with just one hand. Left hand."

He sloshed the gin around in the bottle, then took a drink. "It's hard for her, what I did to her. It's hard. She doesn't mean it."

"I know," said Georges. He sat on the sagging couch beside his father. "Is she okay?"

"Sleeping at last, I think."

Georges studied his father's profile. He had been handsome when he was younger, a proud and confident man, and some of that was still there. But he was broken now, with scars of his own.

"We had lives," his father said suddenly, as if he could read Georges's thoughts. "I was respected. And your mother was so lovely. You should have seen her when I first met her. I knew she could do anything she wanted. Anything in the world."

"It's all right, father," Georges said gently. "It's all right."

"No! You have to know it wasn't like this. Your parents were good people. We were young. We had dreams, and we worked hard."

"I know," Georges said. "I remember. What happened wasn't your fault."

"You know what it was for? Do you?"

Georges said nothing. His father took another long slug of gin and dropped the nearly empty bottle on the floor.

"A degree. For a stupid boy from Adamawa. He was a bad student, but his father was Patrice Kamkuma, a big man among the Tikar there. They wanted me to forge his transcript. Pass him in courses that he never took and get him a degree. With honors! So he could move up in the regional government. That's it. So he could be water commissioner or something. What difference did it make? But I was too proud." He spat the word with disgust. "I had to have my integrity! Where is it now? I'm a bum who drinks on money his son makes working late into the night. What pride in this life? Romy saw it. She wanted none of it, and she was right. And your mother…" he began to sob.

"I know," Georges said. "She was beautiful. I remember."

"She's still beautiful!" his father said suddenly. "But her heart is broken." He waved an arm to take in the shabby living room, and beyond it the worn out, threadbare reach of East Palo Alto. Perhaps the whole world. "This isn't the life I promised her."

Georges put his arm around his father's shoulders and felt him tremble. "It will be all right," he said quietly.

They sat in silence while a police cruiser flew past outside, its red and blue lights flashing through the slits in the blinds, its siren wailing the way his mother had. As the sound faded, his father rose and stumbled off to bed.

CHAPTER 5

Georges had the day shift for most of the next week, though he picked up a couple nights as well to make the rent. He was washing plates during the lunch rush on Friday when his boss, Mr. Malhotra, burst into the kitchen.

"Somebody! You, Georges! I need you to bus the tables in Section two! Come on, come on! People are waiting!"

Georges shut off the water and put the sprayer back on its hook. He turned to Mr. Malhotra and gestured to his stained, water-soaked apron.

"Yes, yes, get that off! Just do the needful. Come!"

A pair of waiters stuffed him into a white collared shirt. Then they gave him a tray and sent him into the front of the house. It was packed. Major technology companies were clustered all around the neighborhood, and Jaipur Masala was a popular lunch spot. Georges cleared an empty table so the hostess could seat the next group. By the time he got those dishes back to the kitchen, there was another. And the work fell into a steady rhythm.

Eventually there were no waiting customers clustered near the front door. Then there were a few empty tables, and Georges figured he'd be sent back to the kitchen soon. He was heading to a rear corner table when he stopped suddenly. In the booth he'd just passed was a young man finishing his Thali platter. His t-shirt said, "There's no place like 127.0.0.1."

That man was Joshua Sulenski.

Georges didn't recognize the two men with him, but there was no mistaking Sulenski. He'd read everything he could find about the man. And now Georges had come halfway around the world and here he was, having lunch at Jaipur Masala.

Georges set his tray down on the corner table and took a deep breath as he approached their booth.

"Good afternoon, gentlemen," he said. "Is everything satisfactory? Is there anything I can bring you?"

"We're good. Thank you," one of the others said. Georges thought he might be a bodyguard.

"Very good. Thank you," said Sulenski, and snapped off a piece of poppadum.

Georges lingered just long enough for them to notice he hadn't left. "I'm sorry," he said, "but you're Joshua Sulenski, aren't you?"

Sulenski smiled. "That's me."

The bodyguard started to shift toward the edge of the booth.

"There's something I have to ask you," Georges said quickly. "How did you synchronize your data streams?"

Sulenski made a subtle wave, and the bodyguard moved back into place. "How did I synchronize my data streams?"

"Feeding into the analytical matrix," Georges said. "Events had to sequence properly, down to the microsecond. Otherwise, the matrix would sort incorrectly, pass bad results to the query engine, and you'd waste time testing bad hypotheses. It just wouldn't work."

Sulenski nodded and smiled up at him. "You've done your homework."

"I built my own version of your architecture back home in Cameroon," Georges said. "Very simple of course. It watched a set of pendulums and derived Newton's laws of motion."

"You did that?" Sulenski said. "It worked?"

"It was just a demonstration model," Georges said. "It had to be simple because I could only synchronize a few inputs, and those only because I controlled them. But I read your paper. You had twelve different intraday and historical feeds, updating at different times, feeding thousands of transactions into the matrix. How did you keep the timing consistent?"

Mr. Malhotra hurried over, but Sulenski was enthused now. Mr. Malhotra pulled up and simply observed.

"Well, that was the problem," Sulenski said. "Each feed had its own delays. They disagreed by half a second sometimes. It was a mess. But the markets would reconcile it all for me after the close, so I had that. Finally, I just ran several days of historical data and kept tweaking my input timing by hand until they predicted what really happened."

Georges felt a rush of revelation. "You cheated!"

"Well," Sulenski said with a grin. "I found a loophole. Sometimes that's the only way to get things done. What's your name?"

"Georges Benly Akema, sir."

Sulenski handed Georges a business card. It was blank except for a phone number.

"It's good to meet you, Georges," he said. "We should talk more. Call this number, and I'll have someone pick you up. Are you working tomorrow?"

"No, sir," said Georges. "I would be honored."

It was only after Sulenski and his party had left that Mr. Malhotra dragged Georges back into the kitchen and screamed at him for ten minutes.

When Georges got home and told his parents what had

happened, they didn't know what to make of it. They seemed torn between hope and suspicion.

"What does this man want from you?" his mother kept asking. "Is he legitimate?"

Even Georges wasn't certain that he wasn't the butt of some esoteric joke. But at the appointed hour, a black Mercedes pulled up outside. Georges took a deep breath, kissed his mother, and shook his father's hand. Then he walked down the crumbling cement walkway with grass growing through the cracks, and a uniformed driver opened the door for him.

The car took him to a gleaming corporate campus with a sign reading "Myria Group" at the entrance. It drove past glass and steel buildings and grassy meadows with walking paths, and finally deposited Georges in front of the main building. There, a man asked Georges's name and spoke quietly into his wristwatch. Then he ushered Georges inside. Josh Sulenski was waiting beneath a large impressionist statue of Albert Einstein.

Sulenski wore jeans and a plaid button-down shirt that wasn't tucked in. Georges felt awkward in his carefully pressed suit, but Sulenski smiled and shook his hand. "Good to see you again," he said. "Can we get you something?"

"No, thank you," said Georges. "I'm very grateful for your kindness, Mr. Sulenski."

"Oh God, call me Josh." He led Georges to glass doors that slid open as they approached.

For three hours, Josh took him everywhere, introducing him to development teams, showing off prototypes, answering his questions. At the end of it, Georges still had no idea what kind of company Myria Group was meant to be. He also couldn't say whether Sulenski meant to offer him a job. He'd certainly talked Georges up to his project leaders. But there was nothing specific. Perhaps Sulenski was known for occasionally sweeping through the office with temporary enthusiasms that never went anywhere. Georges still didn't know what to think as they ended up at a restaurant on the roof of the main building.

They sat in a corner as the sun began to set, looking out over the parklike grounds. Ducks settled onto a pond as waiters brought out a tray of Ethiopian dishes on spongy injera bread. They ate and talked about details of the projects they'd seen.

"So, what do you think?" Josh asked as the meal wound down.

"It's very impressive," Georges said.

Josh laughed. "Did I ever mention my father ran a strip mall print shop? Business cards, birthday invitations, stuff like that. Great dad, not much of a businessman. What I mean is, I wasn't born to this. I know where you're coming from and what's at stake. I did some background on you, too. You've had a shitty year, Georges. Seriously, one for the books. And now you're thinking I can reach down and change everything, get your family out of that crappy apartment in E.P.A. I can turn your whole life around. Or I can just send you home and forget about you. So you're going crazy trying to work out what I want to hear, aren't you?"

Georges said nothing. He could feel his hopes slipping.

"Don't worry, I'm going to give you a job," said Josh. "There's a lot going on here. Any of these projects, you'll do fine. But here's my question. Do you know why I have Albert Einstein in the lobby?"

"What?" Georges had felt a moment of exhilaration, but quickly fell back into uncertainty. What did the statue have to do with anything?

"It's because of the Nobel," Josh said. "I like to keep that in mind."

"The Nobel Prize?"

"Einstein won for physics in 1921. But not for relativity. Relativity freaked people out. Scientists and philosophers lined up to trash it. They gave him the Nobel for the photoelectric effect. That was nothing new. A guy named Fritts built a working solar cell in 1883. He just didn't know why it worked. Einstein just explained something everyone was already familiar with. So that was fine, but relativity was too big and scary. The committee went out of their way to say the prize wasn't for relativity. It's in the presentation speech."

"I see," Georges said. He wasn't sure why Sulenski was so surprised by this. It seemed obvious to him that the world tore you down, that you did your best and it came to nothing.

"Albert in the lobby reminds me, keep your best stuff behind the curtain," Sulenski said. "If you have to go public, for money or whatever, show them your second-rate work. That won't upset them so much."

Sulenski stopped and looked out at the setting sun.

"So you've got a job if you want it," he said. "We're doing an actuarial package for the insurance industry. Boring, but it keeps the lights on. You'd be a great asset. You can walk out of here right now and show up for work Monday morning making six figures with top health coverage for your mom. Or you can ask me the question I'm pretty sure you want to ask me."

"If predicting the stock market was your second-rate work," Georges said, "what have you got behind the curtain?"

Sulenski grinned and pushed back his chair. "Come on," he said.

CHAPTER 6

The room was spacious, but sparsely furnished. Tables and chairs were scattered seemingly at random, loaded with laptops and papers. There were server racks against one wall and a large flat screen monitor on another.

"It's not exactly mission control," said Josh. "But welcome to the skunkworks."

He closed the door behind them. "Over here's what I want to show you."

Josh sat at a desk and gestured for Georges to take the chair beside him. He tapped a few keys on a wireless keyboard and nodded toward the wall monitor.

The screen woke up to an aerial tracking shot of shipping containers. Acres of them stacked high on an enormous cement plain with spaces marked and numbered in yellow paint. Georges saw traffic control arrows on the pavement and huge cranes in the background. The camera was mounted on a drone, he realized after a moment.

The shot closed in until it picked up a figure running fast beside a row of containers. He was tall and lithe, wearing black pants studded with pockets and a gray knit shirt. A small pack was strapped between his shoulders by a leather harness.

"Where is this?" Georges asked. "Who is he?"

"His name's John Crane," said Josh. "He works for me. Sometimes. Sort of. This was shot at the Port of Oakland a little over a week ago. This is kind of special really, having real-time contact and being able to record footage. Usually he's halfway around the world somewhere, out of touch for days."

Crane turned and ran down a narrower space between two rows of containers as the drone kept pace. He crossed an access road and hurdled a metal railing without breaking stride.

A voice — Sulenski's? — crackled over a radio channel. "Two more rows, then right. You're clear to the intersection."

"We're tracking a group of angel investors who've been laundering money for Asian organized crime groups," said Josh. "Chinese mostly, but others from Vietnam, Thailand, all over. They pour money into risky tech startups, turn it into stock, which then gets used to collateralize loans that are reinvested into new startups, on and on. Eventually, it becomes untraceable. Only problem is getting the money back out. Government's pretty good at tracking accounts and wire transfers these days."

On the screen, Crane stopped at a corner then took off to his right.

"I don't understand," said Georges. "How does that relate to this?"

"If you can't move your laundered money electronically, you just have to move it physically. Bulk cash smuggling. It's huge. More than three billion dollars a year, and that's just to Mexico. I'm not sure this operation's even on the radar yet. But we've been trying to disrupt the VC group, and we got a line on a shipment back to their customers in Shanghai. So we thought we'd interfere."

On screen, Crane altered course to avoid being seen by an

approaching forklift driver. He veered down another passage, then turned back toward his original course. Finally, he approached a container sitting alone on a numbered pad.

"Okay, watch," said Josh. "Here's where things start to go wrong."

Crane checked the code numbers on the container, verified it was the one he was looking for. Then he took something from his pocket and leaned over the door latches.

"This thing's not working," he said after a moment. "This isn't the standard mechanism."

"Hang on, coming in," the radio voice replied, and the drone descended. Crane stepped aside as the camera zoomed in on the device that secured the container's heavy locking rods. It had a ruggedized display with keypad and what Georges took to be a signal indicator.

"It's communicating with something," said the voice on the radio. Georges was certain now that it was Josh.

Crane turned and checked his surroundings. "So there are watchdogs nearby," he said. "In case someone tries to do just what we're doing. Eyes on the perimeter please."

The drone climbed back up for a wider view. Crane studied the device for a few more seconds, then announced, "I got no way around this. Can we pull back and work on something?"

"No time. It's scheduled to lift out in a little over three hours."

Georges heard Crane sigh. Then, "Okay, guess I'm going through it."

He pulled something from a pouch on his leg. A moment later, the camera picked up a bright flash. It was a portable cutting torch, Georges realized. He watched as Crane cut through the security bands and then burned through the steel locking rods. He was trespassing at the port, and he was breaking into a shipping container. What had Josh gotten him into? Georges remembered his mother's words: "Is he legitimate?"

"That's problem one," Josh was saying. "We didn't have the right equipment. We've just been buying whatever we need off the shelf. Sometimes that's fine, but sometimes we need more. We need our own workshop and people who can improvise special gadgets."

On the screen, Crane turned off his torch and jerked the locking rods free.

"What's he going to do?" Georges asked Josh. "You said there's money in there. Is he stealing it?"

Josh grinned. "That was my first thought. It's untraceable, right? I was going to take it downtown and spread it around to folks who need it. But, you know, it's a whole shipping container full of money. It's not like he was going to carry it out of there. The main thing was making sure it didn't get back to Shanghai, so we decided to destroy it. There are two phosphorus grenades in John's pack. But it's a moot point," Josh added with a gesture toward the screen. "We're about to run into problem two."

On the screen, Crane pulled the huge double doors open. He stopped and was still for several seconds, standing outside the container with his arms holding the doors apart.

"Uh, guys," he said at last, "this is *not* a hundred and twenty million dollars in small bills."

"What do you mean, John?" Josh's voice asked over the radio.

"You need to see this."

The drone dove until the camera could see over Crane's shoulder into the container. The interior of the container wasn't the rusting steel and stacked bundles Georges had expected. It was bright white plastic with flush lighting panels and rounded corners. It looked like a spaceship, Georges thought. It looked sterile.

In the center sat a raised platform of what appeared to be

heavy foam blocks wrapped in plastic. Georges could just make out where they latched into the floor...

There was a person strapped to it.

"What the hell?" Josh's voice said on the radio.

Crane stepped inside. "He's alive," he said. "There's a heart monitor here, respiration, oxygen saturation. He's on IV drips."

As Crane moved, Georges noticed tanks fastened to the rear wall, and tubes connected to the platform.

"They're shipping a person?" Josh's voice said. "On a container ship?" The drone inched slowly forward.

"Asian male," Crane said, leaning over the foam barriers. "Maybe thirty-five. About five foot eight, one seventy-five." He ducked down. "Come in and get some pictures. See if you can ID him."

The camera zoomed in on the man's face. Georges was struck by how helpless he was, lying in a foam and plastic cocoon inside a container lost among thousands just like it. When the camera pulled back, Crane was detaching one of the foam barriers from the floor. He threw it aside to reveal a wheeled gurney, also latched to the floor.

Crane stood up. "How long since the alarm tripped?"

"Thirty-eight seconds."

"I can't get him out of here," said Crane. "I don't even know if it's safe to remove these drips."

"Get out, John!" Josh's voice said on the radio. "This is pear-shaped."

"No," said Crane. "Get the drone back up. Call 911. Give them this lot number and tell them you've got multiple RTS 3 trauma injuries. That should get a response."

Georges heard Josh's voice telling someone, "Do it," as the drone edged back out of the container and flew up into the afternoon sun. The camera caught a crew cab pickup speeding down the access road.

"John, you need to get out."

"Keep me informed on that ambulance."

As the truck braked to a stop outside, the container doors swung nearly shut, hiding Crane inside. Four men climbed out. They wore uniforms and carried nightsticks on their belts and pistols in their hands. They fanned out around the broken doors, moving in slowly.

Then everything erupted into a whirlwind of motion. Georges couldn't follow every move from above. The door flew open, and he heard the crack of gunshots, saw Crane roll and sweep a guard's legs from under him. As another moved in, Crane locked his arm somehow and spun him. Crane flipped the man onto the pavement and did something that seemed likely to break his arm. Then he pulled the man's nightstick from his belt and used it to disarm another.

The details didn't matter. Georges stared enraptured at the screen. He watched Crane standing between the four attackers and the helpless man in the container, a storm of energy and action. He did things Georges knew he could never do, but in his mind, Georges saw machetes flashing in the sun, and he saw himself transformed into someone powerful and strong.

When it was over, all four men were on the ground, and Crane stood over them. He looked up at the drone. "Ambulance?"

"Just cleared the main gates. Less than a minute."

"Get the drone out of here."

As the camera pulled away from the scene, Crane ran in the opposite direction.

The video ended and Georges sat in silence for a long moment. "What happened?" he said at last. "To the man in the container?"

"EMTs got him out and transported him to Highland Hospital," said Josh. "An hour later, he was checked out, supposedly transferring to a private hospital in Marin County. But that hospital doesn't exist. He just disappeared. We still don't know who he is, why someone put him in a shipping container bound for Shanghai, who took him out of Highland, anything."

Josh got up and made his way around the scattered furniture to a dorm refrigerator in the corner. "Water?"

Georges nodded absently. He was still struck by what he'd seen. He remembered Officer Makoun's words. "If you'd been there, your mother would still be in that room. And you'd be in the room next door." He couldn't argue with that. But if this John Crane had been there…

A water bottle came sailing at him. Georges snatched it out of the air as Josh returned with his own.

"So now you know what I'm doing behind the curtain," Josh said. "And I need help. That was a debacle I don't want to repeat. I need people who can improvise solutions to weird technical problems. But more than that, I need people who can help sort out what's going on out there. Because we're groping in the dark. We got away with it this time, but sooner or later that's going to end badly."

He looked at Georges expectantly. "So you can have an easy job writing actuarial software, or you can be part of the team I'm putting together behind the curtain. What do you say? Can you help me?"

Georges remembered officer Makoun once more. "If you want to help your mother, do something smart."

Georges gestured to the screen. "Him," he said. "John Crane. I want to help that man."

Josh shook his head and sighed. "Yeah, he's okay, too."

―――

As Josh's Mercedes drove him home, Georges imagined his

parents' reaction to his new software development job. That would be the official job description anyway. He didn't think his parents would approve of what he would really be doing.

Myria Group's HR department was already looking for a new apartment for them, somewhere out of their rundown neighborhood. There would be a signing bonus to get them moved in. There would be room for Romy if he could find her and talk her into coming home. There would be therapy for his mother. There would be everything they needed to start putting their lives back together.

Georges saw his parents peering nervously from behind the living room curtains as the car pulled up. They'd suffered, and there was nothing he could do to change that. But now he could help keep it from happening again. John Crane would be his champion, and Georges would arm him for battle with ingenuity and skill. Josh had no idea of the things Georges could do.

Once he had compared his life to the swing of his pendulums. They swung up, but only so far before gravity dragged them back down to the bottom again. But they didn't stay at the bottom either. It was time to swing back up again.

PART II
SNEAKERNET

CHAPTER 7

Iceland, 25 km outside Reykjavik

According to the map, this place had been a farm once. Not a particularly fertile one from the look of it. It lay tucked between a steep hill to the south and the rocky flanks of the Esja volcanic mountains to the north. The land was rocky and rough, swept by cold winds. It offered little to anyone trying to work it. The former owners might have planted some grain, but their main source of food and income would have been sheep. It would have been a hard life.

When the Allies came during the Second World War and built a huge, modern airbase outside the tiny fishing village of Reykjavik, many rural families had abandoned their farms and moved to the new boom town for steady work. John Crane imagined these particular farmers would have been among the first to leave.

Crane lay prone on the hillside. He had carefully made his way to one of the few patches of brush that offered some cover. There were no trees in sight, just thick grasses and the occasional stand of shrubs like these. If he stood up, they'd barely reach above his knees; he'd be readily visible to the guards below.

He swept the slope with a pair of Leica binoculars. The old farmstead had been replaced by an ultra-modern building of stone, steel, and dark glass. It was a black, flat-roofed circle in the middle of carefully maintained grounds, surrounded by a larger circle of chain link fence. Two armed guards manned the gate that commanded the only approach road. There was nothing else along the road. Nobody ever wandered out here to disturb the guards. They had to be bored out of their minds. Crane hoped that made them less observant because this was a terrible place to try to sneak into.

Not only was there no cover, but it was June in Iceland. The sun hung near the horizon to his left, a sullen red ball floating just above the sea. Technically, it would set sometime before midnight, but even then, there would be only a murky twilight. It would never get truly dark. Crane saw no point in waiting.

He had repeatedly timed the security cameras in their arcs. He knew just where he had to be and how long he could be there. He put the binoculars away and prepared his wire cutters. Then he leapt to his feet and sprinted down the hill.

Crane was a figure in black tactical gear with a small pack, running down a hillside in plain view. Any moment he expected to hear alarm sirens, but he made it to the fence. He fell to the ground and quickly snipped through the bottom links until he could slide through. Then he folded the chain links back in place and dashed to a metal access door at the rear of the building. There were two cameras along the roof that swept the grounds. But if he made the wall before they converged on him, he'd be safely out of their field of view. He slammed into the wall and pressed his back against the stone, looking frantically for approaching guards. Nothing.

Crane breathed slowly, forcing his heart rate down. He had a few minutes until one of the workers came out for a smoke. Crane didn't know what the man did, but it happened on a precise schedule. Every night at the same time, the door opened, and the same man leaned against the back wall long enough to finish a cigarette before going back inside.

At least that was the pattern he'd spotted over several nights of watching the compound. Last night, the night Crane meant to make his move, that pattern had been broken. Someone had shown up unannounced, and there had been what Crane took for a security drill. He'd had no choice but to back off.

The coincidence bothered him. Crane wasn't a big believer in coincidence. But they'd given no sign that they suspected he was out there. So far tonight, things seemed to be back to normal.

Crane heard the latch click and rose to a crouch. The door opened and a figure stepped through. Crane grabbed the man's shirt in both hands and hauled him out. Before the door could close behind him, Crane kneed him in the gut. The man wasn't a guard; he'd obviously never been trained to fight. He'd barely registered that something was wrong before Crane put him down.

Crane pulled the man's access card off his belt and swiped it across the reader. The door beeped and Crane opened it. He slid inside and quietly closed the door behind him. So far, so good.

CHAPTER 8

The Ionian Sea, Six Weeks Earlier

The two-seater Dornier flying boat picked John Crane up at the pier in Vola, on the northern Greek coast. The plane sliced through the impossibly blue water and then leapt into an equally blue sky. It was a short flight. Soon the plane descended toward a small island, one of dozens dotting the sea here. This one was perhaps half a dozen acres of green slopes and chalky white cliffs. There was a single building with a long terrace built into the cliff face. They touched down on the water, and the pilot pulled up to a wooden dock.

Josh Sulenski waited at the end of the dock. He wore shorts, boat shoes, and a gray t-shirt that said, "Keep Calm and Activate Bankai." Crane had no idea what that meant, and he'd learned not to ask.

"John! Thanks for coming," said Josh. "What do you think? Is this place great or what? Wait until you see the view from the terrace. Did you eat?"

"I'm fine," said Crane. "Did you buy an island?"

They walked back up the dock toward an arc of beach stretched between two white cliffs.

"Rented it," said Josh. "It's not for sale. Can you imagine? I mean it's probably a bad idea. I'd just disappear here and then nothing would get done. Anyway, I appreciate you going out of your way."

Crane looked around. "Yeah, this is a real hardship, Josh."

"Well, I'm not done imposing on you," Josh answered. So, there was a job. Crane had expected as much.

Josh led him up a staircase carved into one of the cliffs. The terrace had a sweeping arc of glass and sliding doors on one side, and a spectacular view of the sea on the other. Josh led the way to a small table with two glasses, a pitcher of ice, and a bottle of ouzo. He prepared the drinks and they drank in silence, listening to the sounds of the ocean, watching sea birds wheel and dive for fish.

"So where are you sending me?" Crane asked at last.

"We've got a problem in Iceland," said Josh.

"What kind of problem?"

"A company called Gögnfoss Greinandi, hlutafélag," Josh said, and Crane was surprised at how easily his tongue rolled around the complex, Nordic syllables. "Datafall Analytics in English. They do some public facing stuff. Social media, massively multi-player gaming. Less publicly, they do data mining, consumer profiling, and some less savory things. They're responsible for 21 percent of all Internet traffic into Iceland. And apparently, they're up to something. A few months ago, I was contacted by an employee at their supercomputing center outside Reykjavik. They were working on strong crypto, and he was worried about what they meant to do with it."

Crane sipped his ouzo. A gull cried overhead. "So why did he come to you?"

"They're building on my work," Josh said. "Predicting large dataset fluctuations. He'd figured I'd understand. If they pull this off, they'll have the keys to everything. Every government secret, every banking password, right down to my aunt's Facebook page."

"I gather they can't be trusted with it," said Crane. "I'll take a little more of that, by the way."

Josh poured him another glass. "We gotta watch ourselves with this stuff."

They clinked their glasses and drank.

"And nobody can be trusted with that," Josh added. "Not even me. I wanted to see how close they are, so I had my people work up something to tap their data. That part was really cool. They've got 150 racks of blade servers, over 10,000 nodes, something like 200,000 cores altogether. We figured out how to holographically image just one of them over very short intervals to capture the state of the whole system."

Crane had no idea what Josh was talking about, but he gathered it was meant to be impressive. "Really?" he said, leaning in.

If Josh noticed the sarcasm, he didn't acknowledge it. "I haven't been sitting on my ass since I cracked the stock market. If these guys are using my work, I've got a couple years on them."

"So all's well?"

"No," said Josh. "We wanted to bug their system and watch it in real time. But their network security's pinpoint. We couldn't slip a bit through without them noticing it. So we did the next best thing. We made a recorder and sent it over to Iceland. Our contact planted it in one of the servers. Plan was, he'd leave it there for a couple months, then pull it and send it back to us."

"I take it something went wrong."

"Datafall got suspicious. They fired him, walked him out of the building, and that was that. Apparently, they didn't know about the tap. As far as we know, it's still there. But I need you to go in and get it, and sneakernet the data back here."

Crane considered the implications, assembled his questions into some kind of orderly list.

"What do we know about the place? The physical layout? Security?"

"I've got a file for you," said Josh. "We know the basics. Plan of the building, data and power trunks, things like that. We know their security's very good. That's why I have you."

"Flattery won't get me into the heart of a secure supercomputing center, Josh."

"No, but it gives you a warm feeling and makes you want to do things for me." Josh grinned, then waved the issue away. "You can get in. We'll make sure you have what you need."

"What about the device itself? What's it look like? Where's it hidden?"

"Got you some backup for that," said Josh. He tapped his smart watch and spoke into it. "Can you join us on the terrace, please?"

A few moments later, a set of doors slid open and a young black man emerged. He might have been Josh's age, though Crane wouldn't have bet on it. He was a little overdressed for the beach in oxfords, black slacks, and a white shirt open at the collar. He approached rather tentatively, Crane thought, the way you might approach a movie star for an autograph on the street.

They stood and Josh made the introductions. "John, meet Georges Benly Akema. Georges, this is John Crane."

They shook hands and Crane said, "Nice to meet you."

"I've done some of your tech support work, Mr. Crane," said Georges, and Crane heard a lilting African accent in his crisply enunciated English. "It's a pleasure to meet you face-to-face at last."

"Georges was studying electrical engineering in Cameroon. He actually built a smaller version of my prototype system out of cast-off parts as a school project! But his family got caught up in something over there, and they had to leave the country. When I found him, he was busing tables in an Indian restaurant in Palo Alto. Total waste of talent. He'll be your tech support. He knows his way around the hardware, and he has the specs on the data tap. He'll fly into Reykjavik with you, and you'll wear a pair of stereo cameras so he can see what you see. If you have any trouble with the technical setup, he can walk you through it."

Crane glanced over at Georges. "You're comfortable with this?"

"Yes, Mr. Crane," said Georges. He drew up to his full height and tried to look confident. "This is an important job. I look forward to contributing to the success of the mission."

Crane grinned. "Well, you can dial it back a little," he said. "And call me John."

CHAPTER 9

Inside the Datafall building, Crane looked down a darkened hallway lined with closed doors, a bulletin board, and a fire extinguisher. Somewhere, a radio played jangly Europop. Nothing moved. He slipped in his earpiece and put on the glasses they'd given him with its tiny cameras at his temples.

"Georges, you there?"

Georges was aboard Josh's Gulfstream at Keflavik Airport, with the pilots in the cockpit and the engines warm. Crane had told them to be ready to leave on very short notice.

"Coming in now," Georges said in his ear. "I've got your position. The maintenance shaft is about thirty meters up."

Crane moved quickly down the hallway. His keycard could get him through most of the doors. But the plan was to avoid the hallways entirely. In a niche behind the elevators, he found an access panel that opened onto a maintenance crawlspace. Crane slipped inside, closed the panel behind him, and was plunged into darkness. He switched on the flashlight mounted on his shoulder and saw a cement shaft with steel rungs for climbing. He started down.

At the bottom, another panel opened into a narrow tunnel.

He followed it until it ended at a door. The supercomputer chamber would be on the other side. Crane switched off his light and crouched in the blackness, listening. When he heard nothing after thirty seconds, he slid the panel open and stepped through.

"Whoa," Georges said in his ear.

The chamber appeared to be carved out of sandstone, hung with panels of deep burgundy fabric. The stone facade was layered into tiers of false columns and arches that held recessed lights. With the coolness, the dim light, the quiet, the place suggested a medieval basilica.

Suspended in the center of the chamber was a huge metal and plexiglass cube. Inside, server racks stood in orderly rows. They were strung with color coded bundles of cable and glittered with LEDs. In their setting, the racks made Crane think of gravestones.

Crane was at the bottom of the chamber, a sub-floor strung with thick bundles of power cables and hoses for cooling water. Directly above him, a metal mesh deck ran around the outer edge of the chamber, and a narrow bridge crossed to the cube of the supercomputer itself.

Crane heard a door opening, then footsteps echoed on the metal deck. He edged back into the shadows. A few moments later, a guard walked past above him. His black battle dress uniform and MP-5 submachine gun effectively shattered the ecclesiastical feel of the place. He walked around the cube and left by the doors on the opposite side.

When the doors had closed, Crane moved quickly up a metal staircase to the deck. The bridge led to a revolving door of plexiglass panes. Crane passed through it. Inside, he heard the quiet whisper of cooling fans. He scanned the server racks, letting Georges read the code numbers as he moved down the rows.

"We want node 1186, rack 29," said Georges. "Next left."

Crane turned the corner. He spotted rack 29, crouched beside it, and pressed the release button. The rack hissed softly open on pneumatic runners to reveal rows of processors and memory modules. Crane moved aside a thick, orange bundle of cable and scanned the board.

"Where is it?" said Georges, echoing Crane's thought.

Crane had seen photos of the data tap. It was a little smaller than a cigarette pack, built to look like another processor so it would be easy to overlook. But Crane knew what to look for; it just wasn't there.

"Check the board ID," said Georges.

"Where is that?"

"Look left."

Crane did and saw a small code number etched into the board. He heard typing, then, "That's not the right board. That should be in rack 41. Check the next drawer up."

Crane moved up a drawer, pressed the release, and the rack hissed out. He looked at the code number.

"That's wrong too. They must be rotating the nodes! Try…hang on."

Crane heard more typing. He was intimately aware of passing time. At any moment the man he'd attacked could come to or be missed. Someone might come into the chamber, or he might trigger some hardware alarm. Crane's instincts told him to get out, but he wasn't leaving without the data tap.

Georges had him move down the row he was on, checking board numbers and looking for a pattern. Finally, he said, "Okay, got it."

Georges sent Crane down two more aisles to another cabinet. "Same thing. Sixth drawer up."

Crane pressed the button, and the rack slid out. He pushed

aside the bundle of cable and there it was. An extra processor module with a heat sink glued on with thermal paste.

"Bingo," said Georges. "Pull the heat sink and…"

Crane removed the heat sink, but Georges' voice was fading in and out behind harsh static.

"Georges?"

"…getting this, Crane?"

"You're fading."

"Interference," Georges said as the static rose. "Someone's jam…"

Then Georges was gone.

Crane swore. They'd been discovered somehow. Before long, armed guards would storm the chamber.

There was a procedure for disconnecting the data tap, but Georges was supposed to walk him through it, and Crane had no more time to be delicate. He popped the clips holding the board in place and ripped the whole thing free. He positioned it carefully against the edge of the rack and pushed hard until he broke off the corner of the circuit board that held the data tap. He slipped it into a zippered pocket on his pants.

Outside, the lights came up. He noticed a red LED blinking on the frame of the revolving door. It was probably locked down now to trap him inside.

He ran through the rows of cabinets, pressing release buttons at random. Racks slid out into the aisles, making it harder to follow him. Finally, Crane stepped up onto one extended rack near the center of the cube, and pulled himself on top of the cabinet.

A trio of security guards appeared outside, armed with MP-5s. One moved to the revolving door, and the red light went out long enough for him to enter. The other two circled the supercomputer, then took up positions covering the doors leading out of the chamber.

The guard inside the cube moved slowly down the center aisle, sweeping each row with his weapon as he came. He spotted the disturbed processor racks and called that in. He turned down an aisle, checking racks, but didn't close them. Finally, he turned down Crane's aisle. Crane lay flat atop the cabinet, holding his breath, willing the guard to focus on the opened processor nodes instead of looking up. As the man stepped around the rack Crane had used to climb up, Crane pushed off the cabinet and dove onto him.

The impact drove the guard into the rack and knocked the breath out of him. The rack tore loose, and they fell. Cooling water from a broken hose sprayed over them as they struggled.

Crane heard shouting as he slammed the guard's right arm hard against a cabinet. His gun fell to the floor, and Crane knocked the man out.

There were more voices outside now. They'd be calling for the revolving door to be released. They could already cover the central aisle. In the other direction was a gauntlet of servers and the plexiglass wall of the cube. Crane's way out was decided for him. He'd wanted to travel light, so he hadn't prepared for too many contingencies, but he had the basics.

He hurriedly sifted through his pack and took out the compact Sig Sauer P938 pistol he preferred when he wasn't planning to need a gun. From the few other odds and ends, he chose a smoke grenade and a clear plastic tube that held two foil pouches the size of Crane's fist. He removed one and returned the tube to his pack.

The pistol went into a custom thigh holster built into his pants leg. The smoke grenade clipped to his belt. That left the foil pouch. Crane tore it open. Inside was a doughy, white mass the size of a tennis ball that started to hiss on contact with the air. Crane hurled it down the aisle, and it splattered against the plexiglass.

Crane picked up the guard's MP-5, took a deep breath, and counted to three. The panel was already turning milky white, and Crane could hear faint cracking sounds. He leapt to his feet and sprinted down the aisle, firing the MP-5 into the plexiglass. He hit it hard and exploded through the panel in a shower of bright fragments. He cleared the gap and landed on the metal deck with a jarring impact.

One of the guards was already through the revolving door and inside the cube, but the other ran toward him. Crane emptied the rest of the clip at him, and he fell back around the corner. Crane tossed the smoke grenade after him.

He could hear alarms as he stood up and discarded the empty submachine gun. He didn't know where to go. If they'd figured out how he got in, they could have sealed the access shaft.

"Georges?"

There was no response. Crane could taste the chemical tang of his smoke filling the chamber. Whatever he did, he needed to decide now.

Then he heard footsteps and whirled as a figure hurtled at him. He wore a jumpsuit and brandished some kind of long, metal tool. Not a guard, but a technician from somewhere.

Crane drew his pistol, but couldn't bring it to bear before the rod smashed across his wrist and the tech slammed into him. His pistol clattered away across the deck, and their momentum carried them both over the edge.

They hit the cement floor below. The tech lay stunned, the tool on the floor beside him. Crane grabbed it and slammed him in the temple as he tried to rise. The tech went still.

Crane heard shouting above. His gun was out of reach, and he'd lost situational awareness. It was time to leave. Crane ducked beneath the deck and ran.

CHAPTER 10

They finally found Einar Persson at Harpa, the glass honeycomb concert hall perched on Reykjavik's waterfront. He was enjoying a performance of the Iceland Symphony in the company of a very beautiful woman when they set a helicopter down directly in front of the main entrance.

For a moment, Einar indulged himself by pretending the clatter outside had nothing to do with him. He imagined some police emergency that he could gawk at from behind the crime scene tape like everyone else. But he knew better. Then two members of Datafall's security team burst into the hall in tactical uniforms and boots, with unhappy ushers in tow.

Einar leant over to his date and whispered, "I'm terribly sorry for this. Really, I am. I'll call you as soon as I'm able."

Then, over her murmured protestations, he stood up and made his way to the end of the row. The orchestra soldiered on through Debussy's La Mer, and annoyed patrons stared daggers at him as he walked up the aisle to meet the two worried looking men in their battle dress uniforms. Einar was a tall man in a tuxedo with a body builder's physique and a blond buzz cut. He accepted the angry stares and whispered reproaches, but he didn't acknowledge them.

"What's happened?" he asked quietly as they walked out of the concert hall, but he knew what the answer would be. What it could only be.

"There's been a brushfire level event, sir," one of them answered.

Of course there had been. Nothing else would justify this kind of response. Critical company data had been compromised. One or more of Datafall's metaphorical cats was out of its bag. Einar also knew which one it would be.

"Details."

They filled him in as they strode quickly through the main lobby toward the doors. Building security was gathering now, and an older man in a suit followed along behind, protesting how inappropriate this all was. Einar ignored him and took in the facts as they were known. One man had penetrated the supercomputer facility and escaped. He was believed to have removed a foreign device from one of the processor nodes. He'd been in communication with someone outside the facility using a sophisticated spread spectrum system. Two men were injured and there had been minor damage to the supercomputer itself. All this had happened nearly two hours earlier. The men were very apologetic. It had taken them that long to track Einar down.

Outside, his helicopter sat idling on the cobblestones in front of Harpa, its blinking lights reflecting off the building's geometric planes. The blades were spinning, and onlookers were keeping a safe distance. The police had arrived to deal with the unauthorized landing, and one of Einar's men was arguing with them. There was a great deal of gesturing going on. Einar and his escorts cleared a path through the gathering crowd. They swept straight past the improvised police cordon and strode to the helicopter. Einar got the attention of the man keeping the police occupied and curtly gestured for him to get back aboard or be left behind.

His two escorts leapt into the open side door and extended their arms to help him up. Einar climbed in and stood in the doorway. The police had noticed something was happening now. The remaining operative on the ground broke off his argument. He leapt in and took a seat in the cockpit.

A quartet of police officers hurried toward them, waving them down. It wasn't permitted to land a helicopter here, but having done so, it was apparently also not permitted for it to take off again. Einar had bigger things to worry about.

"Let's move!" he called out. The helicopter lifted off and slid quickly away over Reykjavik into a sky that glowed dull orange in the long twilight.

"What's been done?" he snapped, and his crew quickly filled him in. Standard brushfire protocols, of course. But those were designed by men who assumed an attack on their data would be a cyber attack by hackers, not an old school physical penetration of the building.

Einar had not made that assumption. He wasn't entirely unprepared for this. It was unfortunate it happened on a night when he'd gone off the grid and forced his team to hunt him down. He could have done without giving his quarry a two-hour head start. Still, he had certain advantages, not the least of which was Iceland itself. Einar knew perfectly well who their enemies within the country were, and none would have had the motive or the ability to pull off something like this. That meant foreigners. Foreigners who would need to get their stolen data out of the country in some kind of physical volume. In many ways this was better than a hacking incident because, for all practical purposes, there'd been no breach at all if the attackers couldn't get the data out of the country. And Iceland was a remote, isolated place that offered them very few ways to do that.

"Private aircraft arriving in the last week?" he asked.

"Five, sir," one of his operatives read from a tablet. "Only one of which is still on the ground at Keflavik." He read off a tail number.

"Why wasn't I notified?"

"It was just logged as routine, sir," the man said. "It's not on the targets of interest list."

"Well, perhaps we'd better add it, don't you think?"

"Yes, sir."

"Do we have a team heading for Keflavik?"

Another man spoke up. "Mr. Olvirsson dispatched a duty team, sir. They should arrive in..." He checked his watch. "Twenty minutes."

"Olvirsson's giving orders?"

"He assumed command in your absence, sir."

Einar nodded. Good man. He'd had the guts to step up and take control, and he'd made at least one good call. He'd clawed back some of that two-hour head start.

The helicopter was flying fast over the outskirts of Reykjavik. They'd be at the site within minutes and Einar could take over. He toyed with the idea of ordering the pilot to divert to Keflavik. But no. Einar's place in a crisis was at the command center. He was already going to have to explain a brushfire event to the company's directors. They wouldn't be pleased to learn that he'd been deliberately out of pocket for two hours as it developed. He could sweep that under the rug, but only if he was there onsite.

"Get me a channel to the Keflavik team," he said. "I'll direct them from base."

CHAPTER 11

Crane ran with a steady, medium-fast pace, a pace he'd trained at for years and knew he could maintain for long distances. The light was just good enough to see by as he ran over the broken ground. The sun was a glowing wedge along the horizon behind him. He dodged a tussock of long, brown grass and kept on.

He was circling a tall hill that wasn't big enough to have a name on the map, though Crane guessed the locals had a name for it. The Datafall complex was on the other side of that hill, stuck between it and the volcanic mountains to the north. On this side of the hill was a tiny hamlet, a clutch of half a dozen small homes clustered close together as if huddling for warmth once winter came. There was a gravel road leading out toward the main highway. And there was a tiny, ancient church with a sod roof where Crane had left his car.

Again, the situation wasn't ideal. Probably no one but the residents of those half dozen homes and the postman had come down that little road in years. Crane very much doubted that they'd failed to notice a stranger parking his car behind the church and walking off around the hill. But you didn't get to pick the mission parameters. Crane was hoping they'd taken him for a tourist roaming the countryside with a rental car and a day pack. There seemed to be enough of those drifting around Iceland in the summer.

Crane stopped for a moment, listened, and heard nothing. He scanned the slope ahead of him. There were few enough landmarks out here, but he'd stashed his backup bag in an erosion gully along the hillside, a bare scar in the green-brown slope. There was a rock nearby that could be seen from a ways off. He knew he could find the bag. The course was straightforward enough: back out the way he went in. Retrieve the bag, make it back to the car, then hightail it to Keflavik and the Gulfstream.

But there was a lot of distance to cover between him and the jet. A lot could happen between here and there. He set off again, angling up the hillside slightly.

He recovered the bag a few minutes later and checked his watch. Eighteen minutes since he'd left the complex. He wasn't sure what Datafall's response capabilities were or what kind of a cordon they could throw out in that time to stop him. It was another ten minutes to the car. Crane set off again, pushing his pace a little. He decided to see if he could make it eight minutes.

It was just under eight minutes later as Crane approached the clutch of buildings. He knew something was wrong before he knew exactly what. There were lights that hadn't been there when he left. Crane could see the church steeple standing out in the twilight. His car was there, but so was another vehicle. His rented Nissan sat isolated in the pool of its headlights.

Crane crouched down to avoid silhouetting himself on the hillside. He moved forward and knelt beside a small cluster of three-leaved rush. There was no real cover here, but at least it would break up his outline. He took a pair of binoculars from the backup bag and swept the church.

"Damn it," he muttered.

The other vehicle was a Toyota Hilux, dull gray with the Datafall logo on the doors. Two men in black uniforms stood nearby. They were armed. One of the doors of his Nissan was open. They'd been through the car. That wasn't a problem. There was nothing inside that would tell them anything. But they'd found the car, and that was very bad.

Crane thought he might be able to take them if he could maintain surprise. But then what would he do? His choices would be to drive out in his own car, which they'd now be watching for, or in one of their own trucks. That seemed equally unlikely to pass without notice. For all he knew, the Hilux could have a GPS tracer. Either way, he'd have to take the Ring Road, which circled the country and was the only road back to Reykjavik. Then there was one highway out to Keflavik. They'd be able to intercept him almost anywhere they chose to, simply because there weren't any choices he could make. His only chance was to do something unexpected.

Crane moved away, heading back around the hill and leaving the car to them. It was worse than just being able to predict his route, he realized. They'd know he was headed for Keflavik because that was the only international airport and almost the only way out of the country. It wouldn't take a genius to figure out there must be a plane waiting for him there. Georges and the Gulfstream would be a target. Once again it occurred to Crane that Iceland was a singularly bad place for this kind of job, one that gave every advantage to the opposition.

He made his way back around to the west side of the hill, out of sight of the team at the car. When he thought he'd found the point on the hill that was nearest the Ring Road, he sat down, took out the phone he'd been using for the last week, and called Georges.

"Where are you?" Georges said as he picked up. "What happened? Are you all right?"

"I'm fine. What's going on there?"

"Nothing. We just lost you. I've been trying to get you back. They're using some kind of predictive jammer. I could get a packet past it once in a while, but not enough signal integrity to—"

"Get airborne," Crane interrupted. "They've made you."

"What?"

"I have the device and I'm out, but they've got my car. I'm not going to be able to make it back there. You've probably got hostiles inbound. Tell the pilots to get airborne now. Wheels up as fast as they can do it."

"But what about you?"

"I've got a backup plan," said Crane. "I'll get out on my own. You get out of the country immediately. This is the last call you'll get from this phone. Do you understand? If this phone calls you again, don't answer."

"We can't just leave you here!"

"I'll be all right. Go. Now."

Then he hung up and powered down the phone. He pulled the SIM card and buried it in a small depression he dug out of the mossy ground. Then he changed, quickly because it was chilly. He swapped out his black pants and sweater for a pair of hiking pants and a couple layers of light outdoor gear he'd picked up at Cintamani in Reykjavik. He packed everything into his bag, then stood up, hitched the bag up over his shoulder and set out on the long walk back out to the Ring Road.

CHAPTER 12

The pilots had taken Crane's warning seriously and had the Gulfstream accelerating down the runway within minutes. Now they were airborne, climbing to cruise height, and wheeling around to the east, bound for Norway.

Georges sat in the rear of the jet, at the table where he'd set up his laptops and equipment, and felt utterly forlorn. He'd screwed up, badly, and he didn't even know how. The spread spectrum link should have been completely undetectable. But somehow, they'd found it, and that had blown Crane's mission. He didn't even know if Crane was alive.

But for the moment, all he could do was keep himself together and try to help fix things. He dreaded making the call, but Josh needed to be told as soon as possible. The Gulfstream had a Wi-Fi hotspot that connected to a satellite link. Georges took a long look at his phone, then called up Josh's number and hit dial.

Josh picked up immediately. He'd obviously been waiting for a report. Georges told him what had happened.

"It's my fault," he said when he was finished. "They picked

up the link. I thought it was secure, but they found it somehow. I blew his cover."

"Not your fault," said Josh. "And that's not helpful now. Focus on what we can do."

"What can we do? We're not there, and he's cut us off. He wasn't kidding about the phone. I tried calling him back and it's not on the network. He's gone dark."

"We're going to have a talk when he gets back," said Josh, "about keeping me in the loop on his emergency plans. In the meantime, let's figure out what he's doing and how we can help him."

"Right," said Georges. "You're right."

"So is he going to have you fly back in and pick him up somewhere else?"

"I didn't get that impression," said Georges. "He sounded like he just wanted us gone."

"Well, Iceland's an island in the middle of the North Atlantic," said Josh. "There's only so many ways to get off of it. Basically, there's air and there's water. Hang on a sec."

Georges heard keystrokes, then Josh said, "Oh, come on."

"What?"

"I just had my map draw a thousand-kilometer radius circle around Reykjavik," Josh explained. "There's not a lot of land in it. And most of that's glaciers on the Greenland coast. Let me see…there's the Faroe Islands, which is like the one place even more remote than Iceland. And it just, just hits the edge of the Hebrides. That's a thousand kilometers. It's not like he can steal a rowboat. He's got to be planning to fly out. Where else could you fly into? There's got to be somewhere. Ask the pilots."

Georges went forward to the cockpit and had a hurried discussion with the two pilots.

"Not a lot of options," he told Josh a couple minutes later when he came back. "There are plenty of small airfields, but they're made for short range prop planes flying in-country. The runways are too short for a Gulfstream. Besides Keflavik, there are three airports where we could land."

"Seriously? Three?"

"Reykjavik has an airport closer in to the city. Then there's Akureyri on the north coast, and Egilsstadir in the east."

"They could have teams there watching out for him already," Josh mused. "Three airports aren't very many to watch."

"Two, really," said Georges. "If he's right, coming back to Reykjavik is way too dangerous."

Josh sighed. "Okay, what about planes that can fly out of those smaller airfields? Could one of those make it somewhere? Ask the pilots."

"Already did," said Georges. "Short answer is maybe. They say if you had a twin-engine turboprop, you could use the shorter runways, and you could reach airports in Greenland, Scotland, Ireland, parts of Norway."

"I'm hearing a 'but' in your voice," said Josh.

"But there aren't any twin-engine turboprops. We're talking about unmanned airstrips, not even paved, some of them. Locals will have a few smaller planes parked there, but a plane like Crane needs is too expensive. Only place to find a plane like that would be a charter operation."

"Which brings us back to our short list of airports," said Josh. "What about boats? Is there any way he could make it off by boat?"

"Like you said, it's a long way to anywhere. It would have to be a pretty big boat. Not the kind he could handle by himself." A thought occurred to Georges. "I did see a cruise ship in Reykjavik. But he said it was too dangerous to come back to Reykjavik."

"And if he was going to Reykjavik, we already had a perfectly good airplane there," Josh added. "Wait, do the cruise ships dock anywhere else?"

"I don't know," Georges admitted.

"Hang on a sec." Georges heard a furious clatter of keys, then, "Why, yes, they do. Let me run his company credit card."

There was more typing, a pause, then Josh came back. "That son of a bitch! He booked himself on the *Celebrity Eclipse*! In a suite, no less. Peter Drew, VP of Strategic Acquisitions, Myria Group...What the hell, John? He bought the unlimited beverage package! He wasn't even planning to be on the boat!"

Georges smiled. He'd noticed that Crane had a habit of spending more than was strictly necessary, just to tweak Josh. But he didn't care about the particulars right now. "Where's he going?"

"Hang on." Josh typed some more. "The *Eclipse* is at sea right now. It left Reykjavik ten hours ago. It docks in Akureyri at 9:00 tomorrow morning and it's there until 7:00 p.m. when it leaves Iceland for the Faroes and Norway. That little..."

Georges furiously searched through his bag for a map of Iceland and spread it out on the table. Reykjavik was at the southwestern tip of the country. He found Akureyri, more or less in the middle of the northern coast. Route 1, the Ring Road that circled the island, would take Crane there. He could reach Akureyri in something like four and a half hours by car. Plenty of time to catch the ship.

But looking at the map, Georges saw the danger. The Ring Road was effectively the only way to get from one part of Iceland to another. Datafall's people would be watching it to see if he came back to Reykjavik. When he didn't, there was only one other direction he could have gone.

"We're headed for Bergen right now," said Georges. "What do you want us to do?"

Josh thought for a moment. "Divert to Stavanger," he said.

"The Eclipse docks there in four days. If he makes it onboard, he'll call in and you can pick him up."

"What if he doesn't?"

"Then we'll have to figure out what happened and find another way. Keep me posted."

"I will."

After he hung up, Georges settled back in the luxurious leather seat and let out a deep breath. Somehow, hearing about the cruise ship cabin filled Georges with new hope. Crane had a plan. Maybe there was still something he could do to help, to make up for his mistake.

He grabbed the map of Iceland and started tracing the route Crane would have to take.

CHAPTER 13

It was almost midnight as Datafall's helicopter descended toward the supercomputing complex. In the dim twilight, Einar could see trucks parked on the grass, their headlights illuminating the building. His entire security team was there, along with some operations staff who'd apparently been hauled out of bed and called in for the emergency. Soon, word would filter up to the executive board, and they'd want his report. Einar would need plenty of usable information to give them when that happened.

The helicopter touched down on the landing pad, and Einar jumped out the side door. He strode toward the building in his tuxedo, the helicopter powering down behind him. A pair of security men jogged toward him. He recognized one as Ari Olvirsson, the one who'd taken the initiative and dispatched the team to Keflavik. The other he knew vaguely. That one was carrying a radio handset, and Einar assumed he was there to put him in touch with the Keflavik team.

"Sir," Olvirsson said as they met. Einar kept on walking, and Olvirsson and the other man turned and hurried to keep up with him.

"Good work, Ari," he said. "Bring me up to speed."

"I'm afraid he's still on the loose, sir," said Olvirsson. "We found a rental car on the far side of the hill, but he never came back to it. I assume he saw our men and withdrew."

"So he's on foot," said Einar. "Good. He'll make his way to the Ring Road, of course." Where else would he go?

"I sent a truck to patrol the road to the south, between here and Mossfellsbær. And the Reykjavik resources are all activated and in position."

Einar nodded. "Very good." The city was an excellent trap. It channeled an enemy into just a few avenues where he could be located and contained. Einar now had multiple screens in place between the intruder and the airport. He wouldn't slip through.

"The signals team flagged a mobile call through the tower here thirty-three minutes after the event. It went live, made one call, and vanished again."

Einar was considering the implications of that when the timer he had set on his phone hit zero and chimed at him. His team should be arriving at Keflavik. He looked over to the man holding the radio.

"Keflavik?"

"Yes, sir," the man said nervously. "Right here."

Einar took the radio. "This is Security Director Persson," he said, crisply enunciating his syllables. "Who am I speaking with?"

"This is Ingolfsson, sir," came the reply. "We're pulling in now, but I think we're too late."

"Why is that?"

"We have an asset in IFR control," the man explained. "He just notified us that your tail number took off three minutes ago. Flight plan for Bergen, Norway."

Einar hissed through his teeth. That was disappointing. "Understood," he said. "Carry on while you're there. See if they've left us anything interesting." But he knew the team would find nothing.

He handed the radio back to its bearer. "Show me everywhere he was," he said to Olvirsson. "We'll start at the perimeter and work our way down to the catacombs."

They showed him the spot where the intruder had cut through the fence, where he'd attacked a power technician having an unauthorized evening smoke, the route they thought he'd taken to the supercomputer, but Einar was only partly paying attention. That was past. He might be able to glean some clues to the man's thought processes, but Einar was more concerned with the future.

The intruder was still out there, with the device he'd come for. If Einar could run him down before he got that device out of Iceland, he could contain the damage. So where was he? What was he thinking, and what was he doing?

Einar knew the man had arrived by private jet, and he'd planned to escape the same way. But when things went wrong, he'd called and sent the plane away. Why?

As far as Einar knew, only one thing had happened to change the tactical picture after the man had escaped from the complex. He'd learned that Einar's men had found his car. That was a bit clumsy in retrospect. He was on foot now, and less mobile. But if those men had stayed hidden and let him reclaim the car, they could have taken him on the road. Now Einar didn't know where he was. And the intruder would eventually have to acquire a car anyway, except now it could be any car on the road.

But that must have been what triggered the call that warned the jet. Why? It would take him longer to get back to Keflavik without the car. Did he anticipate that they would identify the jet and reach it before he could? Everything the intruder did suggested he was very familiar with their capabilities, more so than Einar was comfortable with.

If the man sent the jet away, he must have a backup plan. What was it? Einar nodded and made attentive noises as his people showed him the molten fragments of the plexiglass panel the intruder had blown out to escape the chamber. But his instincts were triggering. How was the intruder planning to escape without his plane? Almost every foreigner entered and left Iceland through Keflavik; it was hard to do so any other way. But he'd sent his plane away. Did he mean to try and get aboard a commercial flight?

Suddenly, Einar recognized his flawed assumption. It was Reykjavik itself that held the danger for him, not losing the jet. If he meant to take his chances in the city, then it would be best to do it immediately, in hopes he could elude his pursuers before they could close the net. And if he was going to risk Reykjavik anyway, the jet remained his best chance of making it out of the country. Therefore, he wasn't going to try to slip through Reykjavik later. He wasn't going to Reykjavik at all.

"Damn it!" he snapped suddenly, startling the technician trying to show him a damaged board they'd pulled from one of the racks. He strode quickly away to the elevators.

"He's not coming back here," he shouted to Olvirsson. "All those men hanging around upstairs, get them on the roads. Send them north."

"North, sir?"

"North. Keep the southern assets in place, but everyone else moves north."

The elevator opened, and Einar punched for the ground floor. Olvirsson was taking notes as the car rose.

"Tell the signals team to look for police reports of stolen cars. And tell them to flag any new SIM cards registering on the cell network outside of Reykjavik."

"Yes, sir," said Olvirsson. The doors slid open and Einar jogged through the lobby area as Olvirsson followed at his heels.

"Where will you be, sir?"

"Airborne," said Einar. He burst through the front door and signaled to the pilot to spin up the rotors. "I'm going north."

Einar didn't know what the man meant to do. But they already had people in place to intercept the intruder if he tried to make it through Reykjavik after all. He might as well play his hunch.

CHAPTER 14

Crane walked north, along the shoulder of the Ring Road. It was after 1:00 in the morning now, as dark as it was going to get. It was a little brighter than a full moon, with the dull glow of reflected sunlight along the horizon to his right. He'd been walking for more than an hour and hadn't seen anything threatening. He hoped they were still looking for him to the south, around Reykjavik.

He saw the asphalt brighten slightly at his feet before he heard the sound of the engine. He turned and stuck out one hand, thumb raised in the universal gesture. This might be some random motorist who might give him a ride, or it might be Datafall's people searching for him. Either way, his best play was to look like a hitchhiking tourist. Of course, that would only get him so far if this was a Datafall patrol. Again, he cursed himself for losing the Sig Sauer.

The headlights belonged to a Volvo truck, Crane realized as it came closer. FL series, red, marked with some cartoonish brand name Crane wasn't sure how to pronounce. It slowed, creaked to a stop beside him, and the driver leaned over to open the passenger door. He was a gruff looking, middle-aged man with a scraggly beard and a plaid shirt. He said something in Icelandic.

"Do you speak English?" Crane asked.

"Yeah, yeah," said the driver. "Get in, you're letting the warm out."

Crane shrugged off his pack and climbed in. The boxy cab was strewn with papers and empty candy wrappers, but it was warm. It made Crane realize how cold it had gotten outside. He stuffed his pack down behind his legs in the footwell, and the truck lurched forward again.

"Thank you," he said. "I'm John."

"August," said the driver. "Where in hell are you going in the dead of night? Out here in the middle of nowhere?"

Crane laughed. "I'm trying to get to Akureyri," he said. "I was out hiking around Thingvellir, and I got…well, long story, but I missed my ship!"

"Hah! The big cruise ship, eh? Yes, they will go without you. But your luck is getting better. I go to Akureyri. We'll be there by morning." He gestured over his shoulder to the back of the truck. "I make some stops along the way for deliveries, but we'll get you back to your ship, no problem."

"Much appreciated," said Crane. "I'm happy to help unload if you'll show me what goes where."

August grunted in acknowledgment. He drove in silence for a minute, then said, "We all speak English, you know."

"I'm sorry?"

"In Iceland. We learn it in school. And we grow up with American and English TV."

"I see," said Crane. "I noticed I was getting along okay in English. Figured I was just finding the right people to talk to."

"No, no. Everyone," said August. "Because of TV mostly. With the…um, we say 'texti.' What do you call them? The words on the bottom that tell you what they're saying?"

"Subtitles."

"Ah. Subtitles. We're both learning something this trip. It's good."

Crane wasn't sure what good knowing the Icelandic word for subtitles would do him. On the other hand, he decided, he could totally see August at a bar somewhere showing off his new knowledge—pointing at the TV over the bar and bellowing, "Subtitles!"

They made small talk as August drove, and the highway wound between various old volcanic remnants and the ocean. In a small town called Akranes they pulled into a gas station with a convenience store, and August opened the back of the truck to reveal cases of soda, candy, and various unhealthy snack foods. There were a couple battered hand trucks in the back as well, so Crane helped haul the store's order inside.

Then they were back on the highway again. Crane dug a granola bar out of his pack, and they shared it. August wasn't hugely impressed. He produced something called a Kókosbolla and swore Crane would never want to leave Iceland once he'd tried it. It was a thin chocolate shell, rolled in coconut flour with some kind of white paste inside. Crane praised it since August clearly expected him to be impressed, but it wasn't to his taste.

They stopped again in Borgarnes, an even smaller town strung out along a narrow spit of land with the sea on either side. August pulled into a brightly lit gas station with a restaurant and shop attached—a curving, single story building of cast concrete that reminded Crane of a diner.

"Another delivery, and we get some gas," said August. Crane helped him haul the candy and drinks again. When he was finished, Crane saw that August was flirting with the woman behind the counter. He slipped outside to the parking lot and powered up the backup phone he'd bought. He dialed the Celebrity customer service number and introduced himself as

Peter Drew. They looked up his reservation number and noted he'd failed to join the ship in Reykjavik.

"Yes, I'm afraid there was a situation that kept me longer than I planned. It's resolved now, however, and I'll be able to join the ship at Akureyri."

They reassured him that that would be fine, and he hung up just as August emerged from the shop.

"You coming?" August bellowed.

Crane trotted over to the truck and climbed in. His backup plan was in place and working, he thought as August started the engine and pulled back out onto the Ring Road. He was invisible here in the truck. He would make it to Akureyri by morning, thanks to August who was turning out to be a surprisingly pleasant traveling companion. He would simply join the crowd of tourists that would flood the town and then follow them back to the ship.

"So, the woman running the store," said Crane.

"Lilija."

"Yeah, I think she's into you, man."

August roared with laughter, and the truck drove on into the night.

CHAPTER 15

Einar Persson strode back and forth on the ramp in his tuxedo while his crew refueled the helicopter. That had been eight hundred liters of aviation fuel burned for nothing, he thought. The man he was searching for had simply dropped off the map. There had been no reports of movement from the southern teams, the dragnet of people he had around Reykjavik and guarding the highway to Keflavik. His spotters on the Ring Road to the north were reporting nothing. And Einar understood why. He'd burned most of that eight hundred liters of fuel flying around the Ring Road himself, and he'd seen nothing. It was the dead of night. There was no traffic at all. There was nowhere for his quarry to hide.

So then where the hell was he?

Einar glanced up at the sky. Cloud cover was rolling in. It was almost 2:00 a.m. now. The sun would be rising in another hour, but it was going to be a gray day. In more ways than one. The executive board already knew what had happened, of course. They'd have been informed immediately of a brushfire event, even if it meant pulling them out of bed. But they'd be pretending otherwise for the time being. They'd give him a chance to bring the situation under control before they intervened. But by morning, it would be impossible for them to remain uninvolved. He'd have to report on the situation, and it would be better if he had good news for them.

An airport worker glanced over at Einar as he walked by. He realized how out of place he looked standing here in his tuxedo, but he hadn't had time to change yet. He'd have to have a spare duty uniform brought out to him somewhere. Of course, he didn't know where he was going to be. This was a mess, he thought.

His phone buzzed. It was the signals team. Thank God, thought Einar as he answered it. Perhaps some good news at last.

"What have you got?" he said.

"New SIM on the network, sir," said the voice at the other end. "It registered, made one overseas call, then went dark again."

Einar felt a quick rush of adrenaline. That was his man. He had him.

"Where?"

"Call was placed six minutes ago, from Borgarnes."

"Borgarnes? Are we sure about that?"

"Yes, sir, location near the Ring Road in central Borgarnes."

"I'm sorry," he said. "Of course you're sure. Who did he call?"

"Call was placed to an 800 number. It maps to a call center run by Celebrity Cruise Lines."

A cruise ship! Of course! There had been a huge white cruise liner docked at Skarfabakki harbor that morning, but it had left by mid-afternoon. It would be bound for Akureyri where it would spend a day before leaving Icelandic waters. That was his backup plan. He was making for Akureyri.

"Thank you," he told the signals team operator. "Keep

watching and let me know if it activates again. And tell your team they've done well."

"Thank you, sir."

Einar slipped his phone back into his jacket and strode toward the helicopter.

"How soon can we be airborne?" he shouted at the pilot.

"Five minutes, sir!"

Einar nodded and stood impatiently by as the crew topped off the tanks. He wanted to be moving, but he knew it was wise to have as much fuel as he could carry. It gave him more options, especially up north where aviation fuel would be harder to find on short notice.

Something still bothered him. He checked his watch again. What the hell was the man doing in Borgarnes? It didn't make sense. He couldn't have walked all the way there. He must have gotten his hands on a car somehow. But if he had a car, he should be halfway to Akureyri by now. What was keeping him?

As the helicopter lifted off into the pre-dawn twilight, he still couldn't make sense of it. He wished they had a police report of a stolen car someplace. It would at least give them a make and model to look for. But at this time of night, it was likely the car's owner wouldn't notice it missing for hours.

Still, they had a position and a direction now. That was something he could work with. The positions of Einar's men were charted on a ruggedized tablet clipped to the helicopter's bulkhead. He pulled it down. There was a blinking dot on the Ring Road in Bifröst, about 30 kilometers north of Borgarnes. He switched the radio handset to the proper frequency.

"Spotter team eight," he said, "Come in."

A moment later the radio crackled. "Team eight, sir."

"Stay alert. He's coming your way."

"Do you have a vehicle ID, sir?" the spotter asked.

"No," said Einar. "But he just left Borgarnes, headed north. He should reach you in less than 30 minutes."

"He'll be easy to spot, sir. There's been no traffic at all out here but a few commercial trucks."

"When you spot him, contact me. Keep eyes on him and guide us in. We're headed for your position now."

"Yes, sir!"

Einar closed the channel and sat back in his seat, thinking. The spotter team would pick him up. The helicopter would have him on the scene in minutes. By the time he had to report to the executive board, he'd have the man and he would have recovered the data. The brushfire event would be history, and they could focus on damage control and improving their counter-intrusion techniques.

Still, something kept nagging at the back of his mind. What had kept him? Had he been forced to walk farther than Einar expected before he found a car to steal...or a truck?

Commercial delivery trucks. That was what the spotters were seeing because they owned the roads at this time of night. They serviced the little grocery stores and gas stations in the settlements strung around the Ring Road. They drove from one town to the next, and then they stopped to unload cargo. It would take them longer to cover the distance than a man in a car trying to escape from pursuers.

That was why there had been no stolen car reports to track down. He hadn't stolen a car at all. He'd hitched a ride with a trucker. Einar pulled a map book from the pouch on the bulkhead and flipped to the appropriate page. The timing was right, he realized. A trucker who stopped in Akranes, and then again in Borgarnes, for twenty to thirty minutes in both places. Of course! Of course. They were looking for a truck.

CHAPTER 16

Driving north out of Borgarnes, August put on some old pop music and tapped happily along on the Volvo's steering wheel.

"No more work for a while," he said. "No more stops until Blönduós. We can make up some time."

Crane sat back and stretched. Datafall's people were probably looking for him well to the south. If Georges and the pilots had followed his instructions, they'd be out of Icelandic airspace by now. He wasn't home free yet by any means, but he could feel the distance between himself and his pursuers opening up. Things had gone off the rails back inside the complex, but he was close to recovering it and bringing the mission home.

Coming out of Borgarnes, the road turned eastward, and the truck rolled through mostly flat, empty land that had been carved up into large fields separated by long, straight drainage ditches. Beyond them, Crane saw low, broken hills. In the dim light he could see the bare slopes rising to an undulating ridgeline. Nothing broke the smooth line of the hilltops as far as he could see. Beyond them he could make out a line of mountains. They looked equally bare.

"Why aren't there any trees in Iceland?" he asked August. "Not none, but... damn close. Is it the winters?"

"No, no," said August. "Trees will grow. The volcanoes play hell with them." He waved his hand at the landscape. "That's all old lava fields out there. Good farming. But mostly, people just cut them all down back in the old days. Now we're trying to grow them again. The government pays you to grow trees on your land. We'll get the forests back. It will take a while, though."

A sound was breaking through the music, Crane realized, meshing with the beat. It took him a moment to realize what it was. Rotor blades. It was not a good sound.

Crane swept the landscape, but saw no lights, no sign of human habitation at all. If they made him, there was nowhere for him to hide. He considered trying to stash the data tap somewhere in August's truck, but they'd search it.

August heard the helicopter now. He was leaning forward, peering up around the edge of the truck's roof, trying to see it. The sound grew louder, unmistakable.

Then, with a roar, the helicopter swept over them, lights blinking. The rotor wash shook the truck. The helicopter slewed ahead of them, turning perpendicular to the road. Crane saw the side door open, revealing a dark interior.

"What the hell is he doing?" Einar shouted over the roaring engine. The helicopter was no more than twenty feet above the roadway, sliding sideways in front of them. Crane could see movement inside.

Einar slowed and steered toward the shoulder. "This guy's a madman!"

Suddenly Crane knew with a dreadful certainty what was about to happen. He released his seatbelt and slid down into the foot well, behind the metal front of the cab. He grabbed August's arm.

"Get down!"

August looked at him like he was insane, fought him to keep his grip on the wheel. Then the gunner inside the helicopter opened up, and the cab exploded around them. Shattered glass rained down, and smoke filled the cab. August roared in confusion and shock, and Crane felt the truck veer to the left, felt the wheels rumble off the edge of the shoulder, heard the crackle of automatic fire and the bullets slamming into the truck's bodywork.

The truck veered sharply back across the pavement and leaned to one side. Crane felt it start to tip and braced himself against the door and the seat. He caught a glimpse of August and of blood sprayed across the back wall of the cab. Bullets were still slapping into the top of the truck. Then they were rolling. Crane fell on top of August, and the noise of the helicopter engine, even the gunshots, were drowned out by the shriek of metal.

When it stopped, Crane was jammed up against the steering wheel and the dashboard. He was lying on top of August. The dashboard lights were still on, and Crane could just make out August's face, his blank, staring eyes. There was nothing he could do for him.

The shooting had stopped, but he still heard the clatter of the helicopter. He kicked out the safety glass at the bottom of the spider-webbed windshield, making a hole he could crawl through.

"I'm sorry, August," he said. Then he grabbed his pack by one of the straps and pushed his way out onto the cold pavement.

Crane crawled around the wrecked cab until the bulk of the truck shielded him from view, then peered back around a torn fender panel. The helicopter had landed on the road perhaps fifty yards away. The engine was still idling, the blades spinning. It was ready to lift off again on short notice.

Then a figure jumped down from the side door and strode toward the wreck. It was a tall blond man, wearing a tuxedo of all things, and carrying a light machine gun. That was the man who had killed August. Crane studied the cruel features, burning that face into his memory.

As the man with the gun came closer, Crane looked around desperately for some plan of action. The land was flat all around. There was no cover except a deep drainage ditch along the side of the highway. Crane had been seeing them for a while. They ran along the road and between fields, a network of them, like the Icelandic version of barbed wire fences. If he could get to it unnoticed, he could follow it away from the highway.

Crane searched through his pack for the plastic tube with its one remaining foil pouch, then he pulled the pack's straps over his shoulders and got ready to run. He discarded the tube and held the pouch in one hand. The smell of diesel fuel was strong. The Volvo's tanks had ruptured when it rolled, and there was vapor in the air. It would do. Crane tore the pouch open and slapped the doughy, white ball against the nearer tank. He heard the sizzle of water boiling away from the metal, heard the tank creak as it rapidly heated.

He ran straight down the road, away from the truck, keeping it between himself and the man with the machine gun. Then behind him, the truck went up in a loud fireball, and Crane instantly sprinted for the roadside, counting on the flash and the explosion to hide him. He dove into the ditch like he was going into a swimming pool.

He hit the dirt hard and tumbled into cold mud at the bottom. He could hear shouting on the roadway above. Crane ignored it. The only thing he could do now was get as far away as possible and figure out what to do next.

The ditch was maybe six feet deep. He crawled on his hands and knees through the cold, grasping muck at the bottom until he reached another ditch. This one cut off at a right angle, leading away from the road and back into the fields.

Crane followed it. He had no idea where he was going. That would come later. He thought of poor August, whose only crime was picking up a lost hiker. He remembered the face of the man in the tuxedo.

A lot of things would come later.

CHAPTER 17

It was twenty minutes before the volunteer fire department from Bifrost showed up. Einar and his men had gotten the fire under control and combed through the burnt-out wreckage of the truck. It was a dirty and unpleasant task. Einar's throat burned from the thick diesel smoke. His tuxedo was a lost cause. And all just to find the body of a short, doughy man who was obviously the driver. Of the passenger who'd caused so much trouble, there wasn't a trace. They'd searched the area to make sure he hadn't been thrown clear. They'd poked through the charred ruins of the cab for some sign of the device he'd taken. They'd found nothing.

Now Einar had a squad of hurriedly dressed first responders with extinguishers and rescue equipment to deal with.

The first volunteer to reach the scene piled out of a sedate looking family sedan and rushed toward him.

"Is anyone hurt?" he shouted.

"The driver!" Einar shouted back. "He went very quickly. There was nothing we could do for him."

"What happened?"

"I don't know," said Einar. "We saw it burst into flame, and so we landed to see if we could help. But..." he pointed back to the smoking wreck with a gesture of resignation.

"What are you doing out here?" the man asked in confusion.

Einar was already retreating toward his helicopter. The device wasn't here. The intruder had survived and gotten away with it. That was the only way it could have happened. That meant he'd done all he could do here. Any more delay was just giving his target more of a head start.

"Geodetic survey!" he shouted and gestured toward the helicopter. "Interior ministry."

The man looked confused but didn't question it. He didn't seem to know what to think. More firefighters were arriving now, putting out the rest of the scattered fires, the small pools of burning fuel in the road. A bright red pickup with foam tanks in the back pulled up, and men began uncoiling hoses.

Einar waved his men back toward the helicopter.

"Wait," said the volunteer fireman. He followed Einar back toward the helicopter until he decided the whirling blades were too close for comfort. "We called the police station in Borgarnes! They'll want to talk to you."

Einar pointed to the gray sky growing brighter as the sun rose again. He let it vaguely suggest people rising, heading for work. "Have to clear the highway!" he shouted. "Have them contact the ministry!"

"Geodetic survey?"

"Yes, that's exactly right."

Then Einar leapt back aboard the helicopter, and it immediately lifted off into the gray morning. Einar looked down as the ground receded. A cluster of confused firemen looked back up at the helicopter, no doubt wondering why the interior ministry would have sent a man in a tuxedo out in a helicopter to do mapping work by night.

Smoke still rose from the charred wreck of the truck. The

volunteers were spraying the engine compartment with foam. The fire had been intense. Along with the damage from the wreck, Einar hoped the explosion and fire would conceal the damage from gunfire. Datafall's executive board was composed of very powerful people. They would be able to make all this go away. But the idea was to kill the intruder and recover or destroy the stolen data. They wouldn't appreciate having to cover up such a public action that didn't even get them what they wanted.

Einar looked across the broken ground below, at the deep green and brown shades of grass. He was waiting for the pilot to ask where they were going. At the moment, Einar had no idea. He glanced back one last time at the blackened mass of the truck and the tendril of smoke spiraling up from it. What a damn waste. Nothing was going his way.

Then, as expected, the pilot's voice crackled over Einar's headset. "Orders, sir?"

Einar glanced at his map. The Ring Road ran more or less north-northeast here. Out here, there wasn't much in either direction to draw the man. But to the west was nothing but a couple lakes and empty lowlands. To the east were a scattering of remote farms. At least there, he'd find cars he might steal. And there were drainage ditches separating the fields. That had to be how he'd slipped away. Now the day was growing light again, and there was precious little cover for a man on foot.

"We'll search east of the road. Pull everyone out of Reykjavik. Anybody south of us comes up here. I want as many eyes on the ground as we can get."

The man was resourceful, Einar had to admit. Better, he was damned lucky. But that would only take him so far. One man, on foot, out here, against barren ground with nowhere to hide. Luck couldn't help him now.

Einar broke out a pair of binoculars as the helicopter swung east of the Ring Road and settled into a comfortable altitude for searching the ground. They'd have him soon, he thought.

He tapped the headset button to speak to the pilot. "And have somebody bring me a god damn duty uniform!"

CHAPTER 18

Crane ran. He'd traveled more than a mile in the network of ditches before deciding it was safe to climb out. He was cold and wet from the muck and bruised from the wreck. He was hungry, and he hadn't slept. But Crane had been prepared for situations like this. The Hurricane Group had put him through military SERE training—Survival, Evasion, Resistance, and Escape—in eastern Washington in the winter. By comparison, he told himself, this should be a piece of cake.

On the other hand, the woods of eastern Washington were thick with cover. Concealment was easy there. Here, there was nothing.

Crane could hear the distant sound of the helicopter. It was searching methodically, back and forth across a defined search area. They'd missed their guess about which direction he was heading, and had done an even worse job of projecting how far he'd made it since leaving the road. They were well behind him at the moment. But when they didn't find him, they'd move farther out. Eventually they'd spot him.

But he knew they would face difficulties of their own. At some point, they'd have to refuel. Crane's map showed several small airstrips scattered around this part of the country, but those probably consisted of little more than a packed dirt runway and a shed or two. Supplies of aviation fuel would likely be limited out here. They might even have to fly back to Reykjavik to refuel. And of course, the farther they had to go, the more fuel they would burn getting back out here, the sooner they would have to leave again, and the less time they could search for him.

So Crane ran. The steep hills he'd seen from the truck rose up in front of him, tilting up into bare, brown slopes that ultimately vanished into a bank of low cloud. He kept up his pace until the sound of rotors faded away. After another five minutes of silence, Crane slowed to a walk, then sat down and let his body rest.

The land around him was barren. There was little wind today. With the helicopter gone, he was surrounded by a great silence. Nothing moved. The land was beautiful in its desolate way, but uninviting. People living in a land like this would be a stern people, he thought, used to living close to the margins of starvation. They would be accustomed to death, to heroic efforts that still failed because the land gave nothing back. They would celebrate heartily when they could, because they knew what tomorrow might bring. And there would be a grim humor that they didn't reveal often. Looking at the country explained a lot about the Icelanders he had met.

Crane took a GPS receiver, a map, and a compass from a side pocket of his emergency pack and worked out his position. He'd put another couple miles between himself and the Ring Road. The high ridge in front of him ran north-south for several miles. He was near its northern end. The southern end was farther than he cared to hike on foot. That meant he had to go around it to the north, or else over it. His instincts warned him away from the northern course. The Ring Road curved around the end of the ridge and headed on toward Blönduós, the next town. Going around the ridge would force him close to the highway, making it more likely someone would see him. Locals might take him for just another hiker—his emergency pack was planned to help him pass as a backpacking tourist—but Datafall might have concocted some story to put the police on his trail.

According to his map, the land sloped down into a valley on the far side of the ridge. It was perhaps five miles wide, drained by a small river. Across the river, another range of barren hills ran parallel to this one. A road ran along the near side of the river, and the map showed several farmsteads. These were considerably more isolated than those out by the Ring Road. Datafall would be less likely to look for him there. The remote farms might offer a chance to find some supplies and get his hands on a car.

He looked up at the mist-shrouded hills. Near the cloud line, even the grasses faded out, and the hillside was bare dirt and scree. It wasn't very welcoming, and he didn't like the idea of a climb. But there it was.

Crane took a granola bar from his pack—leaving him one more—and ate it as he walked on toward the hills. The land grew rockier and his progress slowed as he made his way up the slope. He was painfully aware of how exposed he was here. He angled south, following a less steep path up the ridge. As he gained altitude, he could see more of the countryside he'd passed through. Behind him to the west, the land stretched away in a patchwork of uncultivated fields with the Ring Road a dark line slicing through it. Eventually the fields gave way to a pair of large lakes with a spit of lowland between them, and finally the dark sea. The colors were muted by the low sun filtering through the overcast.

Crane was focused on keeping his pace steady, paying attention to his breathing and his heart rate. The idea was to exert himself just enough, find the sweet spot that would give him the fastest pace without wearing himself out. So it took him a few seconds to notice the sound of the helicopter. It was closer now. They'd refueled more quickly than he'd hoped. And they were moving farther from the road this time.

He glanced over and saw it, a dark spot moving against the cloud cover. If they hadn't seen him yet, it was just a matter of time. He looked around for someplace to hide but saw only a few scattered rocks. There was only one place he could hope to stay out of sight.

Crane abandoned his careful pace. He turned directly upslope and pushed himself higher, faster, running up the steepest part of the slope. Before long he could feel the burn of lactic acid in his muscles, felt his heart pumping. But he could also hear the clatter of the helicopter searching for him, growing louder until it seemed to thunder in his ears. You're imagining that, he told himself angrily. They haven't seen you. Keep moving.

The fog would conceal him. It offered at least temporary safety, but it seemed to taunt him, always just a few more steps away. Crane kept moving, breathing, climbing as fast as his body would carry him.

When he was sure he was above the cloud line, he stopped and crouched low to the ground. He was right. The green land below him was dim and misty now. Above him was just diffuse gray light and the top of the ridgeline. The helicopter even seemed more distant now, working its way up and down the fields below, searching in vain. Crane resisted the urge to stop here, but he settled down to a recovery pace, letting the mist protect him as he headed south along the ridge.

The workout had given him one benefit; he was warm, even sweating a bit. That wouldn't last though. Crane was tempted to find a sheltered spot to curl up and get some sleep, but he wasn't sure he trusted the weather. The air was calm now, heavy and moist, clinging to the hills. But he'd seen how quickly a strong, cold wind could come up and clear it all away. He needed to take maximum advantage of the low cloud cover while he had it.

A long day's hike, then. With no sleep and little food. It was just like his training again, Crane thought. He aimed for the ridgeline and set out, bound for whatever he could find.

CHAPTER 19

Einar looked at his ringing phone. The call had come, just as he knew it would. It was well into the afternoon. They'd given him as much time as they could.

"Set us down," he shouted to the pilot. "Immediately."

The helicopter slewed to the right, toward a flat area beside a small, gravel road. As it descended, Einar accepted the call.

It was Benediktsson at least. He was the board's most junior member. The signal was clear. Einar still had the board's confidence. They had to take an interest, but were interfering as little as protocol would allow.

Einar went through the motions. He explained the nature of the previous night's brushfire event, the scope of the data leak, the actions he had taken to contain the damage.

Benediktsson did express concern about the high-profile recovery operation, particularly the attack on the delivery truck. That was only what Einar expected. He didn't ask for details of Einar's plans going forward—another good sign. Einar offered the details anyway. It was possible they would be called on to suppress further actions. The man had been on the loose nearly twenty-four hours now. The area to be covered kept getting larger. Eventually it would encompass the entire country. It would be too vast for them to search.

But the man couldn't simply live forever out in the back country. Indeed, if he did, that would be fine. The data leak wasn't even a leak unless the thief could get the data out of Iceland. To get out, simply to move around the country, he still would have to pass through particular choke points. Towns and villages, roadway intersections. There simply weren't that many roads in Iceland. The farther their target tried to go, the fewer choices he would have.

Therefore, he explained to Benediktsson, he was changing his strategy. He would still be searching for his target directly from the air. But beyond that, he would identify those places the man was likely to pass through and move men there to set up a screen and wait for him.

Benediktsson expressed every confidence in him, thanked him for his tireless efforts. They went through all the elements of the ritual. But as he hung up, Einar knew he was on the clock. If he didn't bring the man down soon, the next call would come from someone higher up in the board hierarchy. Already their confidence was shaken, whether they chose to acknowledge it or not. This was the first real brushfire event in the company's history; the few petty hacker attacks that had been given the name previously didn't truly deserve it. And it had happened on his watch. While he was at the damned symphony. This had started badly and every hour it went on, it got noticeably worse.

"Four teams are inbound, sir," one of his men announced.

Einar looked up the road and saw a caravan of large, black American SUVs headed toward them. They drove in a tight line, moving fast. These were just the closest. The rest of the teams were moving up from the south. Enough for him to deploy in a wide net around the area.

He stepped down from the helicopter as the SUVs pulled up

nearby and the eight men inside got out. Einar gathered them around the helicopter. One had brought him a crisply folded black duty uniform and a pair of boots. Finally, he could get out of the ridiculous tuxedo. He ran a fingertip across a lapel; it was a total loss, he thought. Between the wear and tear of the helicopter and the diesel smoke, he doubted he'd ever get it into proper shape again. He doubted he'd be able to recover the woman he'd abandoned at Harpa either. One more thing to blame the son of a bitch for. That had been a promising relationship.

He stripped out of the tuxedo and changed into the fresh uniform as he laid out his orders. Let them see him in his underwear. What did it matter now?

"Our man has been in the countryside for most of a day now," he told them. "He's on foot. He's got only what he can carry. He's cold, he's tired, and he's hungry. We can't turn over every square meter of the country looking for him. But he has to come out of the back country at some point. And when he does, we'll be waiting for him."

He pointed at the teams, one after the other. "You're in charge of First Wing. Second Wing. Third, and Fourth. As other teams arrive from the south, divide them among yourselves. The others will report to you. You'll report directly to me. I want two teams patrolling the Ring Road on either side of Blönduós. Let's assume he's still headed for Akureyri. Otherwise, place your teams at remote intersections. I want regular checkpoints. Stop all traffic, check everything moving on the roads. Tell them you're National Police if you need to. Any remaining teams, send them down the back roads. Put the word out to farmsteads. Tell them he's a dangerous criminal, armed and on the run. Say he'll be looking to steal food, or a car, and he already killed a woman at a farm near Borgarnes. Put the fear of God in them. If some local shoots him on sight, I'll settle for that."

They spent a few more minutes working out the details. When Einar was satisfied, he sent them off. He watched the convoy of SUVs speed away on the narrow road and wondered if his plan would work. Even if it did work, was it enough to save the situation? He was improvising at this point, going way outside the scope of his job description. That description was necessarily vague, but a big part of it was protecting Datafall's assets while keeping a low profile. The fewer people who noticed the company, the better. He wasn't doing either thing very well at the moment.

He climbed back aboard the helicopter, and the pilot started up the rotors. Einar wasn't one to dwell on past mistakes. The way to fix this was to focus on the immediate goal. Stop the bastard before he got out of Iceland. As long as the data didn't make it out, they could deal with any collateral damage created in the process, like the truck driver.

He signaled to the pilot, and the helicopter sprang back into the moist, cool air. He had his net in place. Now to drive his quarry forward into it.

CHAPTER 20

Stavanger Airport, Sola Norway

The Gulfstream sat parked on a ramp in the general aviation area. Georges lay sprawled in the back of the plane with his feet up on the table, listening to music on his phone. He checked his watch. Assuming it was on schedule, the Celebrity Eclipse had sailed from Akureyri more than two hours ago. There was still no word from Crane. It was becoming harder to avoid the inescapable conclusion. Crane had missed the ship.

In his headphones, *Soul Makossa* faded out and the lilting voices of Sir Shina Peters' *Sewele* took its place. Georges noticed and smiled for a moment. It was always this way when he was nervous. He would subconsciously start to shift his playlist from the modern hip-hop he usually favored to the older afrobeat that had surrounded him when he was a boy. Peters, Manu Dibango, Amadou and Mariam, Les Têtes Brûlées. Part of him still found comfort in the remnants of his old life in Cameroon.

It had been a good life, he thought. His father had been a university administrator, his mother a French teacher. His sister, three years younger than Georges, had been breaking hearts in high school, and he'd been studying to be an engineer. He had friends, a career in the wings. It had been a very good life until his father ran afoul of Patrice Kamkuma.

Georges had heard of Patrice's son Yanis. He had a reputation around campus, but they moved in very different circles and had never met. But Patrice was a big man in the north, used to getting what he wanted. What he wanted was an unearned diploma for his lazy, entitled son. His father refused to fix it, and that was when the threats had begun.

It was a month later that his mother was attacked while his father was away in America at a conference. The whole family had fled Cameroon, and none of their lives had ever been the same again.

Rationally, Georges knew that it wasn't his fault. There was nothing he could have done. But another part of him couldn't shake the feeling that he should have been there. That he should have protected his mother. That he'd let her down.

And now he'd done it again. He didn't know how, but the spread spectrum system he'd developed to guide Crane through the mission had failed somehow. It was his system, his responsibility. And now, Crane's backup plan had apparently failed as well. He was still trapped in Iceland.

Georges switched off the music. He didn't want to be comforted right now. He wanted to make it right. He wanted to do something this time.

He pulled out the tactical map of Iceland. There was Akureyri, on the northern coast. The map showed airfields, including one at Akureyri, but he had to assume that Datafall was hunting Crane, and that meant assuming they would be watching the airports that were the most obvious way out of the country.

Except one, he realized, looking at the map. He turned around in his chair and looked forward toward the cockpit. Then he remembered the pilots weren't there. They were inside at a coffee shop, seeing no reason to stay aboard the Gulfstream while they waited. He grabbed the map and made his way to the exit door.

Georges hurried across the ramp to the diner. The pilots were seated at a table by the window. The pilot was the older one, the co-pilot the younger one, who Georges thought was Greek or maybe from the Middle East. They were chatting over coffee and pastry. Georges rushed up and slapped the map down on the table, nearly knocking over the pilot's coffee.

"Grimsey Island," he said, pointing at the map. "Can you get me there?"

"Calm down!" said the pilot. "Start at the beginning."

Georges pulled up a chair and pointed at a tiny white speck on the blue field of the sea. "Grimsey Island. It's about 40 kilometers off the coast. It's not safe to land in Akureyri, but they won't be watching there. It has an airport. We fly there. I take the ferry to the mainland and find Crane. Then we take the ferry back out and we're gone."

"Hold on," said the pilot, looking at the scale of Georges' map and the size of the island. "Hold on. That can't be much of an airport."

The co-pilot took out his phone, fired up an app, and started typing. "... s,e,y?" he asked.

Georges nodded. A moment later the co-pilot shook his head. Then he showed the screen to the pilot.

"There's a reason they won't be looking there," he said. "Because we won't be there."

"Why not?"

"He's right," said the pilot. "That's not an airport; it's a driveway. The book says they've got 3,400 feet of runway. Our takeoff distance is more than 5,000."

Georges felt himself starting to deflate. He fought it off.

"Crane's in danger. Real danger. If they catch him, he's dead. How firm is that distance?"

"It's firm!" said the co-pilot, jabbing his finger at the map. "You cannot land a Gulfstream on that thing. You could crash it, but that's not the same thing."

"I don't know," said the pilot, musing, running figures in his head.

"And you sure as hell couldn't take off again!" protested the co-pilot.

"It's at sea level," said the pilot. "Cold, dense air. Running into a headwind with a light load. We might be able to do it."

Georges turned to him. "Are you saying you'll fly me?"

"No, he isn't!" snapped the co-pilot. "I'll call Mr. Sulenski if you make me. I'm not letting you kill yourselves just because you're worried about Crane."

The pilot sighed and nodded. "Sulenski will definitely not go for it."

Georges turned and fired some side-eye at the copilot. Then a small plane taxied past on the ramp. Georges nodded to the co-pilot's phone.

"How far is it from here to Grimsey?" he asked.

The co-pilot punched in the airport codes and read off the result. "Shade over 900 miles."

"All right," said Georges. "This is an airport. There are airplanes everywhere. What can fly for 1,000 miles and take off in less than 3,400 feet?"

"Twin-engine props," said the co-pilot.

"Sure, all kinds of those," the pilot added. "Skylane will do it."

"King Air or a Baron will do it easy," said the co-pilot.

"Maybe even a Bonanza," suggested the pilot.

"Eh, you'd be cutting it awful close on the range," said the co-pilot. "You pick up a headwind..."

The pilot made a noise that acknowledged the point.

"Okay!" said Georges. "Twin engine propeller plane. Thank you. Enjoy your coffee."

He grabbed his map and set out into the larger terminal. John Crane wasn't the only one that could abuse his company credit card until it screamed.

Hang on, Crane, he thought as he stalked the corridors looking for a charter operator. I'm coming for you.

CHAPTER 21

Crane struggled along the ridge in the gloom. It was nighttime again, though that didn't mean much here. The overcast was less bright than it had been some hours ago. The land seemed timeless. There was only clammy mist and bare earth. The silence was oppressive, broken only by the sound of his footsteps and his breathing. He hadn't heard the helicopter in hours. He supposed that was a good thing, though he knew they hadn't given up.

Crane was miserable. He was cold. He'd eaten the last of his granola bars hours ago, and he was hungry. The water bottle stuffed in his pack was empty. He couldn't stay out here forever. He needed to head down into the valley and find water, a place to sleep, something to eat. According to his GPS, he was running out of ridge anyway. It was time to descend into the valley to his east where there were streams and farms.

Crane veered to his left and started down the slope.

He made his way down into actual darkness. Behind the overcast layer, the sun had descended far enough to put him in the shadow of the ridge behind him. That was a plus, but it wouldn't last. Soon enough the sun would climb higher again.

Already he felt the wind starting to pick up. Eventually the sky would clear, and the helicopter would have much better searching conditions. He needed to find someplace to get out of sight before that happened. The landscape was still horribly uncooperative. As he descended the ridge, he started to see patches of lichen and thin, scrubby bushes that kept low to the ground. There was still nothing remotely like cover.

He checked his watch again. He'd long since missed the ship in Akureyri. As he walked, he reconsidered his plan. What was the best way to get out of Iceland now? He supposed he'd have to get to an airport and charter a plane. It was a much more predictable step. The cruise ship might have taken them by surprise, but they'd be expecting him to make a play for an airport. Still, that was the option left to him. And Akureyri was still the best place to do that outside of Reykjavik itself. It was the second largest city in the country, though that didn't mean much in a place where a third of the population lived in the capital. He would be more likely to find a plane there than anywhere else. And there would be more people around. If he couldn't disappear in a crowd, at least more people would make it harder for Datafall to simply gun him down. As they'd done to August.

Crane remembered the big driver's friendly laugh, the way he'd fought to keep control of his truck as the bullets shredded the cab. Crane remembered the man in the tuxedo, too, stalking out of the glare of the helicopter's lights. His face, his blond buzz cut. The way he walked with the machine gun butted into the crook of his elbow. Crane remembered him very well indeed. His job now was to get himself and the data tap out of Iceland. But he'd make sure he crossed paths with that man again one day. Crane walked on, letting his anger and his discomfort blend into grim determination.

As the slope leveled out into the valley floor, the grass

became thicker, but there was still nothing that could hide him from an aerial search. He saw a small group of horses off in the distance and headed in their direction.

In his week in Iceland, Crane had taken several guided tours between trips to scout out the Datafall complex. They helped him learn about the country and cemented his cover as a tourist. On one tour, the guide had told Crane about the stout, long-haired Icelandic ponies. They were descended from horses the original Viking settlers brought over when they arrived a thousand years ago. They had an extra gait, whatever that meant—Crane was no horseman if he could help it. But after a thousand years of isolation here, they were a distinct breed. The guide had told him that it was forbidden to bring other horses into the country for fear the local population would be wiped out by equine diseases they had no resistance to. And if one of these horses was taken out of Iceland for any reason, it could never return.

The horses noticed his approach and kept their distance, though they didn't seem particularly afraid of him. As he suspected he would, he found a stream they'd been drinking from. He drank and refilled his bottle. It was a start. He held out a hand and clucked his tongue, but the horses weren't interested in making friends. Finally, Crane nodded to them and moved on.

Overhead the sky was growing brighter. The clouds were breaking up and shafts of sunlight broke through at low angles to illuminate patches of meadow and hillside. Crane walked for another half hour, then he stopped and listened. The helicopter was back in the air. He could hear it faintly, the sound drifting off the hills. It was far away still, but it would find him if he didn't do something soon. Crane picked up his pace.

After another half mile or so, he came upon a small stone cairn and a faint trail heading roughly parallel to the ridgeline.

He turned and followed it north. It seemed to head closer to the river in that direction. It would take him someplace, if the helicopter didn't find him first. In the meantime, he could try to pass for a hiker. It wasn't much, but he didn't have anything better. If he were wildly lucky, he might even find a real hiker or two to fall in with. They'd be looking for one man, and a group might deceive them.

He'd been walking another half hour according to his watch when he spotted the faint square outline against the dark green. It was the same color as the surrounding grass; only its linearity and ninety-degree angles made it stand out as artificial. It looked like some kind of building.

It was a sod-roofed shelter, he discovered as he came closer. The walls were hand laid and mortared stone, with heavy, weathered wooden pillars holding up the roof. It had been put out here to provide shelter for hikers caught in a storm or needing a place to camp for the night. It was perfect, Crane thought. It would be practically invisible from the air.

He went in and found a floor of bare packed earth and a fire pit with the remains of some long dead campfire. There was some graffiti on the walls. Crane noticed a heart with initials and a date four years past. For all he knew he could be the first person to come along since then. At any rate, it would do. It would do very well.

He shrugged off his pack and settled onto the bare earth floor. He'd catch some sleep here, then set out again, rested, and look for something to eat. He moved until he was as comfortable as he thought he was likely to get on the ground and tried to relax. He began to realize how exhausted he was. He hadn't slept in nearly thirty-six hours now, and he'd been on the move through rough country for most of that time. He had to sleep. The shelter would hide him from the helicopter.

A stray thought crossed his mind as he dropped into the

outer layers of sleep. There was no door. Was he safe sleeping exposed to the outside? Ah, there were no dangerous animals in Iceland. That was right. The same guide had told him. There were only six wild animal species in the whole country. What were they again? The arctic fox. The only one that was actually indigenous. Rats and mice; they'd come over on the ships along with the first Norse settlers. They were always with us. Reindeer, he remembered, introduced to provide food during a famine in the 18th century. But they were only in the east. What were the others? Certainly nothing dangerous. Mink. That was right. Someone tried to farm mink in the '80s and they got loose. They were the closest thing to a dangerous predator, the guide had told him. They would attack lambs sometimes, and you were allowed to shoot any you found on your land. What the hell was the last one? Rabbits. Pet rabbits that got out. They were starting to be seen around Reykjavik.

No problem. The minks were the worst, and Crane thought he could handle a mink if it came to that.

And then Crane didn't think anything at all. He slept deeply as the sound of the helicopter echoed softly off the hills.

CHAPTER 22

Crane dreamed of his father. They were standing at his mother's grave. Crane was somehow outside himself, watching himself as a young boy, awkward in a small, ill-fitting suit and tie. His father stood beside him, his broad shoulders slumped and his head bowed. Crane was watching the scene from behind and from far away, but he heard his father's voice as if he really were standing beside him, reaching up to lose his hand in his father's larger hand.

"Even though the actions of godly and wise people are in God's hands, no one knows whether God will show them favor," his father said. "Good people receive the same treatment as sinners, and people who make promises to God are treated like people who don't."

"What are you telling me?" he heard his child's voice ask.

"Don't go to Iceland. It doesn't matter that you're doing the right thing. You'll die there, because God doesn't care if you do right. And the world won't care that you ever lived."

"But I can't let them get away with it," Crane heard his child's voice saying. "If I don't go, I'll know."

"The living at least know they will die," said his father. "But the dead know nothing."

Crane heard something else, dimly, faintly. It sounded like pounding, someone pounding as if on the lid of a casket, and then the rising sound of his mother's screams.

"She knows she's dead," Crane said. His father had nothing to say to that.

It was a harsh voice that startled him awake.

Crane bolted upright, tactical drills flashing through his mind. Where were they? How many? Which was the biggest threat? Which should he take down first?

It was a woman's voice, he realized as his brain caught up with events. She stood in the shelter's doorway. A rangy woman, in her fifties Crane guessed. A rangy, middle-aged woman with a rifle pointed at him.

She looked down the barrel, focusing the iron sights on his chest, and said something in Icelandic.

"A minute," said Crane. He held his hands out and blinked. He listened for the helicopter but couldn't hear it. The woman wore faded jeans over a pair of boots and a Helly Hansen jacket that was unzipped to reveal a fleece sweatshirt and the untucked tail of a cotton blouse sticking out from beneath. Her hair was gray and unkempt, her skin windblown, her expression steely. A local farm woman, he concluded. And that wasn't some battered old varmint rifle she was pointing at him, but a Sako 85 Carbonlight. If she'd spent that kind of money on her gun, he assumed she took it seriously and knew how to handle it.

"Do you speak English?" he asked.

"What I said is, so you're the one they're after, then," she replied. "A foreigner. I should have known."

"I'm not armed," he said. "I don't mean any harm."

"I'll keep my rifle on you still, I think. You can push that pack over here. Ah! Use your leg."

Crane shifted around until he could get a foot against the pack and slid it slowly across the dirt floor. Then she had him stand up, turn around, take off his jacket, and run his hands across his torso and down his legs until she was convinced he didn't have a concealed pistol somewhere.

How had she gotten here, he wondered. There were no roads nearby, and a car would have awakened him. Was she out here on foot? Why? Was she specifically looking for him?

"I'm not sure why you think I'm such a threat," said Crane.

"Because the police are putting a lot of effort into hunting for you," she answered. "Now come outside with me."

She gestured toward the door with the Sako's muzzle, and Crane moved slowly outside. Maybe fifty yards away, a horse with a bridle and a light saddle contentedly chomped on the grass. So that's how she got here. Crane wondered what she was planning to do with him now that she had him.

"Haven't heard a helicopter around here for years," she said as she followed Crane outside with his pack slung over one shoulder. "The tourist operators don't fly here. They're all up in the highlands, flying over the glaciers. I figured they had to be out looking for somebody. And here you are."

"You've got it wrong," said Crane. "I'm not a fugitive from justice."

"And the helicopter?"

He considered simply denying any knowledge of it, sticking to his story that he was an innocent hiker. But she didn't seem inclined to believe that.

"They're not the police," he said at last. "They're very dangerous men. I have something they want, and they'll do whatever it takes to get it back. We're not safe out here."

The woman said nothing. She directed him where she wanted him to go with small movements of her rifle. Then she nickered softly, and her horse trotted to her. That was a handy trick, Crane thought, remembering how the wild horses had disregarded him last night. He'd never had any luck with horses.

"We'll go to Blönduós," the woman said. "The police can sort it out."

That could have been worse, Crane thought. Blönduós was where he wanted to go anyway. It was the next major town along the Ring Road. There would be people there, and cars. He couldn't let her deliver him to the police, for any number of reasons. But if she really meant to take him to Blönduós, then he could play along for the time being.

"Okay, how are we getting there?" he asked, nodding to the horse. "He doesn't look like he can carry both of us."

"Smart mouth," she muttered. "First, we'll have to find you a horse."

"You're kidding," said Crane. She climbed into the saddle and sat comfortably with the Sako across it in front of her. She pointed east, toward the river. "That way."

"I'm John Crane, by the way," he said. "What's your name?"

"Halla. Halla Manisdottir."

"Pleased to meet you Halla."

Behind him, Crane heard her laugh. "Liar."

Crane sighed and set out in the direction she indicated.

CHAPTER 23

Halla led Crane down into the lowlands where the land gave way to floodplain and the grass was thicker, sprouting in great hummocks. They traveled for the better part of an hour before Halla spotted a group of horses in the distance. She stopped and dismounted, bringing the Sako with her.

"You don't need that, you know," said Crane. "I'm not going to give you any trouble."

"I know you're not," she said. And she let the rifle's carbon fiber receiver rest on her shoulder.

"Do you ride?" she asked.

"Not well."

"These are easy. You just get on and they know what to do."

This was ridiculous, Crane thought as they moved closer to the small herd of perhaps a dozen horses. If these weren't exactly wild, they were still animals unused to human contact. What the hell did she think they were going to do?

"Come on," she called to her horse and clicked her tongue. The horse followed along like a well-trained dog.

"You really don't know how to ride?"

"The last time I tried," said Crane carefully, "it ended badly."

He didn't mention that things had ended much worse for the rider he'd collided with.

"All right, you'll ride Agnarögn," she said. "I'll get one of these."

"These are wild horses! How are we going to catch one? How are you going to break it?"

"You know about horses now?"

Fair enough, he thought. "Okay. What do you want me to do?"

"Move over there," she said, pointing. "And be friendly."

The horses saw them coming now. They looked curious, not particularly afraid. There was some snorting and whinnying going on between them and Halla's horse. Halla called out to them softly in Icelandic, as if she was calming an upset baby. The horses stood their ground as they approached.

To Crane's amazement, Halla walked up to one of the horses, a dark brown mare, and reached out and let the horse sniff at her fingertips. She kept talking to it in Icelandic and slung the rifle over her shoulder so she had both hands free. Crane watched her talk softly to the horse, stroke its neck, move beside it. The horses didn't seem at all threatened by them. Perhaps because there was nothing dangerous in this land, only people who protected them. Crane wondered if it is was normal to just walk up to one when you needed a ride, like some Icelandic bike share program. The idea seemed outrageous to him.

But then Halla was up on the horse, clutching its body with her thighs. It started and cantered a bit, but soon settled down and she steered it back around toward Crane.

"Like that," she said, and Crane detected a note of pride in her voice. "Easy. Can you manage Agnarögn with a saddle and bridle?"

Crane sighed and shook his head. "I guess so," he said. He

walked slowly toward Halla's horse, and Halla called out to her in Icelandic.

Crane stroked the horse's mane, the color of pale straw. Then he put his foot in the stirrup and hefted himself up. The horse waited patiently.

"See?" said Halla. "Not so hard."

"Her name," said Crane. "What does it mean?"

Halla smiled at him for the first time. "Tiny thing. All right, let's go. I'll still shoot you if you give me any trouble. Don't think I won't."

"Your horse likes me," Crane said, grinning despite himself.

"Pff. She's just well behaved. Let's go."

Crane nudged the horse forward, and Halla fell in beside him. Together they set off across the meadows toward the road and the river.

Their progress was slow, largely because of Crane's inexperience on a horse, but it was faster than walking. It wasn't long before Crane heard the helicopter again. It was louder this time. It must have crossed over to their side of the ridge. Crane glanced over at Halla. She'd heard it as well and was craning around on the back of her horse, looking for it.

"They're not the police," Crane said. "If you want to take me to the police, take me to people you know. At the station. In Blönduós."

Halla didn't answer. They rode on, and the clatter of the helicopter echoed off the hills.

"Who are they?" she asked some minutes later. "If that isn't the police out searching for you, who are they?"

"They work for an Internet company in Reykjavik called Datafall. That's the English name anyway. They have an Icelandic name, but I don't think I can pronounce it."

"And what is an Internet company doing out here, beating up the countryside looking for you?"

He debated for a moment how much to tell her. Keep it simple, he decided. "They're up to some things they shouldn't be," he said at last. "They're breaking the law. Breaking it badly, and they know I have proof. If it gets out, they'll be ruined. So they'll do anything to stop me from getting out of Iceland."

He glanced over and their eyes met. Hers were a steely grey and they were assessing him, weighing what he said against her judgment of him.

"If they find us out here, they'll kill us," he said. "They've already killed one man. A trucker picked me up on the Ring Road. He was taking me to Akureyri. They blew up his truck, and he was killed. Did you hear about a truck fire on the Ring Road? On the radio maybe?"

"I don't listen," she said quietly, half to herself, and Crane wondered if she meant the radio or him.

"That's how desperate they are," he went on. "They won't stop there. They'll kill you, they'll kill the police, anybody that gets in their way."

The helicopter was growing louder, he realized. Had they been spotted? Would they pass by two people on horseback, or would they land? If he thought they'd been made, Crane realized, their only chance would be for him to try to take Halla's rifle away from her.

Halla stopped her horse and looked back. The helicopter was a dot in the distance, but it was definitely heading toward them. What if she didn't believe him? If she really thought Crane was a bank robber or something, and the helicopter was a police manhunt, then she'd signal them.

"You know the police in Blönduós, don't you?" he said. "Trust them."

The horses grew nervous, especially Halla's. It stamped and sidestepped as the helicopter flew over them at a few hundred feet. Whether it was because she was trying to control the horse or because he'd introduced enough doubt to make her cautious, Halla didn't wave them down. The helicopter continued on to the north. Eventually the sound of its rotors faded. Crane let out a long breath. The wind ruffled his hair, and he watched Halla calm her jittery horse.

Eventually the horse settled. She patted its neck reassuringly, then looked over at Crane.

"So those are ruthless killers, and you're the good guy in this," she said. "That's your story?"

"Well, it's a little more complicated than that," said Crane.

She shook her head and laughed. "What a crock of shit. Come on, keep moving. The police will sort it out."

CHAPTER 24

They had to awaken Einar to take the next call. The helicopter was on the ground to refuel, and Einar needed sleep. He'd been in the air for nearly two full days now, and it was counterproductive for him and his crew to continue without rest.

They were at a tiny fuel depot in the middle of nowhere. One of the crew had refueled the helicopter and was keeping watch. Einar was asleep on the sofa in the small, battered building that served as the depot supply office. The rest of the crew had crashed wherever they could find a spot. The man on watch gently shook Einar's shoulder, showed him the phone with its screen lit up in a call. Einar was instantly awake.

He got to his feet, took the phone from the man's outstretched hand, and nodded to the couch. The other man gratefully settled onto the crumpled cushions. Einar walked outside.

"Sir," he said to the phone as he closed the door behind him. It was a crisp day, but clear. The wind was gusting, so he walked around to the lee side of the building to get out of it.

"Can you give us a status update on the brushfire?" This was

Arnason. Einar recognized the voice. That was indeed several steps up the hierarchy of the board. The signal was, as always, clear. The board was growing impatient to have this resolved.

"There've been no changes," he said. "The man is still contained in the backcountry. The data remains isolated from the outside world." That was about the best spin he could put on it.

"But not nearly as secure as we would like, Mr. Persson. What are you doing to recover the data? Your previous strategy has not succeeded."

There was no denying that, Einar thought. It was time for a shift. The board needed to hear something new, a different plan. And it was appropriate, he realized. The area the man might have reached by now had grown too large to effectively search with a single helicopter. He wasn't going to find him that way. It was time for a zone defense.

"The intruder has managed to evade our air search," he said. "Therefore, I am ceasing flight operations."

"Good," said Arnason. "They're beginning to draw unwelcome attention."

"Our data is safe as long as the man remains in Iceland."

"Not exactly. Our data is isolated only as long as the man remains out of communication."

"Correct," said Einar. "I assume the signals team is prepared to intercept any efforts to transmit the data. But I don't believe he'll make such an attempt. The plan was to recover the recording device and physically carry it out of the country. That plan failed, and we disrupted his escape. I don't believe he has access to a communication link that would suffice. Certainly not in the remote countryside where he is."

"Perhaps," said Arnason. But he didn't sound particularly mollified.

"Our new strategy will be to screen the towns and roads. Whether he wants to leave the country himself or make a broadband connection, he must reach a more developed area. That leaves him very few choices. We have resources in Reykjavik. But I still think he's making for Akureyri. I'm headed there to intercept him. My other teams are sweeping the farms and watching major intersections."

"Very well, Persson. The board agrees with your analysis. Keep your men on the roads and set your trap in Akureyri. We will expect regular updates."

"Of course, sir."

And then Arnason was gone. Einar swore and put the phone back in his pocket. The cool wind whipped around the corners of the building and whistled in the eaves. In the distance he could just make out a silver semi trailer moving along the Ring Road the better part of a kilometer away. Between them lay nothing but broken ground and sparse grassland.

Where the hell was the man managing to hide himself?

It didn't matter now. Einar's new plan was sound. There were only so many ways to move in the countryside. He had men patrolling the few road junctions, checking the remote farms. If the intruder somehow made it past them, he would head for Akureyri, and Einar himself would be waiting there for him.

It would work. It had to work. His own personal stakes were growing with each passing hour. He didn't want to think about what would happen to him if he allowed a data breach of this scope on his watch. It wouldn't be good.

Einar made his way back around the building. The helicopter sat waiting beside the fuel tanks, sleek, ominous, gleaming in the sun. Iceland was a small country. Einar could be in Akureyri within an hour if he left now. If his men located the intruder out here somewhere, he could be back on the scene just as quickly. Between the helicopter and the SUVs, his team had the advantage of mobility.

It was just a question of where the man would turn up. He couldn't stay out there forever.

CHAPTER 25

They rode for an hour or more. Crane had nothing to say, and Halla kept her thoughts to herself. They rode through grassland spattered with pale brown and green. The terrain rolled gently. Sometimes they would pass small stands of brush or a lone sapling. Crane could see mountains in the distance—dark, craggy shapes streaked with snow.

The fence was the first human thing he saw. A line of weathered wooden posts strung with rust-colored wire. It looked like it could have been there for decades. There was no obvious indication of why this particular land was fenced off. Beyond it, the terrain rose gently to a low crest. Crane assumed there must be a farmstead on the other side. Halla turned them to the right, and Crane spotted a metal gate.

"Your place?" Crane asked.

"My friend Mori," said Halla. "His sheep graze here. He has a Land Rover."

Crane nodded. Halla was nothing if not simply spoken. She slid down off the wild horse and patted it affectionately. It nickered happily and wandered off to a nearby hummock of grass.

Halla gestured for Crane to dismount as well. He did, feeling odd twinges in muscles he was unaccustomed to using.

Halla took Agnarögn's reins and led her through the gate. When Crane was through, she closed it behind them, and they walked up the slope. From the top, Mori's farm was laid out below them. Crane saw a group of low buildings around a gravel driveway that led out to the road. A few dozen sheep wandered along the fence near the driveway, and a tractor sat parked outside the barn. The small river he'd seen on his map wove a sinuous path down the far side of the road. Crane saw the Land Rover Halla had spoken of. It was an antique. The black Chevy Suburban parked in front of the house, however, was not. It had tinted windows and a deeply polished finish that gleamed in the sunlight. Crane looked for people but saw none.

Halla had stopped cold. Crane put a hand on her arm and murmured, "down." She nodded and led Agnarögn back down the slope until they couldn't see the house any longer.

"Your friend has company," said Crane. "That doesn't look like one of the locals."

Halla said nothing. She was looking at Crane.

"That's not what the police drive around here either, is it?"

"It is not."

There would be two of them, Crane guessed. They would be inside with the owner, asking if he'd seen anything. Strangers moving across the land. Signs someone had been prowling around his farm. They probably had a story about some horrible thing he'd done.

"Does your friend live alone?" he asked.

Halla nodded.

"He'll be okay. He doesn't know anything. If we stay out of sight, they'll figure that out and they'll leave. If they do find us somehow, you hand me over, do you hear me? You pretend to believe whatever they tell you, and you let them take me."

Halla looked shaken for the first time since he'd met her.

Crane moved back up the slope in a low crouch until he could just see the edge of the house and the cement walk out to the driveway where the Suburban was parked. He lay down on the ground and watched. A moment later Halla appeared and lay beside him with her rifle. Neither spoke. The sheep moved along the edge of a pasture in front of the house. The wind rustled through the grass.

Nothing happened for perhaps five minutes. Then Crane heard the front door open. Two men in black Datafall uniforms walked out to the Suburban. It beeped as one of them unlocked the doors with the key fob. They didn't appear to be armed, but Crane knew they would have weapons in ready reach. He glanced over at Halla, but couldn't tell what she was thinking.

They got in, and the Suburban pulled back out to the road and was gone.

"Come on," Halla ordered. She was back in control again, moving him down the slope toward the farmhouse with small motions of the Sako's muzzle.

They stepped up onto the porch and Halla knocked. There was no answer.

"Mori!" she shouted as she rapped at the door again. Then something in Icelandic.

A moment later, the door opened, and an older man in jeans and a battered brown sweater hurried them inside and quickly closed the door. They held a hurried conversation in Icelandic as Crane looked around. They were in a rather threadbare sitting room with a wooden floor, mismatched furniture, and walls painted a pale robin's egg blue. Old family photographs looked sternly down at Crane from the walls—craggy-faced old women, and men with enormous white beards dressed in hand-sewn black suits. Through a doorway, Crane could see into the kitchen where a teapot was starting to whistle.

They were talking about him, obviously, both of them pointing at him from time to time, looking over at him as if he was about to explode.

"Did you kill a woman at a farm?" Halla said at last, in an accusing voice. "For food?"

So that was the role they'd chosen for him, the dangerous wanderer who would steal from you and kill you if you confronted him. He sighed and shook his head.

"I did not," he said. "That is a lie." He kept his words simple to be as unambiguous as possible.

"I didn't believe them," the man said. "They wanted me to think they were National Police. They didn't say it, but that's what they wanted me to think. But I knew better. They were not good men. I felt this. I am Mori," he added, offering Crane his hand.

Crane shook his hand. "You're a good judge of people, Mori," Crane said, with a snarky glance toward Halla. "What was it about them that set off your instincts? What did they do?"

"I am making tea for my lunch when they drove up," Mori said. "They were very..." he searched for a word, finally saying, "dónalegur."

"Rude," said Halla.

"Yes, that's the word," Mori said. "I told them no one was here, but I thought they would search the house. Who are these men?"

"He says they are a company from the city," Halla said. "Doing something bad, and he can prove it."

"It's right there in my pack," Crane said, with a nod. "If you want to see what they're so upset about."

Halla and Mori traded a look, then Halla opened the pack.

"Wrapped in the black cloth," Crane offered.

Halla unwrapped it. They studied the small box epoxied to a

broken piece of circuit board, copper traces ending abruptly at the edge.

"What is it?" Mori finally asked in confusion.

Crane smiled. "It's like a thumb drive."

Mori nodded. He'd heard of those at least.

"The data on there proves they've been working on a system for breaking electronic locks. For reading people's email. Getting into bank accounts. If that thing makes it out of the country, they're finished."

Halla and Mori looked at each other again. Crane could see them trying to decide whether they believed him. It was just a hunk of plastic, after all. He couldn't really prove it was what he said it was.

"This is for the police," Mori said at last.

"That's where we were going," said Halla. "I came for the Land Rover."

Mori nodded and fished a set of keys out of his pocket. "You'll need more gas for Blönduós," he said, handing Halla the keys. "Tank in the small barn," he added. "Just got it filled last week."

Halla nodded. "Keep an eye on him." She set the rifle and Crane's pack down on a chair and went out. Mori watched her leave, then turned to Crane.

"Have a seat, John," he said. "I'm missing my tea."

Crane sat down and studied the sparse, bachelor decor of the place while Mori puttered in the kitchen. He came back a few moments later with two cups of tea. Crane took his with a grateful nod.

"You know you just left me alone in here with the gun, right?"

"Pff," Mori snorted. "You're not going to shoot me. Halla, she..." He nodded toward the outside. "She's just that way."

Crane sipped his tea. "What's her story?"

"She lives on her father's old farm back in the hills," said Mori. "With that horse and some sheep. She's half wild. Always has been. I used to joke her mother went out walking one night and met an elf on the trail, and that's where she came from."

Crane grinned. "You and her..." he said with a conspiratorial tone.

Mori waved him off. "Bah. The times I asked her to marry me. But she never would. When she has to go to town, she comes for the truck. And sometimes, when the winds are harsh..."

Crane heard Halla stomping back up the porch steps. He nodded to Mori. "I won't let anything happen to her."

Mori nodded thanks, and Crane got up, picked up the pack and the Sako. The door opened and Halla's eyes widened when she saw Crane with the gun. But then he handed her the rifle and shrugged his pack over one shoulder.

"We need to move," he said. "Mori, thank you for the tea. It's just what I needed."

Mori watched them from the door as they climbed into the ancient Land Rover and rattled off down the drive. Crane still saw him, a silhouette in the doorway, as they turned onto the main road and headed north.

CHAPTER 26

Georges found the woman running a shoestring charter operation at the far edge of the private aviation area. She spoke no English, and Georges certainly spoke no Norwegian. But she had a smattering of French, and so Georges was able to convey the idea that he needed to get to Grimsey immediately. In turn, she managed to get across that her name was Marit, and that she had a twin-engine Baron G58 that wasn't doing anything to help pay for itself for the foreseeable future.

In the end, money proved the universal language. Georges suspected he had hugely overpaid, even for a zero-notice international charter. But that was what Josh's ridiculous wealth was for.

They flew west into a sun that never truly set, over the dark void of the sea below. Georges sat up front, alongside Marit, with his bag of tricks in his lap. He had assembled what seemed useful from the things he'd brought to Iceland: a tricked-out laptop, a couple programmable radio transceivers, a smartphone that he'd jailbroken and tweaked with some custom apps, a pocket tool kit. At the last moment, he'd added an old Gerber

Mark I boot knife he'd found in a toolbox aboard the Gulfstream. He hoped he wouldn't find a use for it.

It was a long flight, with little to do besides stare out at the endless water and wonder if he'd made a terrible mistake. He knew nothing about Marit or her airplane. Perhaps she'd never flown over open water before. Perhaps she'd taken a job she was completely unqualified to do out of raw financial desperation. How would he know? He imagined them flying around the North Atlantic, searching in vain for Iceland until they ran out of fuel and simply vanished.

But in truth, he knew it was what could be waiting on the ground that had him imagining vague terrors. He was the one rushing into danger that he wasn't really prepared for. He had no idea what he would find in Akureyri. Perhaps nothing at all. It was possible that they'd long since found Crane. He could be lying dead in the highlands someplace right now, waiting for hikers to discover his bones in another twenty years.

No, Georges told himself. He imagined the voice of a math teacher who had terrified him as a boy. He's alive and he needs your help. You will find him and bring him out. Be a man. Go and do it now.

"Islande," Marit said suddenly. Iceland. She pointed off to the left, and Georges could just make out a dark line of land riding on the sea. Georges clutched his bag and smiled at her. She'd gotten him this far, at least.

"Île Grimsey?" he asked.

She shrugged. "Une demi-heure."

Eventually the plane began to descend, and Georges saw the island ahead. Grimsey was a bare, windswept plateau of deep green grass and sheer gray cliffs in the middle of the ocean. Seeing it, he wasn't surprised the Gulfstream couldn't take him there. The island was tiny. The airstrip—3,400 feet long, the pilot had said—appeared to run almost the entire length of the western coast.

Georges didn't see a single tree. The whole island seemed bare. It was flat and tilted slightly so something dropped would roll west, cross the airstrip, and eventually end up in the sea. There was a lighthouse and a village of perhaps two dozen buildings at one end of the island. What kind of people chose to live in a place like this, he wondered. What the hell was he getting himself into?

The Baron hit the runway and rolled down to taxi speed with plenty of room to spare. He was here. Marit taxied back to the "terminal" end of the airstrip, where there was a low, gray, nearly windowless building and a metal frame tower holding a pair of dish-shaped microwave antennas.

There didn't seem to be anyone to direct them, so Marit found a spot off to the side, where a pair of small planes were already tied down and covered in tarps, and slid in beside them.

The wind off the sea was brisk as they climbed out of the plane. It whipped the sides of Georges' jacket away from his body, so he zipped it up and jammed his hands in his pockets. He wasn't well prepared for the climate here, he thought. He wasn't really prepared for any of this. He would have to improvise, the way Crane did. He took his bag from the cockpit and slung it over his shoulder.

"Well, you're here," said Marit in her spotty French. She seemed dubious that anyone needed to get to a place like this with the urgency Georges had claimed.

"I'll take the ferry to the mainland and find my friend," he answered. "We'll be back as soon as we can. You'll wait, right?"

She looked around at the village and shrugged. "They must have a bar here someplace."

They walked toward the town together. A woman on a bicycle appeared as they reached the end of the main street. So the place wasn't abandoned at least. A sudden thought struck Georges.

"If my friend comes back alone, you'll take him back to Stavanger, yes? His name is John Crane. He's white, maybe 30, tall with dark hair."

She looked at him for a long moment, as if unsure she'd understood.

"Are you going to be okay?" she asked eventually. "Are you in trouble?"

He nodded. "I'll be fine. Just... just if he comes back without me..."

They found a restaurant with a bar toward the middle of one of the village's two parallel streets and stopped out front. Marit looked at him, worried. "I can fly to Akureyri," she said.

"No," Georges shook his head. "It's better you stay here. We'll be back."

She nodded. "Good luck," she said. Then Georges hitched his bag up on his shoulder and headed off toward the small harbor and the ferry terminal.

CHAPTER 27

Halla drove along the narrow road by the river. The Land Rover rattled and squeaked. It was long past due for a suspension overhaul if nothing else, Crane thought. He sat in the cracked and scuffed passenger seat and watched the landscape roll by. They passed an occasional farm, but even those were sparse here.

"How far to Blönduós?" he asked after a long silence.

"Half an hour, maybe a little more," said Halla. Then she fell silent again. Crane could see her grappling with uncomfortable thoughts.

Half an hour to Blönduós and the police. He needed a solid plan before then. For all his claims of innocence, he really didn't want to trust his fate to the Icelandic police. He was an outsider here. And he had in fact broken into Datafall's facility, done a significant amount of damage, assaulted several people, and stolen their property. His side of the story wouldn't look especially good to a police officer. If it even got that far. Crane had no idea what level of influence Datafall would have over a small-town police department, but it was entirely possible that they'd place a couple calls up the chain of command and be told to hand Crane over to them.

So letting Halla take him to the police wasn't really an option. But that left the question of how he was going to stop her. He certainly wasn't going to attack her. It might come to taking the Sako away from her and locking her up someplace. But of course that would just convince her that he was exactly the dangerous criminal that Datafall's people were painting him as.

He still didn't have an answer he was happy with when he noticed Halla slowing. He looked up and realized the Land Rover was negotiating a curve at the top of a low rise. The road descended in a gentle sweep past a farm driveway and swept behind another low rise where the river curved in a lazy oxbow to the left. Beyond that, it intersected with another rural road, and at that intersection were two trucks. One was another of Datafall's black Suburbans. The other was an aged Toyota 4Runner that obviously belonged to one of the local farmers. The Suburban was blocking the road, while the Toyota had pulled off and parked on the shoulder.

Halla was braking, looking at the trucks with concern. Crane noted two black-clad figures in the road. At least one carried an automatic weapon.

"Don't stop," he said. "You're visible. Turn into the driveway."

"That's Gunnar Steinsson's truck," she said. "What is going on here? It's like an invasion."

She pulled into the driveway and drove toward the farmhouse.

They were stopping and searching vehicles. It was a logical strategy, Crane thought. They'd lost track of him, so they threw up a net designed to contain him. Iceland's limited road network was perfect for it. There were only so many ways he could go.

"What are we doing here?" Halla said as they pulled up in front of the farmhouse. There were no other vehicles around. It looked like nobody was home. Crane peered out the back windows, and decided they weren't visible from the intersection here.

"We're deciding what to do," said Crane. "They should have searched Gunnar's truck and let him go when they saw I wasn't in it."

Halla grinned. "Oh, Gunnar won't have stood by for that."

Crane shook his head. "Well let's hope he hasn't gotten himself killed."

She looked at him in frank disbelief. "They wouldn't."

"They already have, I told you. We need to find out if your friend's okay and help him. Do you understand me?"

She nodded.

"All right, they've seen the Land Rover. They were at Mori's place, so they've seen it before. They know it doesn't belong here."

They could pull out and head back the way they came. That might make sense to the watchers on the road. Mori had come to see whoever lived here and was now going back home. But it got Crane no closer to escaping the country, and it didn't help this Gunnar Steinsson. Crane didn't know what he'd done to get himself in trouble with Datafall's people, but now they'd effectively kidnapped a local. Crane had seen that they wouldn't hesitate to kill an innocent if necessary to cover up other crimes.

"Drive back out and head to the intersection. When we pass behind that embankment, I'm going to bail out. You drive up slow, you keep them busy. What are you doing here, who do you think you are—just keep them distracted. I'll circle around behind them and see if I can find your friend."

"Or you could just run away and leave us to them," she said.

"No, I can't. They're out here because I stirred them up. They're my mess. Now let's go."

Crane tossed his pack into the back seat and slid down into the foot well.

Halla considered him for a long moment. Then she put the Land Rover noisily into gear and threw it into a three-point turn.

She drove out to the end of the driveway and stopped, as if looking for oncoming traffic. But she was looking down the slope to the pair of trucks. Crane could tell the men guarding the intersection had spotted them. In his mind he kept an image of the road down to the checkpoint at the intersection. He visualized the sweeping curve, the point where they'd be briefly invisible to the armed team, the route down into the river channel.

"John Crane," Halla said, her voice suddenly thick. He looked up and saw her turning to reach into the back seat. She came back holding the Sako and thrust it at him, stock first. "If you play me false, I swear…"

Crane nodded and took the rifle. Then Halla pulled out and drove slowly down the hillside toward the waiting Datafall team.

CHAPTER 28

As they rolled around the curve, Halla hit the brake and slowed to a fast walk.

"Now," she hissed.

Crane opened the door. As he swung out of the Land Rover, he looked back and met her eyes. He saw the fear in them, the hope she wasn't making a mistake by trusting him. Then he hit the pavement, ran a few steps to keep his balance, and dashed for the side of the road. Behind him, the door swung shut again, and Halla hit the gas. The Land Rover sputtered a bit and disappeared around the curve.

Crane crawled over the bank and dropped down into the river channel, landing at the edge of the water. The river looked cold and impossibly pure. He leaned back against the bank and checked the Sako. Halla had taken good care of it. There were five rounds in the magazine. The rifle's carbon fiber stock made it surprisingly light. Crane held it in one hand and made his way down the water's edge.

The river was calm here but quick, fed by dozens of small streams that tumbled down the steep slopes of the valley. Crane walked on bare earth, and occasionally had to wade into the water. It was as cold as he expected. He wished he could hear what was going on up on the road, but the rushing water was like white noise, drowning more distant sounds.

Crane followed the river around a sweeping curve until he was sure he was past the Datafall checkpoint. The steep bank formed a natural rampart. He stood and his eyes were more or less at ground level. He was about thirty yards past the trucks, he realized. The farmer's 4Runner was closest to him, facing him on the other side of the road. The Suburban was farther up and facing away from him.

Halla had stopped her Land Rover several yards from the roadblock and let them come to her. She was still in the driver's seat talking with one of them. That one had only a pistol on his belt. The other one held an MP5 and stood in the middle of the road several yards back. The submachine gun wasn't exactly pointed at her, but it was ready for use, and the man's stance and the way he held the gun sent a clear message.

Halla and the man at her window were arguing in Icelandic, and the one with the gun was watching them closely. Crane quietly lay the rifle down on the bank and pulled himself up. He rolled up over the edge and lay on the ground. From here he had a clear field of fire, but he really didn't want to shoot these men if it could be avoided. He wanted Halla's help, and even though she'd given him the rifle, slaughtering two men was unlikely to ease her fears. If he wounded one or both of them, he couldn't simply leave them here to die. They'd have to summon medical help at that point, which meant police and a lot of difficult questions.

All of which meant the rifle wasn't nearly as much of an asset as it might have been.

In the meantime, Halla was getting angrier in the driver's

seat of the Land Rover. She was giving him a distraction, and he needed to make the most of it. They needed to figure out what had happened to her friend who owned the Toyota. Crane got to his feet and dashed across the road behind the two guards. There he hit the dirt again and crawled as quickly as he could toward the roadblock until the 4Runner's body hid him.

He heard the Land Rover's rattling old engine sputter a few times and stop. Then the door creaked open. He rose up to peer over the Toyota's hood. Halla was out on the road beside the Land Rover now. He couldn't understand either of them, but the tone was growing more tense. The one with the SMG was focused on them.

Crane edged back along the far side of the Toyota. It was well used. Like the Land Rover, the front seats were cracked. There was a coffee-stained plastic travel mug on the dash, and what looked like a day's mail on the passenger seat.

He crept a few more steps until he could see into the back. The rear seats held only a well-used dog blanket. But in the back of the 4Runner, curled up among a set of jumper cables, a plastic bucket, and various other supplies, was a very angry looking farmer. His wrists were secured behind his back with zip ties. They'd secured his ankles as well, meaning they'd either done this to him in the back of the truck, or they'd had to pick him up and throw him back there. His mouth was covered in his own duct tape.

The man—Gunnar, Crane remembered—looked up at Crane in fear. Crane tried to look reassuring and put a finger to his lips. Gunnar furiously cocked his head in the direction of the Land Rover and the Datafall team. He could hear Halla arguing, and if he was her friend, he probably knew her disposition and where things were likely to lead.

Crane nodded and sank back down out of sight. Off this side of the road was an old stone sheep sorting pen. Crane scrambled off the road and rolled over the top of the wall. Here he had better cover. He moved back until he had a better view of the Datafall men between the two vehicles.

It didn't take Halla long to irritate them. Suddenly the one talking to her stepped back and drew his pistol. He started barking orders in Icelandic. The other one slung his submachine gun over his shoulder and pulled a handful of zip ties off his belt. Perfect.

Crane rechecked the rifle as they walked Halla back to the Suburban. One held the pistol on her while the other opened the back door. Apparently, the plan was to put her in the car while they moved the Land Rover off the road.

Crane sighted down the Sako's barrel and pulled the trigger. The rifle cracked and the window of the Suburban's open rear door exploded into glittering fragments of safety glass.

All three of them flinched. The one with the pistol whirled, looking for the shooter. The one with the SMG fumbled his handful of zip ties and scrabbled to get the gun off his shoulder. Crane worked the bolt to chamber another round and fired again. This time he blew out the front side window and spider webbed the windshield.

"That's enough!" he shouted. "Next one goes down the middle."

The one struggling with his slung SMG immediately stopped and put his hands out to his sides. The other one, with the drawn pistol, started to move toward Halla. Crane stood and pointed the Sako at him.

"Stop!" he shouted.

The man considered his chances for a moment. Then he swore in Icelandic—at least Crane assumed that from the tone —and let the gun dangle in his hand. Halla took it from him and backed several steps away. She covered the pair with the pistol while Crane climbed out of the sheep pen and approached.

"Gunnar?" Halla said.

"In back," Crane said, cocking his head toward the 4Runner. "He's okay, but he looks pretty pissed off."

"I bet he does," she said with a laugh.

Once they'd disarmed and searched both men, they trussed them up in the back of the Suburban with their own zip ties. Crane pulled the Suburban off onto the shoulder while Halla freed Gunnar.

They had a quick conversation in Icelandic, then Gunnar turned to Crane and switched to thickly accented English.

"What in God's name is happening?" he asked. "Thank you. I am Gunnar."

"They were looking for me, I'm afraid," said Crane.

"This I know!" Gunnar said pacing around, waving his hands in agitation and rubbing his forearms to get the circulation moving again. "They asked all about a foreign man. Had I seen him? Was anything gone from my farm? Then they want to search my truck! I don't care for this. Strangers with guns telling me to get out, telling me what to do. I don't put up with this."

He gave Crane a sheepish glance. "But you see how that ended up. Thank you for saving me."

"I'm glad to help," said Crane. "I'm just sorry I got them so stirred up. They're criminals, and I have proof of their crimes. That's why they're so desperate to find me."

Gunnar glanced at Halla, perhaps wondering if she believed this.

"Gunnar, do you have your mobile?" she asked.

"Yes, yes. Of course."

"Call Matti. Tell him I'm going to the airfield, and he should meet us there. I need him to fly this man to Akureyri."

They made sure Gunnar was recovered, then said their goodbyes. When they were back in the Land Rover, heading toward Blönduós, Crane asked Halla, "Do you actually believe me now?"

She glanced over at him. "These men chasing you are bad men for certain," said Halla. "I don't know what you are, John Crane. But you said one thing that is true. The sooner you are gone, the safer everyone will be."

CHAPTER 29

Akureyri Airport

Einar swore under his breath. His team's secure handsets weren't working here. Akureyri might be the second largest city in Iceland, but that wasn't saying much. It was a provincial town of fewer than 20,000 people clustered at the end of the country's longest fjord, where open water gave way to marshy river delta. Datafall had never operated here.

He'd been at the outer fringes of the company's private encrypted radio network before. Here, Einar had nothing. No radio network. No waiting Suburbans full of security men. No support at all. He was undermanned and unequipped. The stranger had managed to strip away most of his advantages and level the playing field.

Einar strode around the helicopter and surveyed the airport. There was a single runway, built on landfill extending out into the fjord. There were no gates or jetways. The planes pulled up, and passengers walked to and from the terminal. Air Iceland provided ground handling and there was a maintenance company, a small flight school, a coffee and sandwich shop, and four car rental companies inside the terminal. An arc of old airplanes sat at the far edge of the field surrounding a large hangar called the Icelandic Aviation Museum. That was more or less what there was. It didn't give Einar much to work with.

He had two of his security men, and he had the helicopter's two-man flight crew, though they weren't trained soldiers. The two security men, Nils and Rikard, were the ones who'd come to find him in Harpa. Einar thought back to the music, the scent of the woman at his side. That seemed like a lifetime ago now. Einar had been enjoying the fruits of his position that night, a position he'd put much time and energy into building. Now, that all hung by a thread. Even if he stopped the intruder here and recovered the data, his reputation with the board had taken a major hit. It would take him a long time to rebuild what this man had cost him. He would start repairing his reputation by killing the thief. Slowly, so he could find out all there was to know about who he was and why he had come.

Einar gathered his men near the helicopter and laid out his battle strategy. Without coverage for their radios, they'd have to communicate over the public network using personal mobiles. "Be careful what you say," he told them. "Open channel protocols."

He sent the helicopter's aircrew into the town itself, about three kilometers away, and told them to simply watch the streets. They weren't prepared for this. They'd just get in the way or, more likely given the target's abilities, get themselves killed and cause him even more trouble with the Board of Directors. He'd considered whether to issue them pistols from the helicopter's weapons locker, but ultimately decided that wouldn't help. More eyes on the battlefield was the best he could hope for from them. If he was lucky, one of them would spot the target coming into town and provide some warning.

Einar and his two men would patrol the airport itself. Reaching Akureyri gained the man nothing. If he wanted to get out of the country, he'd have to come to the airport. This was where they'd take him.

The briefing trailed off as Einar realized there wasn't much more he could say. Einar was a strategist, and strategy was about the most effective use of your resources. He simply didn't have very many resources anymore. From here, the battle would come down to his personal skills and instincts and those of his men. He could tell they sensed his mood. This had shaken their confidence in him, too. He'd been an almost mythic figure to them, but now the stranger had bloodied his nose and shown that it could be done.

His only possible response was to fall back on his most basic leadership skills. Project confidence, assume orders will be obeyed without question. Remain calm and assured. Keep the nagging uncertainty and fear of what the worst case could mean well out of sight.

"That's it, then," he told them. "Everyone to your patrol areas. Text me every fifteen minutes."

They hurried off, and Einar watched them leave. They were playing defense now, protecting their goal here at the airport. To get out of Iceland, the stranger would have to get past him. And Einar was prepared to do whatever it took to make sure that didn't happen.

CHAPTER 30

The ferry took Georges to a tiny village on Iceland's northern coast called Dalvik, and from there he caught a bus to Akureyri. Georges suspected they wouldn't have time for all that on the way back out. He made his way to the small harbor and walked along the waterfront, looking for boats. He checked all the piers, talked with anybody with a boat that looked remotely seaworthy, and let Josh's money speak clearly.

Eventually he found a Captain with a fishing boat. His crew had already brought in the day's haul and gone home, but the Captain could operate the boat alone, and for a price he was willing to take them to Grimsey. It was a pretty significant price, and Georges was pretty sure that, once again, he was being taken advantage of. But that was the position he was in, and Josh could afford it.

With the boat settled, he walked around the small town, getting a sense of the place. He tried to work out where Crane might go and how he would get there.

The huge cruise ship pier at the far end of the harbor was empty, and there was no activity around it to suggest another ship would be docking soon. It had to be the airport. Georges circled around the small central shopping district, then walked out toward the airport. There was no mistaking it. The runway was built well out into the water on a long spit of landfill. A road led out of town along the water's edge. Eventually it split, one fork running across the fjord on a causeway, the other continuing on to the airport itself.

As he walked down the approach road toward the parking lots and the small terminal, Georges didn't see much activity. A few people moved around outside. A pair of cab drivers leaned against a fender and gossiped. A car drove past him and headed into the parking lot. It was quiet. He saw some chain link fencing, but no more serious security.

Inside, the terminal was quiet as well. There were ticketing desks, car rental counters, a place to get coffee and sandwiches. But there were very few people. In some ways that was good, Georges thought. It would be easier to spot Crane if he showed up. On the other hand, it was easier to spot him as well. He hadn't seen another black person since he'd landed. It wasn't as if people were pointing and staring, but he'd be remembered if the police started asking questions.

Then Georges suddenly wheeled and walked into the coffee shop. He'd seen a man in uniform at the far end of the concourse—the black tactical uniform the Datafall men had worn at their supercomputing facility. It was as he'd feared. They were here.

Georges hovered over a rack of snack food and pretended to read labels. The guard glanced into the shop and suddenly stopped. Georges started to panic, then realized he'd heard a faint smartphone alert tone. The man took out his phone and checked the screen, then put it away and walked on.

When he had passed, Georges bought a pack of chocolates

and headed down the concourse in the opposite direction. He found a door and walked outside. He walked confidently, as if he belonged there, and eventually found his way onto the tarmac. Small planes and a helicopter were parked in a row near a strip of grass and a fence. A truck passed by on the road to his right. Somewhere a horn sounded. Now that he was here, Georges wasn't sure what to do.

Then the helicopter's side door opened, and Georges felt another rush of adrenaline hit. A tall man with a bright blond crew cut stepped down onto the tarmac and hurried toward the main terminal. There was no mistaking the Datafall uniform. So the helicopter was theirs, Georges thought. That wasn't good. It made them more capable; it made them more dangerous.

The man stopped partway across the tarmac to check his phone, then dictated a message and tapped the screen. He'd seen their people twice now, Georges realized, and each time they'd been sending text messages. Was that how they were communicating? If so, he could do something about that. But first things first.

Georges strolled down the row of aircraft. As far as he could tell, there was no one else aboard the Datafall helicopter. He moved around behind it and found what looked like an electrical access panel. He took a screwdriver from his pack and got to work. The panel came off to reveal a bank of fuses, and Georges began pulling them. He wished he knew more about helicopters. It was entirely possible he was just shutting down the running lights. But he hoped he was disabling the helicopter, locking it down so Datafall's people couldn't use it to pursue them.

His heart was pounding, and he was sweating profusely despite the cool temperature. He was terrified. He was totally exposed out here. All it would take was one person looking in the right direction to notice someone tampering with an aircraft. Memories started flooding back, of Cameroon, of nights huddled in his bed wondering if there would be a knock at the door or a Molotov through the window. Memories of his mother laying bandaged in her hospital bed. He fought them down and kept working. There was nothing he could do about what happened in Cameroon, nothing he could have done then. He was powerless. But here, now, he had the power to do something. Georges clung to that. He pulled another fuse and stuck it in his pocket with the others. He was still terrified, but he also felt stronger.

When all the fuses were removed, he screwed the panel back in place and walked away, forcing himself not to run. Hopefully the helicopter was now grounded, and he'd denied them mobility. Now, on to their communications.

He walked back into the concourse and found the passenger waiting area. There were rows of metal-framed seats padded in vinyl. A few bored passengers were scattered around, waiting for domestic flights. It was the best cover he was likely to get.

Georges took a seat and took his laptop out of his pack. He plugged in a radio module he'd tweaked to operate on frequencies that weren't entirely legal for unlicensed civilian use and began sniffing for local cell coverage. He quickly picked up a cell belonging to Siminn, the local carrier, and began the methodical process of working out its protocols and gaining access.

It took about twenty minutes, but the time seemed to fly. He was on familiar ground now. He knew what he was doing. A light popped up on his interface, and he was into the cell's SMS buffer. He started downloading recent messages and set up a script to run them through Google Translate to turn them into passable English.

Twice, the same Datafall guard he'd seen outside the coffee

shop wandered through the area without paying attention to Georges at all. He felt like he was accomplishing useful things, but he didn't know how long he could keep doing this before someone noticed he was just hanging around the airport for no apparent reason. He hoped Crane would turn up soon.

CHAPTER 31

At a little before three in the afternoon, a Cessna Skyhawk made its approach and touched down on Akureyri's single runway. It didn't brake immediately but continued moving at speed down the runway until it had passed the taxiway turnoff leading to the terminal and hangar areas. Then it gradually slowed, going all the way to the far end of the runway before turning around and taxiing back.

It had been a quiet flight for John Crane. The pilot spoke very little English, but Halla had explained everything to him at Blönduós in considerable detail.

"Ready," said the pilot. "Ready." And he frantically waved one hand at Crane. Crane nodded, hefted his pack over one shoulder and moved up against the passenger side cockpit door.

"Thank you," he said.

The pilot waved his hand at him again and grinned. "Yah, yah," he said. "Halla."

Crane grinned back. He was getting the impression that Halla had a way of suddenly turning up in her friends' lives with strange requests. Lend me your truck. Fly this stranger to Akureyri. And he gathered they'd long since learned there was no sense arguing with her. They just dropped what they were doing and did it.

"Halla," Crane answered. Then the pilot reached the end of the runway and turned the plane around. At the right moment, when the plane was hardly moving and was best positioned to hide him from the terminal, Crane opened the door and leapt out onto the tarmac.

He landed on his feet and sprinted as his momentum carried him the last few yards to the edge of the runway. He half ran, half slid down the steep, grassy bank to the edge of the water. Behind him he heard the drone of the Skyhawk's engine as it taxied back toward the terminal. He had made it to Akureyri.

The runway had been extended out into the water on landfill. Crane stood on a narrow margin of algae-covered rocks, hidden by the steep bank. He might be visible from the tower if someone was looking carefully for a man along the edge of the runway apron, but he couldn't be seen from the ground. He carefully picked his way along the rocks at the water's edge until he reached land and then made his way across a marshy flat to a sidewalk beside what looked like the employee parking lot. The main terminal buildings were ahead of him.

Anyone here would have seen the plane landing, of course. He had to assume they were looking for him. Crane kept moving. Somewhere around here was an airplane that could make Scandinavia or Greenland. Crane just had to find it, and either charter it or steal it. Before the Datafall men he was sure were here somewhere found him.

———

Einar realized something was odd when the Cessna overshot the taxiway and continued its landing run all the way to the far end of the runway. He was on the roof of the main terminal building with a pair of binoculars. From here he had a reasonable view of the ramp area and the runway, as well as a partial view of the general aviation hangars and support area to his right. If he crossed the roof he could sweep the approach road and the parking lots. His plan was to observe from here until the intruder appeared, then direct his men to him by SMS.

He'd seen one other small plane land earlier in the day. It had immediately decelerated and had plenty of time to slow to taxi speed before reaching the turnoff. Why hadn't this one done the same?

He watched it through his binoculars as it slowly made its way back up the runway and turned off to the general aviation ramp. When it stopped, the pilot got out and was clearly not his man. But Einar's instincts were telling him that something was wrong.

He swept the runway with his binoculars again. At the end, the landfill was built up perhaps fifteen or twenty feet above the waterline. The slope was angled, but not so steep it couldn't be climbed. Einar began to form a guess as to what had happened. If someone was on that plane who didn't want to be there when it reached the general aviation ramp, and didn't want to be seen from the terminal, they might have used that turn at the end of the runway to bail out.

From there, he'd only have one way to go—back along the runway toward land. Einar slowly crept the binoculars back along the runway. At about the three quarters point he would reach land and could turn, cross those low flats…

There! A man on the sidewalk. A backpack slung over one shoulder. He was walking quickly toward the terminal from the far end of the sidewalk to the employee parking lot. But it was a large lot, and today was a quiet day. There were no parked cars that far out.

Einar couldn't make out the man's face, but he knew. Every

instinct told him this was the man he'd been hunting for days all across the country.

He grabbed his phone and dictated a text message to his men. They would converge and destroy.

When the plane landed, Georges had hoped Crane would be aboard. But the pilot was an older man, and he was alone. Georges felt a quick rush of disappointment and went back to his work.

It was perhaps five minutes later when his laptop pinged at him. There was a sudden surge in SMS traffic. Since Georges set up his system to capture and log all SMS messages through the airport, he'd counted three different network IDs sending almost all the messages at the airport. Roughly every fifteen minutes, one sent group messages to the other two, and they replied individually. He figured they were just checking in with each other, and his translator software confirmed it.

But now the system was lighting up with traffic. As he was watching, another group message went out. Something was definitely going on.

Georges' fingers flew across the keys as he sent the new messages to the online translator. As the first result came back, his heart leapt into his throat.

"He is here. West end of terminal."

The other two confirmed. One sent back something the translator program rendered as "Transfer." Georges assumed that meant the sender was on his way there.

He'd been right! Crane was here!

Georges pulled up a command file from his library and loaded it into the SMS system. Hold all messages for confirmation before sending, it told the server. Now Georges was in charge of their communications. He could shut them down completely, or he could let some messages get through and block others. Or he could edit them, he realized. He'd have to figure out what he wanted to say and then run it back through the translator to get the Icelandic. It would be crude, but it might fool them for a little while.

Georges paired his smart phone to his laptop so he could operate the whole thing from there. Then he closed his laptop and hurriedly shoved it into his bag. He needed to get moving. He had to find Crane before they did.

CHAPTER 32

The approach road came in from the main highway off to Crane's right and made a teardrop shape as it circled around to the terminal. Crane walked along it and considered whether to go inside the terminal or stay outside. He needed to get to the maintenance and general aviation facilities at the far end of the airport. That was where he would find a small air cargo or charter operation. Outside, he decided. He'd seen nothing suspicious out here so far.

He glanced into the terminal as he passed the front doors and saw a black Datafall uniform. One man, moving fast.

Crane veered toward the temporary parking lot inside the circle of the approach road. Had the man seen him? If so, Crane would try to lead him to the parking lot where the cars would provide at least some cover.

But he hadn't seen Crane. He left the terminal and headed toward the employee lot Crane had just come from.

Crane moved quickly in the other direction, edging close in to the wall of the terminal. A few yards down, there was a heavy metal fire door. As Crane passed it, the door buzzed open, and a shape lurched out and nearly collided with him. Crane let his training take over. He grabbed the man, spun him off balance, and positioned him so he could easily put him on the ground. Then he froze, realizing he was looking into the startled face of Georges Benly Akema. Georges took a moment to process the situation, then laughed with incongruous delight.

"I found you!" he said. "I actually did it! And you're alive!"

Crane pulled Georges away from the door and let it swing shut. "What the hell are you doing? How did you even get here?"

"I got a plane," said Georges. "It's on Grimsey Island. And there's a boat waiting in town. I knew they'd be watching. They know you're here!"

"Yes, but how do you know that?"

Georges' phone beeped and he checked the screen. "Okay," he said after a moment. "They figured out you're not there anymore."

Crane could see the black-clad shape of the guard making his way back toward the main entrance.

"Come on," Crane said, and started back out toward the parking lot. Georges followed, only partly watching where he was going as he tapped at his phone.

"What are you doing?" Crane asked.

"They're communicating by SMS," Georges said, "so I hacked the cell."

They crouched behind a van, and Georges quickly explained that there were three Datafall people here, one directing the other two. He showed Crane how he was translating and reading their messages before sending them on.

"So you can shut them down. Can you send them false messages?"

"Sure. I can translate into Icelandic, but it's probably going to sound a little twonky."

With the adrenaline rush and the fear of a nearby enemy, Crane guessed they wouldn't worry too much about odd phrasings. "Keep it simple," he said. "Tell the one over there where we are. Just him."

"You want him to come here?"

"Yes," said Crane. "Yes, I do."

———

Georges took a deep breath and nodded. He tapped his phone and said "He's in the front parking lot. Go."

A moment later, the phone returned a screen of computer-generated Icelandic. Georges assumed it was technically correct, but was it the way people actually spoke, or would it immediately tell the Datafall people that their communications had been intercepted? How could he know?

He turned the screen to Crane, who looked at it and shrugged. "I don't know. Send it."

Georges sent it. He was breathing hard again, and he could feel himself trembling. Crane looked alert, but calm and ready. How did he do that? Was it just a matter of experience? What made him able to do the things he did? Georges had always been in awe of Crane, but even more so here in the field, where Georges could barely think for the drumbeat of fear and the steady rush of adrenaline. He was not cut out for this.

One of the phones sent back a quick acknowledgement. Georges told the server to delete it instead of forwarding it on to the team leader.

"Stay here, and stay down," Crane hissed. Then he quickly crossed over to the next row of cars and crouched behind a BMW sedan. Georges heard footsteps running down the sidewalk to the lot. They stopped at the first row of cars, one over. Crane peered down, beneath the BMW's chassis. Then he gestured for Georges to move farther back.

Georges was extremely aware of every sound. The footsteps,

moving more cautiously now. The rustle of his clothes as he edged back against the van. His heartbeat—how could the man not hear that?

Crane tensed to spring and rapped the fender of the car he was crouched behind. Georges heard the footsteps rush suddenly forward, saw the black-clad figure emerge from between two cars and turn. But he didn't turn toward Crane and the sound. The man turned toward him instead, and their eyes met.

Georges saw surprise register on the man's face. He saw the split-second decision to fire. He tried to move, but his body refused. He saw the pistol rising, the suppressor on its barrel pointing into his eyes, the yawning black abyss of the muzzle.

Then Crane tackled him from behind as the gun went off. They went down, and the Datafall man's face planted hard into the asphalt not five feet away from him. Georges saw blood. Crane put a knee hard into his back, grabbed his hair with his left hand, and slammed his face into the pavement again. The man spasmed and dropped the gun. Crane snatched it up and hammered the back of his skull with the butt. Georges saw awareness fade from the man's face, and he sank onto the pavement in a pool of his own blood and broken teeth.

It took perhaps five seconds.

———

Crane looked up to Georges. "Are you hit?" he snapped.

Georges didn't answer. Crane scanned him and saw no obvious entry wound. Then he saw the bullet scar in the side of the van, inches from Georges' face.

Georges followed his eyes and saw it as well. He was already barely keeping it together, but this seemed to be too much for him. Crane saw him start to hyperventilate.

He moved in closer, confirmed that Georges was unhurt. "Look at me," he said. "Look at me. Deep breath. Hold it."

After one false start, Georges managed to hold his breath and kept his eyes locked on Crane as Crane counted off with his fingers. He could see Georges struggling to contain his fear. He was a civilian, Crane reminded himself. He should never have plunged into the middle of this, but he'd done it to help him.

"Let it out. Now just keep breathing and focus on that."

Georges' phone softly beeped. A moment later it beeped again. Georges ignored it.

"What are we going to do?" he asked after a moment.

"We're going to get out of here," said Crane. "You said you have a boat in town, right? Let's grab a car and get over there."

CHAPTER 33

"Where the hell are you?" Einar barked at his phone. "Respond."

The phone rendered that into text and Einar sent the message. It had been nearly ten minutes since he'd sent Nils to locate the target, and nothing. Now Rikard wasn't answering either.

He circled the roof, searching the airport. He had good visibility from here, but there were plenty of places a man might hide. Then Einar's phone chirped and displayed Rikard's number.

"What's going on?" Rikard said when Einar answered, "Are you getting my messages?"

"No. Something's wrong," Einar said. "Stand by."

An SMS outage right now was no coincidence, he thought. He hung up and dialed Nils' phone. At least voice still worked. He angrily hung up as the call transferred into voicemail.

Einar ran across the roof. A white van was pulling out of the temporary lot. He scanned it with his binoculars and could just make out a second figure in the passenger seat. But the driver's side window was down, and Einar got a good look at him as the van rounded the curve of the exit road. It was him.

Einar was already running for the stairs as he dialed his pilot.

"Get back to the airport, now!" he shouted. "Be ready to take off fast!"

———

Crane drove back toward town, past houses and an old church. To his right, the water was a dull gray backed by steep hills across the fjord. He glanced at Georges, still processing what he'd seen.

"Is that man dead?" Georges asked.

"No," said Crane. "He's hurt, but he'll make it."

The van apparently belonged to an electrician. "Is there anything back there you can use?" he asked Georges, to distract him as much as anything else.

Georges glanced over his shoulder. "No, no," he said. "I haven't been clearing their text messages," he added. "They'll know I hacked them by now."

"That's okay," said Crane. "You got the job done. We're out of here."

———

Einar's hotwired Volvo fishtailed as he took the corner too fast. He hadn't had to actually steal a car since he was a teenager. This just got better and better.

In the passenger seat Rikard grabbed the handle over the door and steadied the machine gun propped in the foot well. "A white van with blue lettering," Einar told him. "And there are two of them now. No description on the second."

The Volvo rocketed past the causeway that carried the Ring Road across the Eyjafjörður and sped back toward Akureyri itself. Why had they left the airport? Perhaps the second man had offered some new plan? It was the only thing Einar could think of. But it was a small town. They'd find them.

Einar slowed as they came into town. He hung a right onto the Strandgata, drove past the empty cruise ship dock, and then took a left toward the waterfront. He pulled over and let Rikard out. "I'll call if I need you," he said. Then Einar drove off slowly, scanning the streets for the white van, or for pedestrians who didn't belong here. There wasn't much time left, he thought. One way or another, this would end soon.

───────

Crane left the van on the other side of Akureyri, and they walked through town toward the waterfront. If the van was reported stolen and spotted, he didn't want police searching the waterfront. If nothing else, he wanted to approach the boat with caution, to make sure Georges' escape plan hadn't become a trap.

They made their way through the shopping district and into a quiet residential neighborhood. This gave way to light industrial buildings. Crane could see water from here and hear boat engines.

They passed a marine supply company, and a tour operator, closed today since there were no cruise ships. A row of rakish, black 12-passenger inflatable boats lay moored along the pier.

Georges studied the map on his phone. "We can cut through here." He led the way between two corrugated metal warehouses. They found themselves in a maze of storage buildings, chain link fencing, and piles of old crates and empty fuel drums. Crane didn't like it. It was confusing and the sightlines were short. He let his hand fall to the butt of the silenced pistol he'd picked up at the airport.

As they crossed an intersection, Crane looked to his right and saw a black-clad figure step into the alley thirty yards down. The man's reflexes were sharp. He spotted Crane out of the corner of his eye, whirled, and fired. Crane moved around the corner as the suppressed pistol snapped, and he heard the bullet ricochet off metal.

"Go!" he hissed at Georges. "Left."

Georges ran ahead and took the next left, but Crane stopped and drew his pistol. The Datafall man appeared a moment later, and Crane snapped off a shot at him but missed. Then Crane ran right. He heard another shot slam into the wall as he ducked around the corner. Damn, he was fast.

Crane sprinted down the littered path, leading the enemy away from Georges.

Georges' stopped at a corner and gasped, "which way?"

There was no answer. He turned. Crane wasn't there.

Again, the fear, in a jolt like lightning striking. He was alone. He was being hunted. Georges heard footsteps pounding the packed earth, and he ran. He ran with no idea whether he was moving away from danger or closer to it. He just ran, turning at random until he pulled up before a blue metal wall. On his left was another building, this one faded green and marked with incomprehensible graffiti. On his right was a chain link fence topped with razor wire protecting construction machinery and spools of cable. He was trapped.

He backtracked to the last intersection, but the chain link fence beside him suddenly bowed and sang as if struck by something heavy. Georges dove behind a group of old oil drums stacked against the building. He fell back against the cold metal wall and sank to the ground, making himself as small as he could. Somewhere he heard the soft snaps of the pistols, and bullets striking metal.

Knife. He had a knife. Georges frantically dug through his bag until he found it. He unsnapped the hard leather sheath and tossed it away. He clutched the black metal hilt in both hands, holding the knife in front of him with the blade pointed at whatever came around the oil drums.

Georges heard his heartbeat and felt himself trembling. A boat horn sounded somewhere in the distance. Then, closer, two more suppressed gunshots. He held his breath and clutched the knife. There was a sharp clang that trailed off into a shrill, metallic screech, a grunt, the sound of something striking flesh.

Then two bodies flew into view and landed in the dirt a few feet away. Crane fell on his back with his arms over his head, and the other man landed on top of him. The man in the black uniform pressed down hard on Crane's arms and throat with a length of metal rebar. His expression was savage.

Crane had his pistol, but his wrist was pinned by the rebar. His other arm had some movement, but not enough. He scrabbled at the man's black uniform, fighting to pull him off. But he couldn't. Crane was helpless, struggling to breathe.

All the man had to do, Georges knew, was turn slightly and he'd see him. Crane was going to die, right here in front of him, and then he would die, too.

Georges realized he was standing, though he didn't remember getting up. Then he was running forward, the knife held underhand at his side.

The man saw Georges coming in the last instant. Then the blade took him below the armpit, and Georges felt the tip puncture flesh, felt the scrape of bone against the blade, heard the man's gasp. He yanked the blade free.

They locked eyes for a moment and a strangely intimate look passed between them. Then Crane pulled his hand free of the rebar, raised the pistol to the man's temple, and fired.

———

Crane concealed the body, wiped blood from his skin, and cleared the scene as best he could. If anyone had heard the suppressed gunshots, the police would probably have arrived by now. But he didn't want to be here any longer than necessary.

The last thing he did was take the knife from Georges' hand, hanging limp at his side. He wiped the blade clean, found the sheath on the ground, and stuck it in his boot.

Through it all, Georges stood motionless and silent.

"We killed that man," he finally said.

"I killed him," Crane answered.

"No," said Georges. "No. I did what I did."

"You saved my life," said Crane. "And yours. Come on, we have to go."

"Something in me was strong after all," he said. "And cruel." He fell silent for a moment and seemed to be someplace else entirely. Then it was as if a curtain fell over whatever he was thinking. Georges checked his phone.

"This way," he said.

CHAPTER 34

When Einar tried to check in with Rikard, he got no answer. He swore and slammed his fist down on the Volvo's center console. The thought that he might actually fail crossed his mind. It was an unpleasant thought. It had been a long time since he'd failed at something.

Einar turned around and headed back down toward the waterfront. It was quiet this time of day, with few people around. The tour boats weren't running, and the fishing boats had long since come back in.

Except that one.

Einar braked to a halt in the middle of the road and scrabbled in the passenger seat for his binoculars. One boat was heading out from the docks, a white fishing boat with orange trim. Einar swept the deck with the binoculars, and there he was. Standing on the deck was the man he'd chased halfway across the country. The boat churned up a wake as it powered out into the channel and turned north to head up the fjord.

Einar swore and dropped the binoculars in his lap. He grabbed his phone and dialed his pilot. Where could they pick him up here?

The cruise ship dock, he decided. A wide expanse of open concrete with nothing around it but water. He hit the gas.

"Go!" Einar shouted as soon as the call connected. "Get airborne, now! Pick me up at the cruise ship dock!"

"Um, that's going to be a problem," said the pilot.

The fishing boat plowed north through a cold, gray sea beneath a cold, gray sky. Crane stood in the bow, forward of the boat's small radar and instrument mast. He still had the pistol he'd taken from the man at the airport. The one he'd killed a man with. He tossed it over the side.

Georges came forward from the wheelhouse. "Captain says another hour and a half," he shouted.

Crane nodded and shifted his pack on his shoulder. They'd cleared the fjord and were in open ocean now. Another ninety minutes to Grimsey Island. Then a few hours in the air to Norway, and finally back across the Atlantic aboard Josh's Gulfstream. Crane was tired. He was ready for this to be over.

The wheelhouse door opened, and the Captain stuck his head out, shouting something in Icelandic. Then he shook his head in exasperation. "Behind us!" he shouted and gestured over his shoulder with one thumb.

Crane and Georges went to the stern and looked back. In the distance, Crane made out a short black line, like a hyphen on the surface of the sea. It was one of the tourist Zodiacs, he realized, the ones he'd seen lined up at the pier in Akureyri. It would have seating for a dozen in front, a control station for the pilot in the rear, and a pair of powerful outboard motors. The fishing boat could never outrun it.

So apparently it wasn't over yet.

Einar edged the throttles forward, and the boat surged into the next wave. It went airborne for a moment, then slammed hard against the sea. Einar had never been much for boats and sailing, but he found the pounding and the snarl of the engines strangely comforting. They went well with his rage.

Einar's world had been reduced to this. He was alone in the middle of the ocean, in a stolen rubber boat, with a light machine gun lying beside the control pedestal.

Einar saw the fishing boat ahead. Aboard that boat were the stolen data and the man who'd done this to him. As he approached, he made out two figures on the deck, though there had to be at least one more in the wheelhouse. The two on the deck watched him come.

It was only when he pulled along the starboard side, throttled back the engines, and picked up the machine gun that they scattered. Einar sprayed the boat with fire. He couldn't aim effectively in the pitching Zodiac, but that didn't matter. The two men dove for the deck as he stitched a line of bullets across the wheelhouse.

The boat cut its engines, and a moment later the Captain emerged from the wheelhouse, his hands raised. The two passengers on the deck stood as well.

Einar edged the Zodiac closer with angry growls from the outboards. "Throw me a line!" he ordered.

The Captain obeyed, and Einar gestured with the gun. "Everyone into the bow. Where I can see you."

All three went forward and Einar kept an eye on them as he secured the Zodiac to the rail and climbed aboard. First, he checked the wheelhouse. It was empty. There were hatches leading below decks, but they were dogged shut.

Then he went forward and got his first good look at the man he'd chased across half of Iceland. He didn't look like so much.

"Back this way," he said, waving with the gun. He moved them amidships where there was room to move. The device was probably in the dark-haired man's pack, Einar thought, but it might be hidden anywhere on the boat. He would have to kill these people and scuttle the boat regardless. If he found the device, he could return the data to the board in triumph. But all he really needed was to ensure the data never made it out of Iceland. Sending it to the bottom of the sea would be enough.

He separated the dark-haired man from the others. The man had said nothing yet. He simply stood there. Einar could sense him calculating, looking for his opening. Einar stared back at him for a moment, let him see the determination in his eyes, let him remember what this gun had done to a twelve-ton truck.

Einar gestured with the gun. "Off your shoulder," he said. "Slow. Throw it to me."

The man hesitated for a moment, then he carefully slid the strap down his arm until the pack hung from one hand. He swung his arm back and stooped as if to slide the pack across the deck.

But at the last second, as the boat pitched forward in a wave, he hooked it upward.

The pack tumbled up and the strap fell over the machine gun's muzzle. It dragged the barrel down, and then the man was a dark shape flying at him.

They collided and Einar hit the deck on his back. The gun was ripped free and clattered onto the deck beside him. Einar grabbed for it, but the stranger knocked it away. He punched Einar in the kidneys, then scrambled across the deck for the gun. He would reach it first, Einar realized. Then he noticed the pack had landed on his legs, the strap draped over one ankle.

Einar rolled onto his side and kicked with all his strength.

The pack arced high into the air, soaring toward the gunwale, and Einar willed it upward, forward.

Too late, the dark-haired man realized what had happened. He scrambled after it. Too late. The pack cleared the side of the boat and fell gracefully into the sea.

The dark-haired man never broke stride, he bent forward, and Einar realized he actually meant to dive after it.

"No!" the Captain shouted and leaped for him. They collided and fell against the rail.

Einar fell back onto the deck, laughing in triumph. It was a victory barely snatched from defeat at the last possible instant. But it was a victory. He looked up at the young black man who had snatched up the machine gun. He held it leveled at Einar, trembling in fear. Perhaps they would kill him now. Einar realized he no longer cared. He'd won.

———

Crane lay on the deck and watched his pack vanish beneath the water. It was a dark shape, sinking, and then it was gone.

"Too cold," the Captain was saying. "Gasp reflex. You breathe in water, sink like a rock, you die." The Captain picked at the fabric of Crane's shirt. "Go in the water like this, you don't come up. Let it go."

Crane took a deep breath, then nodded.

"All right. I'm all right," he said.

They got up. The Captain looked at Einar lying on the deck, then at Georges covering him with the machine gun. His scowl made it clear he wanted no part of this.

"What do we do with him?" asked Georges.

"Nobody dies today," said the Captain. "It's over."

Crane clapped the Captain on the shoulder. "I'll disable his boat, and then we'll leave him in it. You call it in to the Coast Guard. Let them find him out here in a stolen boat."

"I am Einar Persson," the Datafall man said amiably. "What is your name?"

"Doesn't matter," said Crane.

The man—Einar—laughed. "No. It doesn't matter. In the end, I beat you."

"Congratulations," said Crane.

Georges held the machine gun while Crane climbed into the Zodiac and cut the fuel lines. Then they transferred Einar back aboard the boat and pushed it away. Finally, Georges dumped the machine gun over the side.

"I beat you!" Einar shouted as the fishing boat's engines sputtered back to life and it moved away. "I beat you!"

Crane turned away and smiled. "That's right," he said quietly. "Go back and tell your bosses that."

Einar's shouts faded as the boat powered away toward Grimsey Island and safety.

CHAPTER 35

Palo Alto, California, three weeks later

Josh Sulenski returned from the San Diego Comic-Con to find a stack of mail waiting on his desk. His assistant had carefully separated it into categories. The junk mail was already gone. Here were the bills, here the various obscure print magazines Josh subscribed to, here the personal letters from people seeking money or favors—there were always plenty of those.

And on the bottom, a package wrapped in brown paper and festooned with colorful foreign stamps. Josh turned his attention to that. He read the address label.

"Who the hell is Halla Manisdottir?" he shouted to nobody in particular.

He sliced through the wrapping with a letter opener modeled after Batman's batarangs and opened the package.

"And why is she sending me socks?"

Again, nobody answered. Josh remembered his assistant had today off.

They were nice socks at least. Hand knit from real wool from the looks of them. Then he realized there was something inside one. He reached in and pulled out a broken fragment of circuit board with a storage module epoxied in place.

A wide grin broke across Josh's face as he realized what he was holding. Georges had come back with a story about the data tap ending up in the North Atlantic, and Crane hadn't contradicted him.

There was a letter in the package. Josh unfolded it and read.

"Dear Mr. Sulenski," it began. "Our friend John Crane asked me to send this to you, but it doesn't look like much to me. I live in the country here in Iceland, and there is little to do in the winters. So I make many socks. More than I need. I thought you might like a pair. Please tell John Crane I am grateful for his help. But he was right. It is probably best he is not in Iceland anymore. I hope you are well, and the socks fit you. Sincerely, Halla Manisdottir."

"You bastard," Josh said with a broad grin. He grabbed his phone and texted Crane.

"Why didn't you tell me you gave the data tap to someone to mail back?"

It was several minutes before Crane answered. Apparently, he was up to something. "I didn't know if she'd actually do it or not," his reply read.

"I'm still pissed about that cruise ship cabin," Josh sent back.

"Okay," Crane answered. Josh waited, but he didn't send anything else.

After a minute, Josh sighed. That was the thing about Crane; you couldn't stay mad at him when he kept bringing home such interesting toys.

Josh pulled up Georges contact on his phone and sent another text.

"Meet me at the shop. Let's make some unpleasant people have a really bad day."

Josh tossed the data tap into the air, caught it, and then headed out again. This was going to be fun.

PART III
SOMETHING SMART

CHAPTER 36

Yaoundé, Cameroon

They buried Sam Eyango at two in the afternoon, and by nine that night the party was in full swing. From the ballroom and open bar, the festivities spilled out into the hotel's terrace. In the warm night air, a packed crowd danced to a DJ hired from Paris while waiters served Cristal and Courvoisier. Sam had been a ganger boy, one of the Ibiza Boys, and he died a ganger's death. But it was a fast life while it lasted, and the Ibiza Boys made damn sure everyone saw that part too. They sent Sam off in style. They did him proud.

About to do him a lot prouder, Michel thought as he led the girl across the terrace. He hadn't come to his friend's funeral to get laid, but he wasn't about to pass up a girl like this. He'd seen her earlier, dancing by herself near the end of the terrace, arms over her head and the fringe on her bright red mini-dress shimmering around her hips. He'd watched a couple hangers on take a run at her and get shot down, but when she found out he ran with Yanis and the gang, that he was a friend of the dead man, well that made all the difference. She loved a bad boy, this one.

Michel had seen it before. Some girls, they weren't gangers, they weren't hard. But they liked to play a bit at danger sometimes for a bit of escape from their safe, boring lives. The scent of death—not too close, just a whiff—would melt them like butter.

And this one—her name was Romy, he reminded himself—was melting down. She leaned drunkenly against him as he led her inside. He felt her body slide against him, and she laughed. She leaned over to snatch an open bottle of Cristal from the bar and said, "Let's go upstairs."

Yeah, that was the idea. He steered her through the ballroom.

"You've got a room?" she asked. "Someplace we can be alone?"

Michel smiled. "A suite, baby, all to ourselves. You know Yanis Kamkumo, right? The big man?" He held up two fingers. "We're like this. First class all the way."

He was exaggerating, of course. But this was no time for modesty.

In the elevator, he pulled her around, pressed her against his body, and kissed her hard. He slid a hand down her side and around toward the inside of her thigh, but she caught his wrist and pulled his hand away. She looked into his eyes as she brought his hand up and took his index finger into her mouth. She closed her lips around it and slowly drew it out again. Michel laughed.

"We're going to get along real good," he said.

"Let's drink to that," she said and tipped the bottle into his mouth. He gulped the fine champagne and felt it spill down his chin. It was going to be a good night.

In the suite he locked the door and turned to see her standing at the window, looking out across the teeming city. "Tell me about him," she said. "Your friend. How did he die?"

"Let's not talk about that," he said. "He's gone. We're here. Let's be alive."

He reached for her, and she kissed him again. Then she said, "no, tell me! I want to know."

"It turns you on, doesn't it? You're a bad girl, aren't you? A dirty girl."

She poured the last of the bottle into a glass on the sideboard and handed it to him with a wicked grin. "You got a problem with that?"

"No, baby. Not at all." He drank down the champagne and said, "all right. His name was Sam, but we called him Bullet because he got shot once, and they left it in him. He was a tough man."

"What happened to him?"

Michel's head was swimming. He must have drunk too much too fast. He sat down on the bed. "He got jumped," he said. "They cut him up bad and left him in some woods at Mvolyé Cemetery."

"Do you know who did it?" she asked. He could see her excitement growing. This was a weird girl, but that wouldn't matter. He'd never see her again after tonight. He just had to keep it together long enough to get her in bed. He shouldn't have drunk so much.

"No," he said. "We've got enemies. Some other gang. To cut him up that much..."

"You look tired, baby," she said. She knelt on the bed beside him, and he didn't protest as she laid him down. "Rest a minute. You know what I think?"

"What?"

"I think it must have been a woman that killed him."

"What? Why?" Alarm bells started going off in the back of Michel's head. He felt...wrong somehow.

"To cut someone up the way you say, they must have been

very angry at him. That kind of rage, that takes a woman. He must have done something to bring that out of a woman. Something really horrible."

She pulled her dress off over her head and tossed it onto the nightstand. She wore only a black bra and panties, but Michel saw something strapped around her upper thigh—a black, stretch fabric belt that held something metal.

"Maybe he hurt someone she loved," she said. "Maybe he destroyed her life."

Michel tried to get up, but he could only raise his shoulders a few inches from the bed. He wasn't just drunk. She'd done something to him.

"Shh, shh," she hushed, gently pushing him back down onto the bed. "Stay there," she said softly. With one hand she drew a gleaming medical scalpel from the belt around her thigh.

"You don't remember me at all, do you," she said. "You just saw my picture. And it was a few years ago now. Sam didn't remember me either."

Michel tried to shout for help, but made only a thin, raspy sound. She grabbed his jaw in a fierce, iron grip and forced his head around so he was looking straight up. His eyes watched the scalpel in horror. The light from the nightstand glowed off the small blade.

"This is for my mother," she said, and her voice was cold, the kittenish tone gone, suddenly and completely. She slashed his cheek deep from below his eye down to his chin. He could feel the flesh part beneath the blade. He gasped in pain, and in a flash she leant over and slashed the other cheek. Michel saw his own blood dripping from the blade as she sat back up. She wiped the scalpel on the bedspread and put it away.

Then she drew another blade from inside her thigh. This one was longer and heavier, but it had the same polished gleam and a push handle wrapped in black cord. She held it up for him and locked her eyes on his.

"But this," she said, "this is for me."

Michel tried to scream, but he couldn't. He couldn't move. All he could do was see the cold hatred in her eyes, and watch the blade rise in her hand. "Please," he managed to murmur.

Then the blade sank into his flesh, over and over, until all Michel could feel was pain and fear, and all he could see was his own blood flowing into his eyes.

———

After she cleaned up in the bathroom, Romy walked carefully around the bed and put her dress back on. What was left of Michel soaked blood into the bedspread. She didn't look at him; she didn't think about him at all as she checked once more to make sure she'd left nothing behind. Then she left the room and walked calmly down the hall.

A man passed her, and Romy felt a cold chill of fear down her back. Yanis Kamkuma himself. The man it had always been about. Romy fought down her fear. She had to look normal, give no outward sign of the chaos going on within. He gave her an appraising look and a smile as they passed, but then she saw a flicker of...what? Doubt? Perhaps recognition? Then she was beyond him, and it took all her strength not to break and run for the elevators.

She reached them at last and pressed the call button. Time seemed to stretch out forever. Behind her, Yanis pounded on a door.

"Michel! Come on, god damn it, I know you're in there."

She glanced back and saw him at the door to the suite she'd just left. He fumbled in his pockets.

Shit! He had a key! The elevator doors stood solidly closed.

Romy walked quickly to the stairwell. She had to get out. She had to be gone from here now!

She took the stairs down to the ground level and stopped. To her left was the main lobby, quiet and dim. To her right, the sound and light of the party. Yanis's men were that way, but so was the loud, busy wake. She could lose herself in the crowd. She turned right.

She made her way through the ballroom to the terrace. The DJ still spun his tunes, people still danced. But now she saw Yanis's men moving fast through the crowd. One tapped another on the shoulder and leaned in, speaking urgently. She saw surprise break across the new man's face, and he took off in another direction.

They'd found him. They were looking for her.

Romy kicked off her heels so she could run. She hurried across the dance floor toward the row of pompon trees at the far edge of the terrace. Complaints followed her as she bumped into dancers, but she didn't care. Beyond the trees she could fade into the night. There were a thousand different turns she could take, a thousand dark places where she might disappear. But the time for stealth was past.

Then she spun to avoid a dancer and ran straight into another man. He caught her to keep her from falling. She tensed to push away from him, but then he said, "Romy?"

She froze.

"It is you!"

She looked up into his smiling face. Daniel Massila. A boy she'd dated in school. He realized he was still holding her arms and let her go. God, of all the luck!

"Daniel."

He seemed so happy to see her. "My God, when did you get back?"

Of course, she realized. He saw the old Romy, from before. He had no idea who she was now. "I didn't."

Behind them, someone shouted, "Hey! She's here!"

"Get away from here, Daniel," Romy hissed. "Run. Now!" Then she spun, pushed a dancer out of her way and left him bewildered as she ran for the trees.

CHAPTER 37

Palo Alto, California

Georges's lab at the Myria group was a cavernous, windowless space in the middle of the building, an oddly-shaped artifact forced on the design by some unusual choices by the original designers. Georges had turned it into a maze of shelves, workbenches, and heavy equipment. Power and data cables snaked around the floor like vines.

"We can't do the real demo in here," said Josh, shaking his head in dismay. "Place is a death trap."

"Nonsense," said Georges. "It's perfectly safe."

Georges, Josh, and a young agronomist named Kevin made their way through the dimly lit passage between blinking server racks. Georges had brought Kevin on a week ago to provide specialized expertise for this latest project.

"Safe for you, sure," said Josh. But there's a thousand different ways for a visitor to die in here, depending on what they trip over."

"Kevin's been here a week now. He's fine."

"If he dies, we can get another agronomist," Josh said with a sly grin for Georges. "Nothing personal, Kevin."

"No, sir," Kevin stammered.

"But I'm not bringing the board of the World Bank Food and Agriculture Practice in here and getting someone maimed. And we can't fly a drone in here anyway. We'll set up your test bed outside and do the demo from the roof."

"Sure," said Georges.

He led them into a large open space at the back of the lab with a raised metal platform. They clanked up the stairs and looked down on a thirty-foot square wooden bed full of soil.

"So what's wrong with it exactly?" asked Josh.

Kevin spoke up, suddenly in his element. "It's a typical famine area soil in south Asia, sir. You'll note the reddish tone. Rich in potash but low in nitrogen and phosphates. Could use a little more carbon content as well. Crop yields are low, requiring more acreage of arable land per person."

"South Asia?" said Josh. "Where did we get it?"

"We flew in a couple tons from southeast Maharashtra," said Georges.

There was a pause. "You did say to spend what we needed," Georges added.

"Yes, I did," said Josh. "Eh. It's just money. We'll make more. All right, show me."

From a shelf bolted to the railing, Georges picked up a grenade launcher with a drum magazine and a wide muzzle. He pointed it into the bed of soil and fired. There was a thump from the launcher, and something slammed into the dirt below. It buried itself in the topsoil, leaving only a small cloud of dust and a mark about the size of a mole's hole.

Georges snapped open the launcher and ejected a round from the magazine. It was a stubby shape, rounded at the rear with a smaller rounded point in the front.

"Caseless," he said. "We aren't helping if we litter the whole place with shell casings in the process."

He handed it to Josh, who held it up to the light.

"That darker band at the back is the propellant," Georges explained. "The chemical payload is in front. Nitrogen, carbon, phosphate, a little lime to balance the acidity in the soil. A couple other chemical tricks. That was the real work. But you come back in a week and test that soil, and you'll find very different chemistry in a ten-foot circle around that spot."

Josh nodded. "So we'll want to lay down a grid with one of these every twenty feet."

"In each direction, yes."

"So to cover a square mile, we're taking about..." he did some quick math in his head. "About seventy thousand rounds."

"When production scales up, we estimate they'll cost a little over three cents a round," said Georges. "That's not bad."

Josh shook his head. "And how big does the drone need to be to carry all those rounds? We've got another month before the World Bank shows up. This is a good start, but let's keep working."

After Josh had left for his next meeting, Georges sent Kevin off to do more soil tests and returned to his desk in a hidden corner of the lab. He put on some old De La Soul and leaned back in his chair, staring up into the darkness of the metal trusses in the ceiling. Josh wanted them to save the world. It was a good goal. The best. But it seemed very abstract sometimes. Put more nutrients in the soil in lands plagued by famine. Take a bit of carbon back out of the atmosphere and bury it deep underground. They were nudging things just the tiniest bit and hoping the effects would grow over time. Maybe they would, but Georges couldn't help feeling that the world needed something bigger.

John Crane was in Finland doing God knew what. He hadn't needed any of Georges's technical wizardry apparently, because they hadn't brought him in on this one. Georges wished they had. He felt more effective supporting Crane's field missions. Crane took action. He produced results that changed things now. Georges knew his own work was important, but he couldn't help his impatience, and he felt something missing in his life that couldn't be solved by making better soil.

Then his phone chimed and buzzed. Georges checked the screen and saw an international number, the code for Cameroon. He turned off the music and picked it up.

"Hello?"

"Is this Mr. Akema?" said a man's voice in accented French. "Georges Benly Akema?" The voice was distant, crackling through a dozen sketchy connections and satellite links to reach him. But it sent a shiver through Georges. He knew that voice immediately. It took him back to events he'd worked hard to put behind him.

"This is Officer Makoun of the Yaoundé—"

"I know who you are," Georges said quietly.

Makoun paused. "You remember me?" He sounded pleased.

"You were kind to me at the worst moment of my life."

"I remember you as well," said Makoun. "They told me you were special. A genius. An Einstein right in Cameroon. You would make us all proud."

"And I wanted to take up a weapon and go after the men who hurt my mother. But you said if I wanted justice, I should do something smart."

"And did you?" Makoun asked.

Georges glanced around the lab. He felt the weight of expectation, suddenly heavy on his shoulders. "I'm trying," he said at last.

"I'm afraid your sister did not."

The words hit him like an electric shock. "Romy? What's happened? Do you know where she is?"

"She's here in Yaoundé," said Makoun. "She's in trouble. I remembered you, you see? So when I saw the name—"

"Is she all right?" Georges interrupted. He'd been looking for Romy for months but hadn't found a trace of her. How had she gotten back to Cameroon? What was she doing there?

"She's killed a man," said Makoun. "Probably two. Both were known to us. Gang members."

The pieces all fell into place in an instant. "The men who attacked our mother."

He couldn't believe it. Sweet Romy, her world full of nothing but clothes and boys. How could she... But of course, she could. Georges himself had killed a man now. It could be done. And the attack on their mother had reshaped his life so completely. How could it not change her too?

"A party guest recognized her," Makoun was saying. "An old boyfriend, surprised to see her again. He gave us her name. But the gang found him before officers arrived. They're looking for her too."

Georges said nothing. His mind was racing as he tried to comprehend Romy driven to murder for revenge. He fought back thoughts of her lying dead in a ditch somewhere, hacked to pieces and soaked in blood.

He wondered what he could possibly tell his parents.

"Are you there?" Makoun's distant voice asked through the hiss of line noise.

"Yes. I'm here."

"I'll do what I can to protect her. But you must know there's nothing good for her in this country, whoever finds her."

"No."

There was another pause, then Makoun said, "Best if she were simply gone from Cameroon, where no one can find her," he said, and let the words hang there. He was a police officer. He could say no more. But Georges understood.

"I'm sorry to bring you bad news," said Makoun at last.

"No, thank you. I had to know."

"I'll do what I can," Makoun said once more.

Makoun had to be violating police procedure by telling him about an active case. He'd done what he could. Georges couldn't expect any more special treatment. "My family and I are very grateful," Georges said.

"I have to go," said Makoun. "Remember what I told you before." And the line went dead.

Georges trembled as he set down the phone.

Do something smart.

Yes, he was supposed to be a genius. He should just do something smart and make everything better. But of course, it was never that simple. Maybe he wasn't as smart as people thought. Or maybe being a genius with computers and technology wasn't really all that helpful.

But his sister was lost and in danger. He had to do what he could.

―――

Georges didn't know how to tell his parents, but they immediately saw that something had happened, and he had to tell them everything. They were shocked, and his mother began to cry.

"What will we do? My baby girl!" she wailed.

His father tried to comfort her. "We'll get her back," he said. "We'll borrow money. Pull some strings."

Georges knew there was only one thing to do. On the way home, he'd made his decision—the only decision he could make.

"I'll go to Cameroon," he said.

His parents looked at him in shock.

"There's a flight tomorrow morning. I'll find her and bring her home."

"No!" said his father. "It's too dangerous. I'll go. This is my fault. I will go. I'll need bribe money."

"It's not your fault! And how will you find her?" His father couldn't move in the underworld of youth gangs and crime. He'd get taken for every dollar he had, if not worse. "You can't go into the world she's found there."

"And you can? You're no gangster, Georges!"

Georges nodded. That was fair enough. "No, I know. You're right. But I know her friends. I know young people. And I have resources."

"What do you mean, resources?"

Georges said nothing. His parents still thought he developed actuarial software for the insurance industry. He couldn't tell them what his real job was, or the things he'd done.

He took his father and mother's hands in his. "Trust me," he said. "I know what I'm doing. I'll find her, and I'll bring her home. I promise."

CHAPTER 38

Helsinki, Finland

Russian embassies had certainly gone upscale since the old days. John Crane stood in a bespoke tuxedo with a glass of champagne in one hand and watched the reception swirl around him. Actual Soviet embassies were a little before his time, but he'd seen old intelligence photos of this very room. It had been a dour little place, carved up into dingy cubicles that churned out propaganda about Soviet industrial triumphs. Now it was a palace ballroom, complete with sculpted marble and glittering chandeliers.

He stood in front of tall windows that looked out on the snowy embassy grounds. Hedges blocked the headlights of passing traffic on Tehtaankatu. A small chamber ensemble played a waltz on the far side of the room. It was easy to imagine himself at a ball in some old Russian aristocrat's country dacha.

That's not so far off actually, he thought, given the state of the Russian government. Russia was run by ultra-rich oligarchs these days. Everything could be traced back to some billionaire's control. The diplomatic corps was no different. The various factions struggled to expand their influence, fighting each other for power and wealth. And they fought dirty.

That was why Crane was here. Josh had chosen to intervene in one such struggle, to keep one of the few remaining reform-minded oligarchs from being eliminated by people who were far worse. Crane had warned Josh that getting into this game would be a lot easier than getting out again. But Josh said he was more afraid of what happened when somebody finally won. That was nearly the case now, but there were still a few oligarchs fighting for their independence, and that kept the dominant powers occupied.

And so Crane was here to pass a flash drive to a contact. The information on the drive would help their beneficiary undercut his rivals, whether by blackmail or by general public outrage when it was released. Crane didn't know the details, and he had no idea where Josh had gotten his hands on the information. That worried him a bit as well. Josh had found new sources somewhere and was keeping them to himself for now. Crane knew Josh would confide in him eventually, but it usually didn't take this long.

His thoughts were interrupted as a woman appeared through the crowd of diplomats, financiers, and various political celebrities. She was striking with a ballerina's body in a deep blue satin dress with a slash of embroidered flowers across the midriff and down one leg.

Well, that won't draw attention, Crane thought as eyes turned to follow her. Crane put his glass on a passing waiter's tray as she approached. Then he smiled and took her outstretched hand.

"It's been too long," she said.

"We must catch up," he answered. "Shall we dance?"

"Of course."

He led her toward the center of the room where couples

danced to the orchestra's waltz. Crane took her in his arms, and they made up small talk about imagined lives as they danced. Crane slipped the drive from his fingertips into hers, and he didn't see where it went from there. Not his concern. He'd passed it along.

As the waltz ended, she pretended he'd said something funny and laughed, a soft, inviting sound. "We should both leave," she said softly. "For appearances' sake, let's imagine we're leaving separately to rendezvous someplace more private."

"What a lovely idea," Crane said. He raised her hand to kiss her fingertips, and then they parted. He watched her leave, then followed a few moments later.

Crane returned to the cloakroom to retrieve his overcoat and phone. The phone had been busy in his absence, he noted as he slipped it back into his pocket. At least half a dozen missed calls and voice mails. Something was happening, but he couldn't check in right now.

The air was chill as he stepped outside. The woman was on the far side of the looping drive, passing the guards at the outer gate. He saw her turn left onto Tehtaankatu. Then his phone was buzzing again. He answered it as he walked past the limousines waiting on the drive.

"John? John, are you okay? I've been calling for an hour."

It was Georges Benly Akema, and Crane could hear the tension in his voice.

"I'm fine, Georges. You know I can't always just pick up the phone. What's going on?"

"It's my sister. I know where she is."

Georges had been trying to find his runaway sister as long as Crane had known him. "Well that's good, right?"

He passed through the gate onto the sidewalk. The woman was approaching the corner, walking quickly in high-heeled boots and a fur-trimmed coat.

"Yes, and no," Georges said hesitantly. "She's back in Cameroon…she's in trouble."

Down the block, a figure rose suddenly from between two parked cars and stepped onto the sidewalk.

Crane turned and walked quickly past the embassy's decorative iron fence. The woman turned left again onto Ullankatu. It was a smaller side street, dark and tree lined, a perfect place for a mugging. The figure turned after her.

"Shit," Crane muttered. "Sorry, that wasn't for you, Georges. Go on." He quickened his pace.

"I'm in a car for the airport," Georges was saying. "I connect through New York, then Casablanca…"

"Uh huh." Georges kept talking in the background as Crane closed the distance on the pursuer. Far down the street, he saw headlights approaching.

"I hate to ask you this," Georges was saying, "but I need help. I know what she's done, but she's my sister. Can you help me find her?"

"Hold that thought, Georges."

Crane dropped his phone as the pursuer whirled. It fell into a patch of snow, and Crane spun away. A knife gleamed dully in the streetlight's yellow glow. Crane's coat flared as he dodged the attack, and the tip of the blade sliced into the lining.

The attacker corrected and came back for another pass. Crane trapped the arm and forced the blade up. They were face to face now, the attacker in a tuxedo as well. Crane recognized him from the reception. He must have been following the contact and left while they danced.

Crane grunted as the attacker thrust a knee up into his midsection but kept his grip on the man's wrist and forced him back against a parked Renault sedan. He slammed the wrist against the car until the knife flew free and skittered away across the roof. The attacker swung a fierce left against Crane's temple and staggered him. Crane fell back and barely blocked a follow-up strike to his throat.

Crane heard the woman's heels clattering on the sidewalk as she ran away, into the approaching headlights. Then the attacker feinted and lunged. Crane caught his arm and turned with him. He guided the lunging man past himself, adding his own energy to the movement, and drove him hard into the metal uprights of the embassy fence. The man grunted in pain and reeled back, dazed. Crane took his collar, spun him a quarter turn and smashed his face into the corner of one of the fence's stone columns. The man went limp, and Crane dropped him to the ground, blood streaming from his forehead.

A black Escalade lurched to a stop in the street, and the passenger door flew open. The woman looked back as she climbed in, and Crane saw the fear in her eyes. Then the door closed, and the Escalade took off in a squeal of protesting tires and disappeared around the corner.

Crane went back to retrieve his phone. On the far sidewalk, a passerby looked across the street in shock, talking on his own phone. To the police, no doubt. It was time to get out of Helsinki.

As he dug his phone from the snow, Crane heard Georges calling frantically to him.

"Talk to me, John! Are you all right? John?"

He brushed away the snow.

"I'm fine, Georges. I got distracted."

"I thought I heard—"

Crane walked quickly back toward Tehtaankatu. There was a cab stand there. He could be at the airport inside thirty minutes.

"It's okay, Georges. I'm fine. And of course I'll help you. Where are we going?"

CHAPTER 39

Yaoundé, Cameroon

Georges waited at a gate at Yaoundé Nsimalen as passengers filed off into the terminal. He'd been back in Cameroon for not quite twenty-four hours now, and it still didn't feel right. The heat, the sounds and smells, that specific accent of French spoken everywhere, the hustle of people trying to eke out a living in a hard city. This should have been natural to him. This was the country of his birth, where he grew up. He was home.

But it didn't feel like home. It hadn't since the day he saw his mother in a bloody, medicated heap at Central Hospital. Georges knew this city intimately, and yet somehow it was still strange to him. It had never occurred to him to come back. He had a new life in America now. It had been a hard start, but he'd made it better. But Romy. He had no idea what had happened to her after she left home. He'd pulled himself and his parents out of their slum apartment in East Palo Alto. But his sister had slipped through his fingers, and he had no idea what had happened to her since then. Whatever it was, it had brought her back here in search of revenge.

It wasn't a path that suited her. She wasn't supposed to be running for her life, hunted by men hardened by poverty into brutal cruelty. It was a path that ended in the cold dark of a grave.

He looked up and saw John Crane emerge from the jetway. He had a bag over one shoulder and a heavy overcoat draped over his arm. He was dressed for Finland, not equatorial Africa. Georges waved, and Crane nodded back. They met at the end of the security barrier and shook hands.

"Thank you," Georges said, "Thank you. I'm so sorry to bring you into this."

"Don't be ridiculous," said Crane. "You need help. I'm here."

They walked through the crowded concourse. Apparently, Crane had no luggage beyond the bag on his shoulder.

"I'm going to need to do some shopping," he said.

Georges nodded. "I got us a car, a couple of hotel rooms. I made some calls."

Crane glanced around as they stepped out into the heat of the tropical afternoon. "Weapons?" he asked softly.

"Not a problem in Cameroon. Not if you know the right people."

"Don't take this the wrong way, but you don't strike me as the right people."

"I was a good kid," Georges admitted, "but maybe not always *that* good. I had some friends my parents didn't approve of."

"Oh," said Crane, "bad influences? From the wrong side of the tracks?"

"This is Cameroon," said Georges. "It's all the wrong side of the tracks."

———

Crane sat in the passenger seat of the rented Toyota crossover and soaked in the atmosphere of the city. He hadn't been to Africa in some time, and never to Cameroon. Yaoundé was the capital, a boomtown with Chinese money pouring into the oil industry. New towers were going up in the central business district. The bank they visited had readily converted Crane's Euros into Central African Francs. He'd found a very upscale shop to replace the clothes he'd packed for Helsinki, and they'd passed a Porsche Cayman a few minutes ago, parked outside an elegant French restaurant.

Now, less than a mile away, Crane saw how most of the city's residents lived. They drove slowly down a crowded street behind a jitney bus that belched smoke from its tailpipe. Women in bright colors carried groceries. A man pedaled past on a crumbling bicycle, a huge pile of flattened cardboard boxes strapped to his back. There was a sense of grim desperation about the place despite all the color and the snatches of music. This was a place where it took all someone had just to keep from falling back. It took a lot to carve a path out of this place to the other city of cafes and Porsches. Most people would never make it, and the ones that tried would be hardened and sharpened by the effort. This was a place that would breed dangerous men, Crane thought. This was where they would find Yanis Kamkuma.

Georges had briefed him with what little he knew. Yanis was the son of Patrice Kamkuma, a powerful man in the country's unsettled north. He'd proven adept at terrorizing local farmers into signing punitive resource leases, so he was useful to the corporations busily squeezing the north for oil. He'd developed a power base there, and this had all started because he wanted his son Yanis to build on that. Putting his son into a position in the regional government would give him direct access to the flow of corrupt money moving through Cameroon.

By all reports, Yanis was completely unsuited to run a

government department, but Patrice was used to getting what he wanted. When Georges's father had refused to play along and fake college transcripts, Patrice did what he always did. He put Georges's mother in the hospital. But this time the old tactics hadn't worked. Georges's family had fled to America, and for whatever reason, Patrice had never managed to get Yanis into the regional government.

Instead, Yanis had come to the capital with his father's reputation and some money behind him. He'd gathered his own gang of hardened young men ready to do what it took to get ahead in Yaoundé, and he'd done what his father did. Yanis's gang was well known among the city's youth. They lived fast and high. They funded themselves through robbery and extortion. They charged through these lawless parts of the city with their elbows out, knocking over anyone who blundered into in their way.

Georges's sister had chosen very dangerous prey. Now she was hunted herself, by both the police and Yanis's gang of thugs, the Ibiza Boys. They had to find her first, in a teeming city that was new to Crane, but home turf for their adversaries. Hopefully Georges knew more about the grimier side of Yaoundé than Crane would have guessed.

"Down here," Georges said, taking a left onto a dirt packed side street. They glided slowly past a pack of children playing football. Houses lined both sides of the street, brightly painted cinder block structures surrounded by corrugated metal fencing. Ahead of them, someone fought a gate open and a car edged out.

"My friend Ntone," said Georges, pointing to a house. "He loved school. He was good at drawing. But…you know."

They pulled up in front of the house. As they got out a lanky teenage boy approached. He looked warily at Crane for a moment, then turned to Georges.

"Watch your car, boss?"

Georges flipped him a coin, then led Crane to a small gate beside the driveway gate. He pulled it open with a screech.

"Ntone! It's Georges. You home, man?"

They crossed the narrow, dirt-packed yard and Georges knocked at the door.

"Ntone?"

The door opened, and a young man looked out. He was about Georges's age, with close cropped hair and a tank top that hung off his lean frame. He scowled out the narrow crack in the doorway and eyed Crane. His left hand held the door while his right was behind his back. Crane positioned himself to push Georges out of the way if it came to that.

"Georges? I thought you went to America," he said in French. His tone was more cautious than happy.

"Yeah. First time back."

"So you got an American," Ntone said, still eyeing Crane.

"He's okay," said Georges.

"What are you doing back here, Georges? You didn't come all this way to see your old mate from school."

"No," Georges agreed. "We need to talk to you. We need to buy some things."

Georges let that hang there for a moment, then added, "But it is good to see you Ntone. Too long."

Finally, Ntone nodded and his expression relaxed a bit. "Come in. Come in."

They entered a small, tidy living room. Charcoal sketches and paintings lined the wall. Ntone's work, Crane assumed. Georges was right. He had talent. Ntone took a remote from a coffee table—a wooden platform laid atop a bulky metal trunk—and switched off the TV.

"Your ma?" Georges asked.

Ntone shook his head. "Just me now."

"Sorry, man."

They sat down, Ntone and Georges on the sofa, Crane on a chair to one side.

"You got out," said Ntone. "All the way to America." He nodded toward Crane. "Who's this? Your bodyguard?"

"John Crane," Georges said, turning to him and switching to English, "this is Ntone Esua. Ntone, my *friend* John Crane."

"Nice to meet you," Crane said in English over a perfunctory handshake. He'd decided to let the man believe he didn't speak French.

"I guess you really made it, huh?" Ntone said to Georges. "You got white American *friends* now. Good for you."

"Ntone, have you heard anything from Romy?"

"She's back too?" Crane could see Ntone's surprise. He hadn't known she was here.

"She's in trouble. We're trying to find her. I've been calling her old friends, but nobody knows anything. Some I can't find."

"You're back looking for her. What's she doing..."

Then Crane saw realization dawn across Ntone's face. "Holy shit," he murmured. "I heard some girl killed a couple of Kamkuma's boys...Romy? Damn."

"They're looking for her. And the police. I have to find her first."

"I can't believe it," said Ntone. "Little Romy. She was...damn. I can call a couple people from the old days. Word will spread, maybe make it back to them."

"They already know it's her."

"Georges," Crane said in English, "does he know where Kamkuma and his gang hang out?"

Georges translated the question, and Ntone nodded. "They're not hard to find. The Kamkumas have a place over in Bastos that they use. Some other hangouts too. You going after them with just your white American? Bad move, my friend."

"He's more than you think," said Georges. "But we're going to need guns."

"Yeah, you got that right," said Ntone. "You got money?"

"We've got money."

Ntone stood up and took one end of the coffee table in both hands. "Okay, then. Help me move this off."

CHAPTER 40

St. Petersburg, Russia

The night air was heavy and damp, and the alley smelled of alcohol and piss. Einar Persson pressed himself into a niche beside a rack of overflowing trash cans, cold cement against his back, and waited.

Einar put his hand into his thick overcoat pocket and felt the reassuring weight of the gun. He'd been here almost four hours now, waiting for Alexei Kuznetsov to return home. When he finally did, Einar would put two bullets in the back of his skull and then get the hell out of here. It wouldn't be difficult. The apartment building had no security to speak of. The neighbors were either smart enough to mind their own business or too drunk to notice what was going on. He wasn't assassinating a head of state, or some corporate titan with a bulletproof limousine and a flock of armed bodyguards. Alexei Kuznetsov was a grimy little nobody who had inherited a laundry service catering to corporate clients. For some reason his new masters wanted it, and Kuznetsov was too stupid to play ball.

Einar spat on the pavement in disgust. This was what he was reduced to, all he'd been able to salvage from the old life that had collapsed beneath him. As head of security for Datafall, he'd had money, prestige, and authority. When he snapped his fingers, things happened. But Datafall was no more. At first, he thought he'd contained the brushfire incident, kept the company's secrets safe. He'd told the board as much, and they'd believed him. But as time went on, and things started to come apart, it became clear that he'd been wrong.

At least Einar was smart enough to see the writing on the wall early. He'd resigned his position in disgrace and gotten out before the government investigation got into full swing, and things got really bad. He was able to slip out of the country and disappear. He wasn't in prison now, which was more than he could say for much of Datafall's senior leadership.

Eventually, out of money and traveling on a forged Danish passport, he'd washed up here. Einar didn't like Russia. He didn't like Russians. But he knew that here he would at least find someone ready to pay for his particular skills without asking questions. Einar didn't mind killing people. He'd done it before. But starting over again at the bottom, that galled him.

Einar checked his watch. It was after midnight. Where the hell was Kuznetsov? Out drinking, no doubt. When he got here—

"Mr. Persson?"

Einar's heart rate leapt as he drew his pistol. The voice had come from the darkness at the far end of the alley. Who knew he was here? Who knew his real name?

"I know this is a surprise to you," the voice said. It spoke in crisp Icelandic. "I know you're armed and planning violence, so I want to assure you that I am not here to arrest or kill you."

Einar had some cover in the niche. If he moved out, he'd be silhouetted to someone at that end of the alley by the streetlights behind him.

"I've brought you a small gift to show my good intentions,"

the voice said. Something came flying out of the darkness and slapped against the pavement a few feet away. A wallet.

"I will step into the light now to show myself."

A figure emerged from the darkness. A man in an overcoat, his arms out to his sides and hands empty. Einar leveled his pistol at him. He took a few more steps, until Einar could see his face in the dim light. He was Asian, perhaps thirty, an expensive suit beneath the equally expensive overcoat. He smiled and nodded toward the wallet.

Einar glanced around the alley. No one else. He kept the pistol trained on the man as he edged out and crouched down to retrieve the wallet. He flipped it open. It was Kuznetsov's.

"You need not wait here in the cold any longer, Mr. Persson," the man said. "Mr. Kuznetsov won't be coming. Right now, he's in his car at the bottom of the Neva."

"Why?"

"As I said, as a show of good faith. I come with a proposition. We have a mutual enemy, Mr. Persson. I believe we can help each other."

Einar considered the situation for a long moment. If someone wanted to kill him, there were certainly less complicated ways to go about it. He put Kuznetsov's wallet in his coat pocket and lowered the gun.

"All right," he said. "You know me. Who are you?"

"I'm Andrew Choi. I represent a multinational business organization headquartered in China, but with operations around the world. These operations are, of course, not always legal."

"In other words, a triad."

"Not exactly. Though our business often requires us to deal with them."

"So why do you need me? It sounds like you have plenty of people who could do anything I can do."

Choi smiled. "I mentioned a mutual enemy. A man who

penetrated Datafall Analytics' supercomputing center and exposed damning information about the company's activities. This led directly to the company's downfall, and indirectly to your current reduced circumstances."

"You don't need to remind me," said Einar. Oh, he remembered the man well enough. He'd hunted him across Iceland before finally catching up to him at sea. The man had gotten the best of Einar and left him adrift in a small boat, but at least Einar had completed his mission and destroyed the stolen data. Or at least he'd thought so.

"What did he do to you?" Einar asked.

"Much the same as he did to you," said Choi. "He disrupted an important operation that had been underway for nearly a year. We had finally tracked down and captured a high-value target and were returning him to China though covert channels. Somehow, this man managed to find and liberate him. This set us back greatly, as well as causing...considerable embarrassment in certain circles."

Choi reached slowly into his coat and took out an envelope.

"This man has harmed us both. I'm sure you'd like to take revenge as much as we would."

He opened the envelope and handed Einar a photo. It was him. Einar remembered everything about that man—his face, his voice, the way he moved.

"His name is John Crane," said Choi. "We want him dead. And yes, we have people who can kill an enemy. But you are highly motivated. This envelope contains what we know about him, as well as travel and identity documents for you. We'll provide transportation, weapons, whatever you need. We'll put John Crane in front of you, and you won't fail. When he's dead, there will be other work more suited to your skills than this. Do we have an agreement, Mr. Persson?"

Einar didn't have to think about it. This was a way out of

Russia, a step back up in the world, toward the spot on the ladder he'd lost. Maybe higher if he read this man correctly. And all he had to do was kill the one man in the world he most wanted to kill. John Crane. He ran the name back and forth in his mind. Oh yes, he would have killed John Crane for nothing. He didn't have to think about it at all.

"Yes, we do."

"Excellent," said Choi. "Then let's get out of this miserable alley and figure out what you'll need for Central Africa."

CHAPTER 41

Yaoundé, Cameroon

Yanis Kamkumo had a well-earned reputation for sudden outbursts and fits of rage. His crew learned to read the signs and keep a safe distance. Yanis was not a happy man even at the best of times. This was not the best of times.

Yanis sat in the back of his Land Cruiser as Bili drove. Bili was one of the newer recruits, relegated to driving Yanis around. There was no escaping his anger in the Land Cruiser, so the more senior members avoided the job. Bili sat quietly behind the wheel and steered carefully through the crowded streets. Yanis was in no mood for conversation today.

His phone buzzed against his chest, and he pulled it from his shirt pocket.

"Shit."

"Boss?" Bili ventured from the front.

"Shit. Pull over here. And get out."

It was his father, Patrice, calling. He must have heard about the second death. Of course he had. His father was endlessly on his back. Even two hundred miles away in Adamawa, it was like he was right there.

Bili found a place to stop on the side of the street and slipped out as Yanis answered the phone.

"Hello, father."

"What the hell is going on down there, boy?" Patrice Kamkumo had always gotten what he wanted through bluster and intimidation, followed up with brutal violence if that didn't work. Yanis had heard this tone from him every day growing up. It was the voice he used with incompetent underlings or those who tried to resist his will.

"I'm on top of it."

"Oh! Oh, good! Because what I heard is one of your boys tried to screw some piece of fluff and got himself sliced up! And maybe it was her who killed the first one. So that would mean you've lost two of your men to a girl! I'm glad to hear that's just gossip!"

Yanis sighed.

"At least we know that now," said Yanis. "It's not some other crew. There's no war to fight."

"Better if it was," Patrice snapped.

"And I know who she is. It's Romy Akema."

Patrice was silent on the other end. That was something he hadn't known.

"Akema?"

"Yes, father. The old professor's girl. Do you remember?"

"Ah, yes. So it's revenge," said Patrice. "For the mother. How did you learn this?"

"A friend recognized her. He wasn't part of it. We made sure."

"Where's this friend now?"

"I've got eyes on him. We can bring him back in anytime."

"He'll tell you who her other friends are. Track her down that way."

"I'm already doing it, father! I have names and numbers. I

have men on the street. We'll find her. If that doesn't work, we'll bring her to us."

"Oh?"

"If she wants to kill us, she has to come to us," said Yanis. "She tries again, we'll be ready for her."

"Not good enough!" Patrice snapped. "If she knows you're after her now, she'll run. It's not enough. If she just vanishes, then she killed two of your men and got away with it. It makes you look weak—makes *us* look weak! Word gets around, even back here. You have to get this under control fast, or I'll do it myself, do you hear me?"

Yanis put a hand over the mouthpiece and let out an exasperated sigh. As if his father was going to come down to the capital and magically point her out among more than a million people. He'd been yelling to get what he wanted for so long, it seemed he thought yelling could accomplish anything.

"We're going to throw a party," said Yanis. "A big one, public invited. Booze and girls. Show everyone we're not afraid."

"Yes, that's good," Patrice admitted.

"She'll come, and we'll catch her."

"What makes you think so?"

Yanis remembered Michel's body splayed out across the bed in his hotel room, hacked apart and soaked in blood. Yanis had seen violence before. He'd dished out plenty of it himself when it was called for. He'd seen dead men who died badly. Michel's killing had been up there with the worst of them.

Neither Michel nor Sam would have been easy to kill, especially for a young girl. The safe way would be from a distance, with a gun. But she didn't do that. She got close. She butchered them like goats. She kept slashing away well after she'd killed them. She must have been bathed in their blood—so much blood she'd had to wash herself off in the room's shower before she left. She hated them enough to do all that. But she'd smiled and flirted, let them touch her, kiss her, feel her up. She did what it took to get their guard down, and then she struck.

If she could do all that, then her revenge had to be a cold fire burning away her heart, burning itself into the deep corners of her soul. She was driven by it, consumed by it. She wasn't going to stop.

"Trust me," Yanis told his father. "She'll come."

CHAPTER 42

High school was pretty much high school anywhere in the world, Crane thought as they headed across town to find the next name on Georges's list. Romy Akema had been part of a circle of girlfriends who shared everything. They dated the same gaggle of boys and kept each other's secrets. They helped each other deal with the thousand little hurdles of adolescence. Shared challenges forged friendships that they swore would last forever.

Then they graduated, and all went their separate ways. No longer yoked together in the narrow track of high school, their differences suddenly emerged. The old ties faded, and they spun off into individual lives.

One of Romy's friends was in medical school now. One was a receptionist at an insurance company. Another was raising an infant daughter and living with her parents. None of them had heard anything from Romy since she suddenly disappeared. None had any idea she was back in Cameroon.

"Who's this next one?" Crane asked.

Georges took his notebook from his shirt pocket and handed it over to Crane. Crane skimmed down the list.

"Odila Bassong," he read. "Did you know her?"

"I remember her," said Georges. He made a show of concentrating on the traffic, braking and taking a corner. "Her last name was Foncha then."

"So she's married."

"Yeah."

Crane backed off. He sensed a bit of history there, perhaps. Georges wouldn't have been the first young man to get his heart broken by one of his sister's friends.

They pulled into the parking lot of an apartment tower. This was an affluent neighborhood. The building was new and well-maintained, and armed security guards patrolled the sidewalk. The weaponry he'd picked up from Ntone Esua would be more trouble than help here. He slipped the Beretta pistol beneath the seat alongside the compact Mossberg Shockwave shotgun.

A pair of guards at the door carefully checked their IDs and called up to make sure they were expected. As they got off the elevator, Odila was waiting at the door of her apartment. She was a striking young woman in a sleeveless ivory dress with swirling blue trim. He suspected she'd dressed to impress Georges.

"Georges Akema!" she said. "Let me look at you!" She scanned him up and down, then laughed and embraced him. "You turned out all right," she said, and kissed his cheek.

Georges introduced Crane without explaining why he was there, and they went inside. The apartment was tastefully furnished, with a view across the city. A photo of Odila with her husband sat on a side table. They looked well put together, careful about appearances, successful.

Odila offered them a drink, but they declined. They sat around a coffee table and she began to make small talk about their past, but Georges nervously interrupted.

"Have you seen Romy?" he asked. "Have you heard from her at all?"

Odila stopped, and Crane could see her trying to work out what was going on.

"You didn't come back to Cameroon together? When you called, I thought—"

"I haven't seen her in two years," said Georges. "I'm trying to find her."

She looked at Crane with new suspicion. "Is Romy in trouble? Are you—"

"A private detective," said Crane. "She's not in communication with the family, and I'm afraid her father's in very serious condition."

Georges looked at him in surprise. Crane thought he was about to object, but then he settled back into his chair. He looked even more upset, which Crane thought worked to their advantage.

"Oh no!" said Odila. "Is he..."

"We need to find her quickly."

Odila nodded gravely. "She was here. A week ago, now. She called me out of the blue and said she was back in Yaoundé, so I asked her over. We hadn't talked since you left for America. There was a lot to catch up on."

"Did she tell you where she's been?" Georges asked urgently. Crane gave him a quick scowl. He needed her to keep talking, not start thinking about how or why Romy had lost touch with her family.

Odila thought for a moment. "You know, she didn't say much about that. She said she'd been working. Saving to come back home. That you were doing well for yourself. But mostly we talked about old friends. Who's still in town. Who got married. What they're doing. You know."

Crane nodded. "How long was she here?"

"Oh, a couple of days!" said Odila. "We talked until late. My husband gave up and went to bed. We'd had a couple bottles of wine. And then there was some problem with her hotel reservation. They gave her room to someone else. I said she should stay here. It was fun, like the old days when we used to sleep over. Then she stayed another night until the hotel got things sorted."

"Which nights were these?"

"Last Tuesday and Wednesday, I think. That's right. My husband has his study group Thursday nights, and I was alone.

"So on Thursday she moved to the hotel. Which hotel was that?"

Odila thought for a moment. "Huh. I don't know. That's funny. She must have said."

Crane tried a few more questions, but Odila knew nothing else. They thanked her, and Crane left the number of his burner phone with a request to call if she heard from Romy again. Then he got Georges out of the apartment before he said something to break the illusion they were trying to create.

"Why did you tell her that?" Georges asked as the elevator doors closed. "About my father?"

"Because we needed some reason for you to be frantically looking all over Cameroon for her," Crane explained. "With me."

"Those girls were always gossiping like a bunch of clucking hens. She'll tell everyone she knows."

"Good. We want her to. All we've got to go on is the names of some people you remember from her school days, and most of those are getting us nowhere. She's your little sister. How much did you really know about what she did and who she hung out with?"

"Not enough," Georges admitted.

"This one is part of her inner circle. She knows other people your sister's close to, people she'll trust when she's in trouble."

"That's what she's doing, isn't it?" said Georges. "Moving around, from one old friend to the next, crashing on couches. The hotel's just a story, right?"

"That's right," said Crane. "She'd be too easy to find in a hotel. She's covering her tracks. She's cool too. She was here after the first murder. The second was Thursday. She hung out here a couple days, caught up with her old girlfriend, then went off and killed a man."

The elevator deposited them on the ground floor, and they headed back out into the afternoon heat.

"I still can't believe it," said Georges. "I know she's smart enough to get away with it. But..."

"Don't worry," said Crane. "We'll find her. Now we've got an in into her network. That story about your father will spread. They'll want to help her. If we're lucky someone will call us."

They got into the car, and Georges sighed. "More likely they'll just tell her," he said.

"Probably," said Crane. "What will she do then? She took off two years ago and hasn't been in touch since. What's left of the relationship? If she thinks your father might be dying, will that get her to surface?"

"If she believes it," Georges said after a moment. "I think so. But she'll be suspicious."

That made sense, Crane thought. She'd have to wonder why Georges had followed her here now, after two years, and with a private detective no less. That detail would surely be part of the story as it spread. Having them show up searching for her just as she was running for her life was a lot of coincidence to swallow.

If she didn't believe the story they'd set out for her, what would she believe? Why would she think they'd come? She had no reason to think they knew what she was doing. But if they didn't, how did they know to look for her in Yaoundé instead of back in the States?

Perhaps his private detective persona could help there. She might believe he'd been able to turn up her travel documents somewhere, in a State Department or airline database. Of course, a regular PI wouldn't be able to do that, but she might not know that.

Ultimately, she'd either believe the story or she wouldn't. If she didn't, she might break contact with her old friends and go deeper underground. On the other hand, learning they were searching for her, that they knew about the killings, might bring home just how much trouble she was in. Perhaps she just wanted to get safely out of Yaoundé ahead of Kamkuma and the police. If they were very lucky, Romy might call them for help herself.

"What are you thinking?" Georges asked in the driver's seat.

"I'm just figuring the odds," said Crane.

"You know what Josh would say right now."

Crane grinned. "Never tell me the odds."

Georges started the car, and they headed out toward the next name on the list.

CHAPTER 43

After the cold of St. Petersburg, Yaoundé's tropical heat was oppressive. But Einar was used to being uncomfortable. And he had bigger things on his mind.

He'd easily cleared customs with the forged documents Choi had given him. They hadn't gotten a second look. Now he was on the street outside the terminal, his one small bag at his feet, waiting. Around him, travelers wrestled luggage, and cabs jostled for position to scoop them up. Every so often someone would swoop down on Einar, offering him the safest, cheapest, or most luxurious ride into the city. He sent them off with a growled obscenity or two. He was waiting for someone in particular, though he wasn't entirely clear on who. He assumed they would make themselves known.

Here came another one, stepping out of a nondescript Korean sedan. He was a bit better dressed than the others, Einar noticed. He left the car idling at the curb and headed straight for Einar.

"I don't want a fucking ride," Einar snarled.

"Actually, this one, I think you do want, Mr. Persson," the man said in faintly accented English.

Einar gave a vaguely apologetic nod. "Yes, I suppose I do."

They walked back to the car, and the man opened the front passenger door for him. Einar glimpsed a couple hard cases on the back seat. One had the unmistakable dimensions of a long gun case.

His contact got in and drove smoothly out of the airport.

"Are those for me?" Einar asked, with a nod toward the hardware in the back.

"Yes. So is the car."

Einar nodded. "What's back there?"

The driver accelerated around a rattling jitney bus. "Springfield M1A carbine with a Nikon scope and one hundred rounds of .308. The pistol is a Sig Sauer P226 in .40 Smith and Wesson. Laser sight and two hundred rounds."

Einar nodded. It would do. It would do very well. "Good."

"You'll also find a stun gun, a camera with telephoto lens, as well as a phone with some custom software loaded."

"What kind of software?"

"Your target is traveling with someone. He seems to be a local fixer, but —"

"A black man? Young?"

His driver gave a wry smile. "It's Africa, Mr. Persson. We're all black here."

"But this one's not from here, is he? He flew in as well?"

"That's right. You know him?"

"He was in Iceland too."

"Is it a problem?"

Einar remembered the other one as well. He'd appeared suddenly in Akureyri and begun wreaking havoc. He'd been the one to sabotage the helicopter, Einar had realized later, and to hack his team's communications. He'd been there at the end, on the boat. John Crane was mainly responsible for the stolen data recorder making it out of Iceland and destroying his life. But the other one had played his part too.

"No," he said. "No problem at all."

"The fixer got hotel rooms and a car," said the driver. "They don't know someone is looking for them, so they weren't careful enough. Their rental has a tracker installed. There's a lot of car theft in Yaoundé. We've penetrated the company's servers. The car pings the servers with its location every thirty minutes, and your phone will tell you where they are."

"Very convenient."

They were in the city now, in heavier traffic. They stopped at a light, beside a black SUV.

"You've a hotel room as well. Address is in the car's satnav. Is there anything else you need?"

Einar smiled. "You've been very thorough."

The driver nodded. "Then I will leave you here. Good hunting, Mr. Persson."

He put the car in park, got out, and climbed into the passenger side of the SUV. The light changed, and the SUV pulled away. Einar got out and hurried around to the driver's side as the cars behind him honked impatiently.

On the center console, the smartphone chimed, and the map refreshed the blue pin that showed the location of the rental car. Thirty minutes on the dot. Einar's contact had been as good as his word. He didn't really need the tracker now. He'd closed in long enough to get a visual on the car. Now he followed from a distance and observed as his targets crossed the teeming city.

Still, he was grateful for the tracker. Yaoundé was a bewildering patchwork of mismatched roads, noise, strange smells, and most of all, people. People everywhere, jamming their battered and scraped vehicles through overcrowded streets or walking among the idling cars. Poorly muffled motorbikes spat smoke into the air. Hawkers sat on corners shouting about clothes, cigarettes, and bootleg DVDs. Einar drove through a roundabout, past a group of young men doing bicycle stunts on the center island while a video crew filmed them. The city was a swirling, chaotic cauldron of humanity in all its glory and all its squalor. It would be easy to lose his targets in this place.

A block away, their car pulled out of a shining luxury high rise, and they drove past him on their way somewhere else. He turned around at a gas station and followed. They were meandering around the city with no apparent pattern, but Einar knew there was purpose to this. They were looking for something, or perhaps someone. If he knew what they were seeking out, he could hunt them more effectively. He wondered if his new employers knew what had brought Crane and his sidekick to Yaoundé. He could always call and ask them. The phone's contact directory had a single stored number with no name attached. But he knew his performance was being evaluated, and he meant to prove his worth. He would call the number only if it meant the difference between success and failure. It was too bad, he thought as he followed the Toyota through the city's maddening road network. He would have liked a chance at another clue to who he was working for.

Einar had been asking himself that from the moment the man calling himself Andrew Choi had disappeared into the St. Petersburg night. More recently, he'd wondered why they needed him at all since they clearly had sophisticated assets on the ground here, and all the equipment a hunter could ask for. They'd carefully told him almost nothing about themselves, just enough to convince him of their shared intentions.

They were using him to maintain distance, he had decided. Plausible deniability. If something went wrong, there would be nothing to connect him back to them. That was the only thing that made sense. Einar didn't like being expendable, but he was in no position to complain at the moment. And it was true that he wanted John Crane dead as much as they did.

Ahead of him, the car pulled over and parked. Einar turned into a side street, parked, and got out, slinging the camera bag over his shoulder. He reached the corner in time to see Crane and the other man crossing the street. The neighborhood was sketchy, even by Yaoundé's standards, the streets unusually empty. He watched them enter a shop that appeared to sell used electronics. In any European city, Einar would have assumed the place was a front for fencing stolen property. But he was still developing his sense of this new city. Perhaps it was legitimate after all.

Down the street was the mouth of an alley. From there, he might be able to see through the windows. Einar quickly circled the block and found the other end of the alley. The packed dirt was strewn with broken bottles and smelled of cheap beer and vomit. Flies buzzed in the heat. Einar made his way to the far end until he could see the shop's windows across the street. He crouched down and removed the camera from its bag. He powered it up and zoomed in with the telephoto lens until he could see the interior of the shop.

Crane and the other man stood at the counter, talking to the clerk. There was no one else in the shop. The clerk didn't seem intimidated. This was a friendly conversation. Einar let the lens drift over John Crane, his hair, his face, his build. He carefully expanded his mental picture of the man, deciding who he was, how he would move and fight. The man who traveled with him had useful talents, Einar knew, but he'd be no threat in combat. But Crane held himself like a fighter. Einar had underestimated him at Akureyri. Never again.

Then there was a voice behind him, low and hissing. Einar

turned to see a man threatening him with a knife, speaking in rapid French. Einar didn't understand him, but he got the message well enough. He wanted the camera, and anything else of value. Einar picked up the twitchy eye movements and small pupils that came with heroin use.

"Okay, okay, just be cool," he said in English, trying to sound afraid. The man waved the knife and barked something back in French.

Einar pulled the camera strap over his head and slowly held it out. As the man reached for it with his free hand, Einar suddenly dropped it. The man's eyes were still following the camera down when Einar slapped the knife away and punched him in the throat. He took the right wrist and spun the man against the wall, his arm behind his back. The mugger protested in French, his voice a frustrated wail. Einar ignored him and twisted the knife from his grasp. A moment later, the man let out a final groan as the blade slid between his ribs and into his heart.

Einar held him against the wall until the trembling ceased, then lowered him to the ground. There was very little blood with the knife still pressed tightly into his side. Einar snatched up the camera and prepared to flee, but as he looked around, he realized no one had seen or heard them. He was alone with the body. The only sound was the traffic a block over. He glanced back at the electronics shop and saw Crane and his companion leaving. They headed not toward the alley but toward their car. A few moments later, the Toyota rolled past the alley mouth. John Crane was in the passenger seat, but he didn't look in Einar's direction as they passed. Then the car was gone. He would lose track of them by the time he got back to his car, but the tracker would tell him where to go.

In the meantime, there was something else he could do here to help himself. The store clerk would know what Crane and his friend were looking for. He might even know where to find it. Einar knelt down again and pulled the crude knife from the would-be mugger's side. He wiped it on the dead man's filthy shirt, then concealed it against his leg as he strode out of the alley and crossed the street.

The clerk's second conversation would have to be a lot less friendly than the first.

CHAPTER 44

Club Paradis was at the edge of the Emombo district, on a street being gradually turned into a commercial and entertainment strip by foreign investment. The club was on the ground floor of its two-story building. The second floor held a double row of hotel rooms, though Yanis knew they were used more for prostitution than by travelers. Yanis sat in the owner's office at the rear of the building with his feet up on the owner's desk. The owner himself cowered in a corner, trying not to move or make a sound that might bring Yanis's attention back to him. A trickle of blood dripped from his nose. There had been a disagreement about the cost to rent the club for a private function, but it had been settled quickly enough.

"Party's tonight, man," Yanis said. "You going to have plenty of 33 on hand?" 33 Export was a popular local beer.

"Yes, yes," the owner said. "It'll be here. The truck comes this morning."

"I'm counting on you, you hear? This is a special night. Everything needs to be right."

"It will be!"

"You don't want to embarrass me tonight."

"No. No. Club Paradis is the top. Best in Yaoundé. You'll be happy."

Yanis didn't actually care. True, the party was meant to show the locals that all was well with his crew despite the murders, and they'd built a reputation for doing everything first class. But their public image was easy enough to repair. They could knock a few heads around any time to remind people to take the Ibiza Boys seriously. The important thing tonight was to take down Romy Akema before she did any more damage.

To make sure of that, he'd effectively taken over the club. It would be his boys on the door and patrolling the floor. They would control movement in and out of the club and the upstairs rooms. Once she came into the club, she wouldn't leave again. And he'd done his best to make sure she'd come. It was just the kind of setup she liked. Drinks flowing and music. Dim light and a crowd to hide in. The smell of sex in the air to get her victim thinking with his dick. For the last two days they'd papered the city with flyers and put out the word. Come party with the Ibiza Boys at Club Paradis. If she were smart, she'd know it was a trap. But she had no way of knowing they'd made her. And if she was smart, she'd have stayed far away from him and his boys in the first place. No, something was driving her. The need for revenge had soaked deep into her soul and wouldn't let her go. She'd come. She'd come to him tonight, and she'd die.

"Wait here," he told the manager as he stood up. "Deliveries show up, you take them. Any of your staff show up, you keep them here. It's a normal day, you understand?"

"Yes, yes."

"I've got to get ready. I can't be watching you all day. Anything happens..." He threw a slap in the man's direction, and he flinched.

"It won't! I won't...please don't hurt me. I'll do what you want."

Yes, Yanis told himself as he walked out to the front of the house, restoring his reputation would be no problem at all, despite his father's fears. Just kill the girl, and everything would be back to normal in no time.

His crew had taken over the main floor. They'd found the bar, and Manu was playing at bartender while the others laughed and drank.

"Cut that shit out!" he barked. Faces turned in sudden surprise.

"Manu, get out from there. What the hell are you all doing? Over here, over here!"

He gathered them on the open dance floor. The place looked grim and dreary by daylight, he thought. His crew gathered there didn't look much better. Nzo had actually brought his drink over with him, the idiot. Yanis smacked it out of his hand.

"What the hell is wrong with you?"

"Sorry, Yanis."

"I don't need you all drunk off your asses by tonight. This isn't a party! We're here to kill someone. Act like it."

He looked over their sheepish faces. They were idiots, most of them. But they were hard. Growing up in Yaoundé's slums or the desperately poor back country of Cameroon had ground out any softness in them. They were something he could mold into a weapon for his own uses. A blunt weapon, to be sure, but a deadly one.

"Manu, Christian, you'll be on the door. They've got walkies for the bouncers. Use them. Bili, I want you on the back stairs. Nobody goes up or down."

He pointed over to the main stairway up to the second floor. There was a narrow balcony that overlooked the dance floor and stage, and beyond that the hallway to the six bedrooms.

"I'll be up there. Henri and Coco, you're with me."

They nodded. "Right, boss," said Coco.

"Up there, it happens in Room Three. She goes for someone, you tell her you've got a room upstairs. You take her there. Martin and Diboue, you'll be in Room Two for backup. Other rooms stay locked tight, you got that? I don't want some stranger taking a piece of tail up there and getting in our way."

"So how do we know this girl, boss?" Christian asked. "Gonna be a lot of girls. And what do we do when she show herself?"

"We'll have a spotter," said Yanis. "Up on the balcony, so he can get a good look down here. The rest of you, be on the floor. Move around, show yourself. It's a party and you're having a good old time. But keep your eyes open, hear me? Some girl moves fast on you, go with it. If she's good to go, bring her upstairs. If it's not her, we'll wave you off and send you back down."

There was a bit of groaning at that. He picked one of them at random and snarled, "Get her fucking number, Simon! You can call her up tomorrow night! When this is done you can get laid until your balls shrivel up. Tonight, you be on point, or maybe you end up a pile of wet meat like Sammy and Michel. You hearing me?"

The boys nodded and murmured, cowed for now.

"If it's her, you take her into Room Three." He gestured toward Henri and Coco. "We'll be right behind you, and Martin and Diboue will come through from next door. That's six of us. That should be enough to take one little girl."

He heard the front doors open and Maurice called out.

"Back here, Maurice," Yanis called, and a moment later Maurice appeared, strong-arming the girl's friend alongside, the one who recognized her at Sam's wake. Yanis thought until the name came to him. Daniel Massila. "Daniel!" he said, with a warm smile that wasn't meant to convince.

"What do you want from me? I told you all I know already!"

Yanis patted his back and put an arm around him. "I know, I know. Thank you. Don't worry, Daniel, it's going to be all right. You're going to a party. There'll be dancing and drinks. And you're going to see an old friend."

———

Crane edged the Toyota through the streets as the late afternoon sun glared through the windshield. Georges was on his phone in the passenger seat. Their networking had paid off. Whoever had called had obviously seen Romy.

"Right. I've got it, thank you," Georges said. He kept asking questions, punctuated with an occasional nod or "uh huh." Then he was quiet for some time, listening. Crane glanced over and saw from his expression that something was wrong.

"Oh no," Georges said quietly. "When? No, thank you for telling me."

When he hung up, Georges said nothing for a moment.

"I'll take the good news first," said Crane.

Georges let out a breath and put his phone back in his pocket.

"That was Alice Nydo, from her old singing club. I'd forgotten about her. She wasn't on my list. But she heard from someone who heard from Odila. Romy stayed at her place last night. She left just a few hours ago. We just missed her."

"Did she know where your sister was going?"

"Maybe," said Georges. "She left behind a flyer. Kamkuma's throwing a big party tonight. Someplace called Club Paradis over in Emombo. DJ, open bar, all of it. All are welcome. Come celebrate with the Ibiza Boys. It's a trap."

"Of course, it is," said Crane. "Will she fall for it?"

Georges thought. "I don't know. She's very stubborn once she sets her mind to something. If she thinks they still don't know who she is…"

"Either way, that's where we're going," said Crane. "If she doesn't show up, then she's safe. If she does, we'll be there. Now what else?"

"Antoine? The clerk we spoke to? He's dead."

"How?"

"Alice didn't know much. Just what the gossip network told her. The police say it was a robbery. They found the killer dead in an alley across the street. It must have happened right after we left."

That was too much coincidence for Crane. Apparently for Georges as well.

"It was them, wasn't it? Kamkuma's thugs."

"Probably," said Crane. "They had the same idea we had. Beat the bushes, work through her friends, find out who's seen her. We need to wrap this up."

Georges looked up the address of Club Paradis and punched it into the car's GPS. Crane followed the instructions as the sun began to set over Yaoundé. He'd begun this intending to just find Romy and get her out of Cameroon. But the stakes were rising now. It was looking more and more like it was going to end up being more than that, that the only way to protect innocent lives was to take down Yanis Kamkuma.

The most likely explanation for the store clerk's death was that Kamkuma had had him tortured to reveal what he knew about Romy Akema, then killed to keep him quiet. But he'd apparently done a fine job of throwing the police off his trail, complete with another dead body to serve as the patsy.

Yes, Crane thought, he was definitely going to have to take this fight to Kamkuma before it was done. And it sounded like Yanis might be more formidable than he'd thought.

CHAPTER 45

The flyers blanketing the city had done their job. The street was packed with cars, bikes, the youth of Yaoundé in their cruising finery. Taxis honked and young men shouted at the girls walking in small clusters. Romy moved through it all with quiet efficiency. She watched the crowd for threats and scanned the alleys and surrounding buildings, identifying the escape routes she'd mapped out earlier on her phone.

Romy was dressed to fit the party in a bright yellow cocktail dress, a purse hanging from her shoulder by a chain. The purse held nothing but a chunk of flagstone she'd picked up on the way here. It was just a part of her costume and a backup weapon she could drop if necessary. Her clothes, makeup, all the things she didn't need right now were in her traveling bag, stashed in a utility shed near Alice Nydo's house. The things that really mattered she wore close to her body. She carried the phone in a stretchy fabric underarm pouch beneath her dress. Her primary tools—the syringe and her two small, sharp blades—were strapped to her thigh, easily reachable under the dress's short hemline.

The party was already in full swing as she approached Club

Paradis. House music spilled from the neon-lit entry. A few people were dancing in the street. A couple big men in suits manned the doors. Romy stopped short as she recognized them. They were Kamkuma's boys. They'd taken the place over. This was indeed the trap she'd assumed. They were hoping to draw her in. She scanned the street but didn't see any more members of the gang. The bouncers were the outer line of defense.

For a moment she wondered whether she should just keep walking and never look back. This was crazy of her. Surely, she was insane. But no, the wound in her was still there, gaping and painful. If anything, coming home had made it worse. Reconnecting with old friends showed her the outlines of the life she should have had. These men tore that life from her with their stupid greed and brutality. Nothing had been right since that day. She wanted her life back, or at least a new one free from the fear and rage that burned everything she tried to build. She couldn't live at peace in a world that included them. They had to die. Even if it made her a killer, someone she barely recognized in the mirror. The person she'd been was long gone anyway. If the new Romy was vengeful and deadly, with blood on her hands, it was because they'd made her that way.

"Hey," she called out to the men guarding the door. "There a cover tonight? This a private party?"

They looked up and she felt their eyes sweep her.

"Nah, darling," one of them said. "Open house tonight. Compliments of the Ibiza Boys."

"Come in and party with us, pretty girl!" the other one called.

She studied their faces for tension, a trace of recognition, but saw none. They knew someone was hunting them, and they'd set a trap. She knew it would get harder with each one as they learned her methods. She would have to adapt. But they didn't know who she was. Not yet, at least. This could still work.

Romy smiled and walked between them into the club.

Inside, she moved through the press of people, scanning faces. The music was loud, and she felt the thick bass beat in her bones. It was a fast beat, urging her on. She spotted more of Kamkuma's boys scattered around the place. She looked for the exits and memorized the routes. Main stairway to the rooms upstairs. Doors to restrooms, the kitchen, the service stairway. She closed her eyes and visualized the ways out if something went wrong. Then she edged around the crowded dance floor and headed for the bar. She'd play it cool for a while, get the vibe of the place, see if any of them approached her. If not, she'd decide who looked like the easiest target and move in herself.

She found a spot at the bar and ordered a drink. The DJ faded into a new track. Someone tried to chat her up, but she quickly shot him down. He was cute, but he wasn't what she'd come here for. The gangers were on alert, she realized as she studied the place. They were positioned in zones around the floor, acting friendly, but watching.

A crack of doubt appeared in her confidence. Would she be able to peel one of them off and get him away? This wasn't a real party like the last one. They were on the job. If she tried to approach one, she'd have to overcome suspicion. Even if she did, she'd have to get him away from the others, and they'd be watching.

Perhaps seduction had outlived its usefulness. Perhaps the time had come for direct attack.

Then her heart leapt as she spotted another familiar face on the balcony. Daniel Massila. Their eyes met and she saw him flinch as they recognized each other.

Shit!

That was Kamkuma beside him, a tight grip on Daniel's arm. They'd made her, she realized with a terrible certainty. They knew exactly who they were looking for.

Romy slid off the bar stool and started toward the front. She cut into the dance floor, threading between the bodies. Adrenaline rushed through her system until her heart beat faster than the music. Then she saw one of the gang angling toward her, one hand inside his jacket. She turned and moved away, but there was another. This one had an earpiece. Kamkuma would be directing them from the balcony.

Keep your cool. Stay ahead of them.

She turned and headed back the way she'd come. At the back end of the bar was the fire door to the service stairs. That would get her off the floor at least. Upstairs, she could look for another way out of the building. There should be a fire escape at the rear. If she could make the roof, the buildings on either side were the same height as this one.

She pulled the fire door open and slid through into pale light and gray cement walls. She started for the stairs, but then a shape hurtled in from the side and slammed into her. A powerful arm pinned her right arm against her chest, and she felt hot breath on her neck.

"Come on," his voice grunted in her ear. "You coming with me." He was strong, the arm like a vise around her chest. He dragged her up the steps as she struggled in vain to break his grip. The purse slid from her shoulder and fell with a heavy thump on the stairs. She stomped back against his calf, but the blow slid ineffectually off his leg.

She fought back the rising panic that threatened to overwhelm her. Her left hand reached beneath the hem of her dress, and she felt for the syringe strapped there. She was pulled two more steps up. Off balance, her fingers slipped off the hard plastic. Finally, she managed to pull the syringe free. She caught the edge of the cap on the strap and popped it off. Then she thrust back hard and jammed the long needle deep into his groin.

He shouted out in pain and she felt the grip on her chest loosen.

"You bitch!" he shouted and shoved her against the wall. Then he punched her in the face. The shock was like nothing she'd ever known. He threw another punch and her head slammed back against the cement wall. Her vision blurred, and she grabbed at the gritty metal railing to keep from falling.

He was drawing back to hit her again when he stopped. His eyes lost focus, and he sank in a heap on the stairs. Romy shook off the fog in her head and knelt beside him. She ran her hands over his body and felt the hard outline of a pistol in his pocket. She pulled it out. It was a cheap revolver. She took it and looked up the stairs. He'd been taking her upstairs, not back out to the floor. That was where they meant to kill her. She had to change the situation, break the trap.

She kicked off her shoes and ran down. As she opened the fire door, the muffled pulse of the music exploded into the stairwell. One of Kamkuma's boys was there, just about to open the door himself. He looked at her in surprise, and Romy shot him point blank in the heart. He collapsed and didn't move.

She kept firing up over the heads of the dancers until the pistol clicked dry. Panic swept through the club like fire through dry brush. She heard screams through the pulsing music. She glimpsed people running, falling over each other. Then the fire door swung closed, and Romy turned and dashed up the stairs. At the top, she dropped the empty pistol and yanked one of the blades from the strap around her thigh. Then she pushed through the door.

She could hear sounds of panic from below—screams, something heavy falling over. Two men blocked the far end of the corridor. One was Yanis Kamkuma. They started toward her, and then she saw a room door open halfway down on her right. Another gang member looked out.

"What's going on?" he asked in confusion.

"Get her!" Yanis shouted.

She was going to die here, she thought for an instant. But then she banished that thought. She let everything fall away but the rage that drove her. The one in the doorway looked unsettled. This wasn't the plan. There was an open door behind him, a way forward.

She was pure animal instinct, the last shreds of the schoolgirl she'd once been pushed away. Romy clutched the knife in her hand and charged.

CHAPTER 46

Crane didn't know if Kamkuma's party would lure Romy Akema, but it had certainly drawn a crowd. The streets around Club Paradis were thronged with people and cars. They parked the Toyota two blocks away and walked. Both sides of the street were lined with low buildings. Crane noted small shops, a restaurant, and a dental office. Club Paradis was at the middle of its block, two stories of poured cement coated in bright lights and neon. Dance music hung in the humid night air, heavy on the bass.

"Stick close to me inside," he told Georges. It would be easy to get separated in the crowded club. He would have preferred to leave Georges in the car. There was a slight possibility that Kamkuma or one of his men would recognize him. But if Romy was here, he'd need Georges to get her out. She didn't know him, and she'd hardly leave with some stranger in a nightclub because he said she was in danger.

They passed two men at the door who were only watching the women and paid no attention to them. Inside, the club was hot. Music throbbed and colored lights swept the packed dance floor. Crane scanned the floor, getting the layout of the place and looking for the gang members he knew would be here. They weren't hard to spot. It was in the way they carried themselves.

But it was more than that, he quickly realized. They were moving through the crowd with purpose, homing in on the bar at the far end of the dance floor. At least one of them had his hand cupped over an earpiece.

They'd found her. Or at least they thought they had. Georges picked up on it too. Crane saw him tense. Then there was a gunshot, nearly drowned by the music. A moment later, five more shots followed in quick succession. Crane heard screams. Around him, people looked about, startled and unsure what was happening. That wouldn't last long.

"Romy!" Georges shouted, and started forward. Crane quickly grabbed him and pulled him back.

"This way!"

He could already hear the wave of panic coming toward them. In another moment there would be a stampede for the doors. He dragged Georges back the way they'd come as the screams engulfed them. He elbowed his way through the crowd, trying to stay ahead of the worst of it. Georges followed in his wake. As they neared the door, a young woman stumbled on her high heels and fell in Crane's path. He swept her up before she was trampled. In her panic she tried to fight him off. Crane kept her moving and managed to push her through the front doors. Then she whirled and was gone.

Georges was in the doorway, looking back over his shoulder and calling, "Romy! Romy!" Crane pulled him clear as the crowd started to spill out onto the sidewalk.

"I'll find her!" he shouted over the screams and cries. "Go! Get the car!"

It took a moment, but then Georges nodded and hurried away down the street. Crane pushed his way through running bodies to a spot up the sidewalk. He pressed his back against a parked car and watched the crowd streaming out the front doors. If Romy came out, he'd see her. If not, then once the crowd thinned out, he'd head back in and look for her. He kept one hand on the Beretta under his shirt.

People kept streaming out the doors. Some were hurt now. Crane saw ripped clothing, a man with blood streaming from a wound to his forehead. The crowd had flooded the street. People searched for friends. Cars honked as they tried to move through the throng.

Crane was just about to try and press his way back toward the doors when he heard glass shattering above him. Something exploded out of a second-floor window, plummeting down in a glittering shower of fragments, and slammed into the hood of a parked car. It was a nightstand, Crane realized. The car's alarm added its shriek to the din in the street. The crowd looked up, momentarily distracted. Then two figures hurtled from the window, caught briefly in the shaft of light from inside. They pinwheeled toward the sidewalk, clutching each other. Crane saw a woman's bare legs.

Then they slammed into the cement, and the screaming started again.

———

Einar sat in his car, well back from the chaos, watching as people swarmed out of the club and milled about in confused panic. He knew what he was watching now. The black man was Georges Benly Akema. He didn't know how he was connected to Crane, but that didn't matter. They'd come to Cameroon looking for Georges's sister, Romy. Apparently, they expected to find her here at the nightclub.

Something had clearly gone awry.

Here came Akema now, hurrying back toward their parked car. He ran right past Einar's window, and Einar briefly considered getting out and simply killing him in the street. He would be an easy target here, in the confusion and separated from Crane. But no, that would just tell Crane that he was here. Right now, they had no idea he was stalking them. Best to keep it that way until he knew more.

He spotted Crane, an island of stillness in the swarming crowd. Einar grabbed the camera from the passenger seat and zoomed in on him. He was scanning the people fleeing from the club, no doubt looking for the girl. Which meant it wasn't Crane who had caused the panic. That was interesting. What else was going on here?

Movement caught his eye, and he shifted his focus up just in time to see two bodies hurtle out of a window and plunge to the street. They slammed into the sidewalk and didn't move. Crane moved quickly toward them. Another figure appeared in the shattered window. He leaned out, looking down, and Einar saw a gun in his hand. Then there were two more shots, and the gunman staggered back out of view.

Einar panned down to the street again. It was Crane that had shot the man. He put his pistol away, then he bent down over the two fallen bodies. After a moment he stood up again with one of them—the girl—slung over his shoulders.

Einar clucked his tongue. That must be the sister. This was turning into much more than just searching for a missing person. What had Mr. Crane gotten himself into now?

The shattered window, the falling bodies, and the gunshots had set off another wave of panic. Crane checked the window. The man he'd shot had stumbled back into the room, though his gun had fallen nearby. The window was clear. He stuck the Beretta back into his waistband and knelt beside Romy.

She'd landed on top of the other man, thankfully. She was dazed from the fall but seemed otherwise unhurt. He wasn't so sure about the man she'd landed on. Blood oozed from the back of his skull onto the sidewalk. A serious concussion at best. He didn't have time to determine whether the man was dead, and frankly he didn't care. He was surprised there had been no police presence around the party to begin with. They would certainly launch a heavy response to something like this. He needed to get the girl out of here.

Crane hauled her up and got her into a fireman's carry. He looked around for Georges and the car. All around him was a chaos of frightened people and honking horns. A crying girl hurried past, shouting into her cellphone. On the street, a car lurched forward and crunched into the rear of a taxi. A motorcycle roared up onto the sidewalk and swept past him as people dove out of the way. Georges wasn't going to be able to make it through this. He'd have to meet him halfway.

Crane oriented himself and headed down the street with Romy slung over his shoulders. She was starting to groan and squirm.

"It's okay," he called over his shoulder. "I'm with Georges. I'll take you to him." He had no idea if she understood him. Even if she had, in her position Crane wasn't sure he'd believe it. He was a stranger carrying her off through the streets in the middle of a near-riot.

He could feel a belt around her thigh as it pressed against his forearm and what felt like a small knife. He couldn't take it from her at the moment, but at least she couldn't reach it in this position. The last thing he needed was the girl he was trying to rescue plunging a blade into his spine.

A horn honked and he looked up to see their rented Toyota

twenty yards ahead. Georges was on the wrong side of the street, waving at him from the car window.

"Unlock the back!" Crane shouted as he carried Romy between two cars. He shoved someone out of the way and hauled the door open. He dumped the girl into the back seat and fell in after her.

"Go!"

Romy started to struggle as Crane landed on her. He managed to yank the door closed. Then he reached between her legs to grab the knife she carried there and tossed it into the front.

"What the hell?" Georges said over the continuous, frantic beeping of the car's collision sensors.

"She's all right! Get us out of here. And talk to her. Let her hear your voice."

The car lurched forward a bit and stopped again. Crane saw people pushing past all around.

"It's me, Romy," Georges was saying over and over. "It's Georges. You're okay. I found you. You're okay."

She had been flailing and struggling against Crane as he tried to get them both upright in the seat. Gradually she came back to herself. Their eyes met, and Crane saw the terror in them as she cringed back against the door. She scrabbled for the door handle, but the child safety lock was engaged, and the door wouldn't open. Then her brother's voice seemed to break through her panic.

"Georges?" she said weakly.

"It's okay, Romy," he said. "It's me. You're okay."

"How are you here? Who is this?" she said, looking at Crane.

"He's a friend. You're okay. We're here to take you home."

Then, somehow, Georges found a route out of the chaos, and the car was moving. They sped away into the night as the first sirens started to wail behind them. Crane moved as far from her as he could in the back seat. He kept his arms at his side and tried not to agitate her. They'd found her, alive, and gotten her safely away from the gangsters searching for her.

Now all they had to do was get her out of Cameroon.

CHAPTER 47

The morning sun filtered through the gap in the curtains and fell across the foot of the bed. Georges sat in the room's armchair and watched Romy sleep. As the sun rose, the narrow shaft of light angled slowly up toward her face. Soon it would fall across her eyes and wake her.

Georges wasn't sure he was looking forward to that.

They'd gotten her back to the room, cleaned her up, and confirmed she wasn't badly hurt. She hadn't wanted to talk then. Georges had given her his bed, and she'd finally gotten to sleep a few hours ago. For Georges, sleep was out of the question. He'd passed the time looking through the phone Romy had strapped under one arm. He dumped its memory to his laptop and sifted through the call records and position data to reconstruct her actions over the last several days. She'd stalked the Ibiza Boys like a hunter, snapping covert photos and taking notes. She'd collected addresses and descriptions of cars. She'd clearly put a lot of thought and planning into her vendetta. Crane had actually said that, for someone without any training, he was impressed by her instinct for fieldcraft.

She'd tagged a spot near Alice Nydo's home as "bag."

Georges assumed that was where the rest of her things would be found, presumably including her passport. They'd need that to get her out of Cameroon, and Crane had driven off to retrieve it. Georges kept vigil over her while his thoughts raced, and he tried to come to terms with what he'd learned.

He hadn't seen Romy since her eighteenth birthday. What had happened to her since then? How had the sweet little sister he'd known turned into a killer? What would happen when he took her home? Would she stay? Was it even safe to take her home?

So many questions he'd never imagined needing to ask. The answers could only come from her. But it didn't matter in the end. He'd found her, and she was safe. He'd promised his parents that he would bring her home, and he would keep that promise. The rest they could work out later.

In the end, the beam of sunlight didn't wake Romy. It was still edging over her forearm when she rolled over and looked up at him.

"Georges."

"Hey."

"Where am I? No, I remember now. Hotel."

Georges nodded.

"Who's the other man? Where did he go?"

"His name's John. He went to get your stuff. You can trust him, Romy. He's a friend."

Romy sat up on the edge of the bed. She was in her underwear. "Where are my clothes?"

"Your dress was a wreck. I've got something you can put on for now."

"I had a knife."

"You don't need it, Romy! You're safe." He got up and tossed her a pair of canvas slacks and a shirt. She shook her head at them but pulled on the pants. She took her phone from the nightstand and stuffed it into a pocket.

"John will be back with your bag soon. Or we can get you something better to wear once we're out of here," said Georges. "We'll have a couple layovers."

She paused for a moment, then resumed pulling the navy t-shirt over her shoulders.

"I got in trouble last night," she said, "and I appreciate you getting me out. I do. But why are you here, Georges?"

"Why do you think? You're my sister! I've been looking for you for two years. Private detectives all over America. Running all around Yaoundé lying to your friends. We just needed to know you're all right."

"I'm fine."

"And you can come home."

She looked at him like he'd just stepped out of a flying saucer. "You mean America? I'm not going back there," she said. "*This* is home."

"It's not like it was before," he said. "I got a job. A good job. We're doing all right. Things are better now."

She looked across the bed at him, and for a moment her expression softened. "Mom and Dad?"

"They're okay. Dad's tutoring kids in French. It gives him something so he feels worthwhile again. Mom's in therapy. She's doing better. I'm working on a prosthetic hand for her. They miss you. They just need you to come back, and we can be a family again. You can't stay here, Romy. Not after this."

The softness was gone as quickly as it had come. She stalked around the bed and confronted him. "You got it all figured out, don't you? Of course you got a good job. You're a genius! They can use that. You can do tricks for them. Me, I'm just a black girl with a funny accent. You get that, Georges? I'm *black* there! With all the shit that comes with it that's nothing to do with me. You don't know what I've had to do."

"I told you, it's different—"

"I don't want that life," she snarled. "I don't want to be black anymore. Do you hear? I want to just be Romy again. Like it used to be here. But I don't have a life here anymore either, do I? I used to. It was a good life here, wasn't it?"

"It was."

"And those bastards took it away! They took everything. They took away my mama! They took my family, my school, my friends, everything. And they made me run away to a place that never wanted me! I'm glad there's a life for you there, and for Mom and Dad. But there's nothing there for me."

"That's not true, Romy!"

She ignored him. "I want to make a life here, and I can't do that with those monsters here. Always knowing they're out there, knowing they could take it away again whenever they want. No. No. They have to die for what they did. They have to die so I can be free of them."

"You're not...you got lucky!" He'd wanted to say she wasn't a killer, but God help him, she was. "You took them by surprise, and you got lucky. But they know who you are now. That party last night was all for you. To draw you in and kill you. And how do you think we knew to look for you in Cameroon? The police called me! They know what you've done too. But it's all right. They can't prove anything. If we get you back to America, we can make all this go away. But you've got no future in Cameroon. You made sure of that when you killed those men!"

"Then I've got no future anywhere, have I?" she snapped. "I'll make a new one. Go back to your home, Georges. Tell them I'm all right."

She pushed past him, and he stumbled against the chair and fell backwards to the floor.

"Romy! What are you—wait!"

She threw the door open and disappeared into the hallway without another word.

Shit. Georges scrambled to his feet and ran after her. The hallway was empty. There hadn't been time for the elevator. He dashed down the hall, turned a corner, and found the door to the fire stairs. He threw it open, and he could hear her footsteps echoing in the stairwell, hurrying down.

"Romy!" His voice echoed off the cement, but her footsteps never faltered. Then another door creaked open. Georges rushed after her. At the ground floor, he emerged into a back corner of the lobby. He saw Romy running out the front doors, silhouetted against the bright morning sun. She turned right and disappeared.

By the time Georges reached the street, she was half a block ahead. The street was quiet this time of morning. Romy dodged around a woman heading for market. A few bicycles rolled by. Then a car suddenly lurched across the street, leapt onto the sidewalk, and cut her off.

Romy stopped and looked around for a way out as the driver's door flew open and a man dove out. It was a white man with a close-cropped shock of blonde hair.

Georges shouted, "Romy!" He sprinted down the street, arms pumping. But he knew he was too late. Romy tried to dodge away, but the man caught her arm and swung her around. She slammed hard into the side of the car with a gasp, and the man punched her once, twice. Then he opened the rear door and threw her into the back seat.

The man looked up at him as he got back into the car and their eyes met for a moment. Then the car reversed into the street, nearly hitting a man on a bicycle as it went. Its momentum swung the rear door shut. Georges's fingertips just brushed the fender as it accelerated away. Through the window he caught a glimpse of Romy's terrified eyes looking back at him.

Then the car sped away, and the tires screamed as it took a corner and was gone.

Georges stood in the street, breathing hard, and a terrible realization swept over him. He knew that man. He would never forget that face. He felt his whole world falling in on him. This was his fault now. One after another he'd drawn the attention of evil forces, and now they were piling up around him, deeper than he could see over, too deep to climb out of. They would overwhelm him and everyone he cared about.

Another car lurched to a stop beside him. The Toyota. Crane looked at him from the driver's seat with obvious concern.

"Georges! What happened? Where's Romy?"

"She ran. He took her."

Crane got out of the car and turned Georges to face him. "Who took her? Kamkuma?"

"No," Georges said, and his voice sounded very weak and far away. "It was the man from Iceland. From the boat."

Crane stopped and looked at him. "You're sure?"

Georges nodded. "I'm sure."

Crane thought for a moment. "All right," he said at last. "Let's get back to the room and wait for his call."

CHAPTER 48

Patrice Kamkuma owned a home in the Bastos neighborhood, an upscale part of town surrounded by European expatriates and foreign embassies. Patrice seldom came to the capital anymore, and the place had become Yanis's home base.

Of course, his father still kept an eye on the place, and on him.

Yanis paced the living room like a caged tiger. He was alone. The others knew better than to be around him right now. He'd put the phone on speaker and left it on the coffee table. His father's angry tones slid off him. He'd long since stopped saying anything new and simply repeated old points. Yes, Yanis understood he'd had to pull strings to keep the police out of it. Yes, he understood that cost them in terms of favors owed and general clout. Yes, he understood that two more of his men were dead, and two in hospital.

"Who were they?" Patrice barked over the phone.

"I told you already," Yanis called from across the room. "It was the brother. And there was a white man with him."

"What did he look like? The white man?"

Yanis sighed. "A white man. With a gun. I told you, I didn't see him. I was in the back getting Bili out. She drugged him with something." That was how she'd overcome the others, he understood now. It wouldn't have been hard at the wake with the alcohol flowing. And she probably picked up Sam at a bar and slipped whatever it was into his drink.

His father was still yelling at him. "I'm sending some more men down. My men! They know what to do."

He wished his father would stop explaining things that he understood perfectly well. Of course this was bad! He was short of men, and their reputation had taken another big hit. That was done. It was what it was. The only thing left to do was stop the bleeding. Then they could rebuild. The last thing he needed was his father sending down a bunch of ignorant country oafs to stir things up. They didn't know the city at all, and they owed their loyalty to his father so they wouldn't take orders from him. But there was no telling his father that. His father always did the shouting. He never listened.

"They all have to die!" Patrice was saying. "The girl, the brother, this white man. All of them. You have to make an example, Yanis. Or the rest of your men will lose respect. They'll drift away one by one until you don't have shit!"

"I know, father, I know. We're out looking for them now."

"Well stop screwing around and find them!" Patrice snapped. "And when you do, make it showy. People have to see what happens when they cross the Kamkumas."

"I know," he said, placating. "They'll all see." He calmed his father down as best he could, and when his father finally hung up, he settled back on the couch and took several deep breaths.

The frenzy at the club had stayed with him. He could still hear the frightened voices, almost feel the crush of pushing bodies. He remembered the sound of light bulbs exploding as one of the effects bars was knocked over. And the gunshots.

He pieced it together in his mind. She'd managed to drug

Bili and left him unconscious on the stairs. Then she'd taken his gun and shot Simon as he came after her. That set off the panic. Yanis had been on the mezzanine when it happened, trying to spot her on the floor. Then she came upstairs and charged Diboue when he opened the door to see what was going on.

He wasn't sure what had happened in the room, but somehow the girl and Martin had gone out the window together. She'd caused a lot of damage, but she'd been out of the fight at that point. They could have finished her. But then the stranger appeared on the street outside. He'd shot Diboue dead as he looked down from the window.

And it could have been him.

Yanis had no idea what instinct had kept him from going into the room after her. Coco and Henri had gone in. With five men and the girl in the cramped room, they'd have been in each other's way, falling all over themselves. So he stayed out and hurried down the back stairs to check on Bili and the others. Would he be dead now if he'd chosen differently? Diboue was. Martin was in the hospital with a cracked skull, and Coco had a couple nasty knife wounds. Anything could have happened to him. Yanis took a deep breath. It didn't bear thinking about. They just needed to get this over with. End it and get back to the way it was.

The door opened, and Manu came in. He must have heard the lack of shouting and realized the phone call was over.

"You okay, boss?"

"No, Manu. I'm way far from okay. Tell me something new."

Manu nodded. "Stephane says one of the girl's friends saw the white man. Him and the brother been asking around town after her. They say the father's sick, and they need her to come home. The white man's a detective from America."

"So what?"

"They gave a phone number," said Manu. He handed over a

slip of paper. "To call if they see the girl. And we know their car now. White Toyota."

Yanis sighed. As if there weren't a thousand white Toyotas running around Yaoundé. But it was something at least.

"Got a plate on the car?"

"The friend didn't pay attention."

Yanis nodded. Why would she? He looked at the scrawled phone number on the torn piece of paper. He didn't know what good it would do. There was nothing to gain from calling them. They had what they came for. The girl would be scared half to death, and the brother and his detective would get her back to America so fast she'd think it was still yesterday. But he had to do something. Just as important, his crew had to see him doing something. Even if it didn't accomplish anything.

"Get a couple boys to the airport," he said at last. "Look for them there. Call me the second they see anything."

"Okay, boss."

Manu left, and Yanis started pacing again. That wouldn't be a bad thing, actually, if they just left Cameroon and never looked back. It would solve the immediate problem. But there would still be his father, and the damage to their reputation if someone killed a bunch of his men and got away clean. No, he had to kill...someone. Someone had to die badly, and it had to be seen as the Kamkumas' terrible vengeance. But nobody really knew who it was that attacked his crew. Nobody would question it when they took their revenge.

It would be best if he could actually kill the Akemas and their detective. But if it came to it, anyone would do.

———

Einar parked the car in a secluded alley behind a street cafe and hauled the girl out. She'd put up more fight than he'd anticipated when he threw her into the car, but the stun gun had settled her. He patted her down, but she had nothing but a phone in her pocket, not even any identification. The clothes she wore looked like they belonged to the brother. She was barefoot. He didn't know what had happened since they'd found her, but it looked like it had ended badly. She'd left in a hurry, with no preparation and her brother chasing her down the street.

He opened the trunk and dumped her in, then bound her wrists and ankles with a roll of duct tape. Now that he had her, he could get to the bottom of this. She'd tell him what was going on, and she would bring John Crane and her brother to him. He just needed a place to set it up, somewhere outside the teeming city where they could have a little privacy.

She was starting to groan and struggle as he slammed the trunk shut. Einar got back in the car and picked up the smartphone they'd given him. Now was the time to contact his mysterious patrons. He tapped the single contact number, and the call connected. It was answered immediately.

"Good morning, Mr. Persson," said a woman's voice in an accent he didn't recognize. "Have you made progress?"

"I have something they want," he said. "They'll come to me now. I just need a place to set the trap. Somewhere remote and quiet. Can you recommend a place?"

As it turned out, they could.

CHAPTER 49

"Anything yet?"

Across the room, Georges sat with his face buried in his laptop screen. He shook his head. "No."

"Keep looking."

Crane stood at the window letting the morning sun bathe him in warmth. But inside he still felt cold. Einar Persson was here. There was only one reason for the former Datafall security chief to turn up here. Him. And now he had Georges's sister. As if it weren't enough to have the police and this Yanis Kamkuma and his gang looking for her, he'd brought yet another enemy, the most dangerous of the lot. Georges had looked to him for help but involving him had just put his sister in much greater danger.

None of this would be happening if he'd just killed the man in Iceland when he had the chance. He certainly deserved it, for killing the innocent trucker who'd picked Crane up on the highway if nothing else. But he'd needed Einar alive to go back to his employers and convince them they were safe, that the incriminating data Crane had stolen from them was destroyed.

Even if that weren't part of the plan, Crane knew he wouldn't have killed him that day. He didn't need to, and he didn't want to kill if he didn't have to. He'd wanted to keep his conscience clean.

But there was a price for that, and right now it was being paid by someone else.

"He won't hurt her, right?" said Georges for what seemed the fiftieth time.

Crane turned from the window. Georges was looking up at him from the laptop. Data streamed past on the screen representing every cellphone in Yaoundé, each call, each location ping. None of them were Romy's phone. It had gone dark on the network somewhere in the same cell that covered the hotel. Einar had found it and turned it off almost immediately.

They couldn't find her that way. Not until Einar decided he was ready to be found.

"It's us he wants, right?" said Georges. "So he'll keep her safe. And he'll get in touch with us."

"That's right."

Of course, what happened after that was very much in question. He wasn't going to demand a sincere apology and then return Romy safely to her family. Einar would want him dead, probably Georges as well. And after that, there was little reason to keep Romy alive as a witness. So Crane found little reassurance in the knowledge that Romy was safe for now. But Georges needed something to hold onto.

And Georges probably believed Romy would be okay once they found her because Crane would be there to save her. He was Georges's hero who could do anything. There was a lot of past trauma to unpack around that. It all went back to the attack on Georges's mother, right here in Yaoundé. Without that, he probably never would have met Georges. Romy wouldn't be on her own destructive quest for vengeance. All their lives would be very different. Now they'd come full circle, back to where it all began. But Georges had picked him up along the way, and he'd brought a deadly new player into the mix.

That much of it was on him.

Crane didn't really care what happened to Yanis Kamkuma. He was here to extract Romy and get her to safety. If that meant taking Kamkuma down, so be it. If it didn't, Crane was perfectly content to let him go on extorting protection money from shopkeepers or whatever he did when he wasn't being hunted by vengeful young women. He was a problem for the local police.

But Einar Persson was another story. Einar's vengeance was personal. It would follow him to the next mission after this, and the next, until Crane dealt with it. This time there was no reason to keep Einar alive. When he found Einar this time, they would end it.

Then, Crane thought, he would have to find out how Einar was able to track him to Yaoundé.

―――

Georges watched the handset pings scroll past on his screen. He didn't really need to watch them. The program he'd inserted into Camtel's system would spot Romy's phone as soon as it logged onto the network and alert him. But he found something soothing in the steady flow of numbers.

And Georges needed calm. He needed to push down the storm of emotions and think. His sister was in danger. Crane was in danger. And it was all his fault.

He'd failed in Iceland. The communication system he'd designed wasn't good enough. It had been detected, and he'd turned what was meant to be a stealth insertion into a desperate manhunt. He'd been the one to unleash Einar Persson on Crane.

He'd taken on a karmic debt in Iceland. And now the bill had come due.

"Anything yet?" Crane asked from across the room.

"No."

"Keep looking."

Of course he would keep looking. What else could he do? He felt powerless in a way he hadn't felt since the day his mother was attacked. Then he'd raged uselessly against the men who hurt her. He'd fantasized about finding and killing them. It was the policeman who'd set him on the right track. Officer Makoun. "Don't try to fight your enemy on his ground, with his weapons," he'd said that day in the hospital waiting room. "If you want to help your mother, do something smart."

He thought he'd done that when Josh hired him and introduced him to John Crane. He'd turned his talents to equipping Crane for the field. Crane had become his champion, fighting the darkness in the world, doing the things Georges himself couldn't do. But over time his failures kept building up like a slow poison. And now he'd caught Crane between them. Einar Persson on one side, representing his failure in Iceland. And on the other side, Yanis Kamkuma and his gang, representing his weakness, his inability to protect his family.

John Crane was about to be crushed between them, and it would all be his doing.

On his screen, a line of data popped up from the stream and flashed at him. Romy's phone had just registered with the network. It had been turned on and connected to a tower. He looked up the cell site identifier. The tower was southeast of Yaoundé, at the very edge of the city's coverage area. It covered a lot of ground, but he could pin her down more precisely.

He told the carrier's system to request a GPS fix from the phone. Within moments, it came back, a series of coordinates that he transferred into a mapping program. The phone was near Mfou, a small farming town. The area was sparsely populated, with scattered farms and cocoa orchards. Georges switched his map to satellite view and zoomed in on the coordinates. Orchard, he decided. There were long rows of trees set amid high grass. A single red clay road wound through them to a cleared area with a low building. That was where the phone was signaling from.

As he watched, the locator disappeared. The phone had been turned off again. Its message had been sent clearly enough. Romy was being held at an orchard near Mfou. If they wanted her, they could come there and try to take her back.

Georges sat quietly for a long moment. He had no doubt that Crane would go there and take on Persson to save his sister. He would go without hesitation. It was who John Crane was. But what if he got killed? What if Romy was killed? The blame would land on his shoulders.

No, it was time for him to stop asking Crane to solve his problems. It was time to take responsibility himself. He was no warrior, but he had strengths of his own. He heard Officer Makoun's voice in the back of his mind.

"Do something smart."

But what was that? On one side, Kamkuma and his gang of vicious thugs. On the other, Einar Persson on his quest for blood. Both closing in on them.

And suddenly Georges knew what the smart play was.

He closed the laptop. "I've got her."

Crane turned from the window. "Her phone checked in?"

"Right."

"Okay," said Crane. "He wants us to come and get her. Where are they?"

"I assume you're going on your own?"

Crane nodded. "Right. I needed you at the club because

Romy wouldn't trust me. I think we're past that point now. I need you safe here. I'll bring her back."

Georges took a deep breath. He was afraid, but he knew it was the right thing to do.

"Okay," he said, taking a pen and notepad from the desk drawer. "I'll write it down for you."

CHAPTER 50

Crane let the car's GPS navigate toward the address Georges had given him. As he drove, he reassessed his resources and considered how he would take down Einar Persson. He had the pistol and Mossberg shotgun he'd bought from Georges's friend Ntone. He'd been expecting a different kind of fight; he'd have chosen differently for this one. But there was no time to rearm himself. It would have to do.

More important than the weaponry was figuring out how Einar would expect him to come, and then doing something he wouldn't be ready for. He would get close, then park the car reconnoiter the site on foot. He'd try to locate Einar and Romy, then figure out Einar's lines of fire. From there, he'd have to improvise.

His Hurricane Group handlers had hated improvisation. Crane found that kind of ironic, since he always seemed to be doing it in the field.

Doubt started nagging at the back of Crane's mind as the GPS reported him closing in on the address. He was heading deeper into Yaoundé's more upscale quarter. He would have expected Einar to choose someplace more remote and less patrolled for his ambush. What was he up to?

Crane pulled over and checked the address again. It was right. He keyed it into his phone, and it came back with the same location. He was less than a block away, and the GPS was pointing him onto the campus of the École Nationale Polytechnique.

Something was very wrong. Crane slipped the pistol into his waistband and got out. The street was shaded, and a comfortable breeze ruffled Crane's hair. He passed students walking in small groups or sitting under trees with books open. Young men and women posed and flirted. A campus patrol officer gave Crane a curious look as he passed, but then moved on.

This was not someplace you brought a struggling hostage and set up a death trap. Not by a long shot.

What's going on, Georges?

The taxi dropped Georges off in Bastos, outside Patrice Kamkuma's walled compound. Georges steeled his nerve as the car drove away. This place had been in the Kamkuma family since before Georges was born. If Yanis himself wasn't here, someone would know where he was.

Two security guards stood at the gate, watching him with suspicion. Georges fought down his fear. There was no going back now. Romy's life was in the balance. He slung his laptop bag over his shoulder and walked steadily across the street.

The guards were big men in ill-fitting suits. He could see the radio handsets on their belts and what he knew were guns beneath their jackets. They looked him over as he approached, sized him up. They clearly didn't consider him much of a threat.

"What you want here?" one of them said gruffly.

"I'm Georges Benly Akema," he said, and he saw the reaction. These men knew that name. He was in the right place. "I need to speak to Yanis."

"Arrived at Destination," said the phone. Crane looked up at an imposing masonry facade. The main doors opened, and a student came out, loaded down with a heavy backpack and carrying a laptop.

The sign beside the doors gave the building number. In French, it read, "Computer Engineering Building."

There was no mistake, Crane realized. This was the place. This was where Georges had studied before Kamkuma's attack on his mother shattered his old life. It was an address he knew by heart, easy to recall in the moment.

He cancelled the navigation app and called Georges's number. The phone rang just once, then rolled immediately over to voicemail. The phone was switched off.

Son of a bitch.

Georges had lied to him, sent him on a wild goose chase. There was only one reason. Georges wanted him safely out of the way so he could do something fiercely brave and very stupid. He was going to get himself killed, and probably his sister as well.

Crane had to find him, and fast. But he had no idea where to look.

"Damn it, Georges," he muttered.

It was about two in the afternoon right now. That meant it was five in the morning in California. Crane sighed and punched in the priority access number for the war room at Myria Group. He just hoped someone was awake over there.

The guards had strong-armed Georges through the gates and hurried him inside. They'd rifled through his laptop bag and kept it. Then they'd brought him here, into a well-furnished study. The walls were lined with books Georges was sure Yanis Kamkuma had never opened. His father probably never had either. They were meant for show, like the ornate wooden desk where his bag now lay and the portrait of Ruben Um Nyobé, the murdered father of Cameroonian independence.

Two different guards stood behind him, members of Yanis' gang. And behind the desk stood Yanis Kamkuma himself. Georges had never actually seen Yanis before. For someone who had had such an enormous impact on his life, that seemed wrong. They should have met. For a moment he had the wild thought that if he'd just tutored this man in college, all their lives could have turned out so very differently.

"What do you think you're doing?" Yanis asked finally. "Just walking in here. Alone. Unarmed." He gestured toward the laptop bag. "But you made sure to bring that. What's going on?"

"I came to ask for my sister's life," said Georges. "You hurt us. She's hurt you. Let's call it even. A clean slate. Let her go, and I'll take her away from here. You'll never see us again."

For a moment, Yanis just stood there. Georges could see the raw disbelief on his face. Then Yanis laughed, a short, bitter laugh, and the gang members standing behind him laughed with him.

"Pathetic," said Yanis. "Your sister, her at least I understand. We cut up your mother. She wants revenge. I'll kill her for that, but I respect it. But you. You're the elder son. The man. If there's to be revenge, that's on you to do. You step up like a man and fight. You don't send your baby sister to kiss up like a whore and then stab a man in the back!"

Georges took a breath and kept his calm. He couldn't afford to let Yanis rattle him. "I didn't send her. She's been away; we didn't know where she was 'til now. I just want to take her home."

"I heard of you," Yanis said, stalking around the desk toward him. "Before all this. They say you're some kind of genius with computers. You were going to get out of Cameroon, be a big man in America. So much smarter than me."

Georges said nothing. Yanis leaned in, studying his face. "Bullshit!" he shouted, and Georges felt a fleck of spittle hit his cheek. "You're nothing! You're weak! Coming here to beg for your sister."

"I'm not begging," said Georges. "I'm here to make a deal."

"Oh," said Yanis. "Oh! A deal is it? You're crazy too, man! What have you got to deal with, smart boy? What do you think will make me just let your sister go after what she's done?"

"Two things," said Georges. "One. Money."

Yanis scoffed. "Look around. I got money."

"Not like this," said Georges. "They were right about me. I *am* a genius with a computer. I can get into any system anywhere and do anything I want. You got your father's nice house. You take spending money from shopkeepers. You run a couple small time rackets. That's little league. With nothing but that laptop right there on your desk, I can rob a bank without ever walking inside. No cops. No trouble. I can take as much as I want, and they'll never even know what happened. I can get you real money."

He could see Yanis imagining the possibilities despite himself. "You can do that?"

"I already did," said Georges. "Just a sample. To show good faith."

The two men guarding him traded a look. He had them hooked. Now he needed to reel them in.

Yanis shook his head. "I can't let her do what she did to me and walk away. Can't let that stand. Your sister has to die."

"*Someone* has to die," Georges said.

Yanis had been walking away across the room. Now he stopped and turned around.

"What are you saying?"

"It doesn't look good," said Georges. "One girl killing a whole bunch of your gang. Even if you get her, it still looks bad. But there's someone else. That's the second thing. The man who came with me."

"The white man? The detective from America?"

"He killed one of your men. He was seen outside the club with a gun. What's to say he didn't kill the others as well?"

Yanis was looking at him in frank disbelief now. He was reassessing the situation, re-evaluating the man who'd walked into his compound alone and unarmed.

"They'll buy it on the street," said Georges. "A whole crowd saw him shoot down one of your men. And that's a different story, isn't it? It's not about how the Ibiza Boys are small time, weak enough that one girl cut them up all on her own and got away with it. Now you're big time. Big enough that someone went all the way to America for a professional killer to take you down. And he got some of you, but in the end, you killed him and put his head on a stake so everyone would know not to mess with you."

Georges fell silent, waiting. He was terrified, but he didn't dare show it. This was the crucial moment. This was where it would either work or...he didn't want to think about what would happen next if it didn't work.

"You giving up your friend to me?" Yanis said quietly.

"He's hired help. She's family. Blood. I'll do what I have to do."

Yanis let out a slow whistle. "Damn, smart boy. You're harder than I thought."

Yanis glanced over at the laptop bag laying on his desk, then back to Georges.

"Tell me more about the money."

CHAPTER 51

It took a little more than half an hour for Coco to return from the Afriland First Bank with the briefcase. Even before he said a word, Yanis knew it was true. Coco looked thunderstruck, and he carried the briefcase like he was afraid it would slip through his fingers and evaporate into mist.

"Ten million francs," Coco murmured as he handed Yanis the case. He nodded toward Akema, still sitting in the same chair with his two guards at his back. "I told them the password he said, and they just gave it to me. No questions."

Yanis turned and set the case down on the desk beside Akema's laptop. He snapped it open and looked at the tight bundles of purple 10,000 Central African Franc notes. This was a year's income for a working man in Yaoundé. A fortune in the farm country back in Adamawa. He closed the case again and looked back at Akema, who smiled.

"That's just a taste," Akema said. "I can get more. But only when my sister's back safe."

"You already have your sister," Yanis said. "What aren't you telling me, smart boy?" The answer dawned on him even as he spoke. "Wait, I know! Your detective's not your friend anymore, is he? He figured out how you're getting the money to pay him, and he wants more, am I right?" The boy was like the goose that laid golden eggs. It made sense that the American wouldn't settle for just an egg or two. Yanis certainly didn't intend to.

Akema looked down at the floor. "We argued," he said quietly. "He took her. I couldn't stop him. He wants me to bring the money to a farm in Mfou."

"So why not pay him? It's nothing to you. You can get all the money you want."

Akema looked up at him. "If I pay him off, I've still got to worry about you. But if I pay you instead…"

Yanis grinned. The boy thought he was doing the smart thing. He had no idea how far over his head he was. "You pay me off, I take out the American for you, and you and your sister are home free."

"Something like that," said Akema. "You need him to be the killer. I need my sister. I'll throw in enough money to make you forget she was ever here."

Yanis turned and paced the room. Akema sat quietly. Coco and the pair of men behind Akema watched him to see what he would do. The boy wanted to make him his hired hand, someone to go do the dirty work of getting the girl back. Maybe it was because he could rustle up money whenever he needed it, or maybe he'd just spent too much time in America. But he assumed he could just buy his way out of whatever problem he fell into. He just had to flash his money, and people would do whatever he wanted. Yanis would teach him otherwise. But this had to be handled carefully. He knew the fairy tale. The goose would keep laying golden eggs as long as you were patient. But if you got too greedy and killed it, you got nothing.

And Akema was right about him needing the American. The American hit man story would indeed play much better than the truth. It would instantly repair his reputation on the streets. It would even satisfy his father.

But there was more to this. He still knew the truth. The girl had to pay for what she'd done. But once he had her and her brother, and the dead American to take the blame in public, then they could both pay for a long time.

He looked back to Akema. "One hundred million francs."

Akema didn't blink. "When I have my sister back unharmed."

Yanis smiled. It was a predator's smile, like a great cat ready to pounce.

"Tell me where we can find her."

As it turned out, the war room was staffed, even at five in the morning local time. Someone picked up immediately. A man's voice Crane didn't recognize.

"How can I help you, Mr. Crane?"

Crane looked at the Computer Engineering Building one more time, then shook his head and set off quickly toward the car.

"Georges has ditched me. I need to find him before he gets himself hurt. Do you have a location on him?"

"You're in Cameroon, right?" said the voice. The man sounded nervous, like a student who'd just been called on by the professor and didn't know the answer. "This is all kind of ad hoc. We don't have coverage on either of you. We did the transfer. Could he be at the bank?"

"What transfer?"

"He called in about an hour ago. He asked us to wire ten million Central African Francs to a password-coded bank account in Yaoundé. He said you needed it."

Crane glanced at his watch. Georges must have made that call right after he left. Why did he need...

"How much is that in dollars?"

He heard keystrokes, then, "a little over seventeen thousand."

Why did Georges need seventeen thousand dollars?

"And you've got nothing else on him?"

"I'm sorry, sir. No."

"Do whatever you can. If you pick up anything at all, call me immediately."

"Understood. Good luck, Mr. Crane."

Crane slipped the phone back in his pocket. When he reached the car, he headed back toward the hotel. Perhaps Georges had left some kind of clue behind that would tell Crane what the hell he thought he was doing.

CHAPTER 52

Things moved quickly once Georges gave them the location, Yanis had assembled the men he had at the house. He'd called in a few others who were away on various errands. Within minutes, he had a dozen men ready to converge on the orchard in Mfou. They left one man behind to watch him and took off in a battered commercial van.

Georges hoped he'd done the right thing. He was smashing two dangerous enemies against each other, and Romy was in the middle. But he didn't know what else to do. He couldn't send Crane into an ambush and get him killed. Persson wouldn't be expecting this. Yanis and his gang should be enough of a match for one man, but it would be violent. He could only hope his sister came through it unhurt. Persson had nothing to gain by hurting her, and Yanis now had a very good reason to keep her safe. She would be all right, he told himself. She had to be.

He sat with his arms tied to the arms of the chair and writhed with nervous energy. The waiting was killing him. Through the casement window across the room, he saw a squirrel dash up the trunk of an Iroko tree outside. Another one followed, and they chased each other around the tree. Georges wanted to get up, move, pace the room, hit something.

The man they'd left to watch him was doing a fine job of it. He leaned against the bookshelves and stared at Georges in naked fascination.

"Hey, what's your name?" Georges asked.

"Manu."

"Could I have some water, Manu? While we're waiting here?"

Manu pushed off the shelves and walked slowly toward him. Georges could see the wheels turning behind his eyes.

"You just..." he made little typing motions with his fingers, "on your laptop, and boom. The bank gives you money? That must be something."

Georges said nothing. He couldn't really just type his way into the local banks. Ironically, that was because they weren't sophisticated enough. Too much was still done by hand instead of by computer. He'd faked it once, for people ready to believe computers were magic and that he was some kind of wizard. But he couldn't do it again.

"Do it for me," said Manu. "Ten million francs. You set it up and give me the password."

"That wasn't the deal."

"Forget the deal! We got you! You and your bitch sister! We don't work for you. You work for us now, until we're done with you."

Manu slapped his face hard. A shock raced through him, and he tensed against the cords binding him to the chair.

"Yanis won't like it if you hurt me," he gasped in desperation.

Manu leaned in until his face was just inches from Georges's own. He grinned.

"Boss said to soften you up a little."

Then the beating started in earnest. Blows fell around his face until he couldn't tell one from the next. He tasted blood, then felt it fly from his mouth as a hard slap spun his head to one side. When Manu tired of hitting him, he bent Georges's fingers back until he wailed with the pain in spite of himself.

He was no hero. He shouldn't have come here. He wasn't made for this.

Manu stomped hard on the top of his foot, and Georges cried out again. His body insisted that he react to what was happening. He had to move, protect himself, but he couldn't, and the frustration grew almost as intense as the pain.

Through it, Georges tried to focus on one thing: the IP address of the alert station back in the war room in Palo Alto. It became the lifeline he clung to. If he could just make it through this...

At last it stopped. He didn't know how long it had gone on. He'd lost all track of time. There was nothing but pain and an IP address. He heard himself whispering the numbers to himself over and over.

Then a hand grabbed Georges by the hair and pulled his head back off his chest. He saw Manu breathing hard, glaring into his bleary eyes.

"You ready to do what I say now?"

Georges tried to speak but all that came out was a pained squawk. He swallowed blood and tried again.

"I'll need my laptop."

―――

Crane tossed the room quickly and efficiently. Georges had taken his laptop but left everything else. There was nothing to suggest what he'd done or where he'd gone. No note explaining his plans, no scrap of paper in the trash with an address or a phone number. There was nothing. He checked his own room in case Georges had left something for him there, but again found nothing.

He swore and threw himself into the armchair beside the desk. He tried Georges number again, but again the call immediately went to voice mail. There was nothing he could do.

A moment later, his phone rang. It was the war room.

"We've got him," said the voice.

Crane was instantly on his feet.

"Tell me."

"His laptop just phoned home with an SOS. He asked for you. He needs help."

No kidding, thought Crane.

"He gave a Yaoundé address. Sending it now. He's being held there. One man on him, maybe more in the house. He said to tell you to hurry."

Crane was already at the door. As he hurried down the hall, a text message pinged with the address Georges had sent.

"I'm on it," he said, and hung up. At least Georges had managed to call for help when the trouble got too deep. That was something.

Of course, he could have just told him what he was going to do from the beginning. The fact that he hadn't meant he thought Crane wouldn't have let him do it.

And he was probably right, Crane told himself as he ran for the car.

———

Across the room, Manu paced back and forth like an angry cat. "What do you mean, nothing?" he said. He was on his phone with his sister again. He'd sent her to the Afriland First Bank with a passcode, expecting her to come out with another magical ten million Francs.

"You give them the password I said? Say it back to me."

He went to the desk and checked the nonsense string Georges had given him. He looked back at Georges in suspicion.

Georges knew he was running out of time.

"What did they say?"

Manu took a deep breath and let it out. "Okay," he said. "No, stay there. I'll call you back."

He put down the phone and turned to Georges.

"You messing with me? You play me for a fool? There's no goddamn money!"

"There has to be!" Georges said, knowing perfectly well that there wasn't. "You must have got the passcode wrong."

"She didn't get the passcode wrong!" Manu snapped. "There's no account. Passcode or no! You lie to me and I'll cut you up good." He pulled up his pant leg and drew a long, thin blade from an ankle sheath. He held it in front of Georges's face.

"You see this? You gonna see it real close if you're fucking with me."

Georges said nothing. He just wanted to lie down somewhere, curl up on his side, and ride out the pain. But he knew it would just get worse from here. He hadn't thought this out well enough. Someone would have to be left standing at the end, either Einar Persson or someone from Yanis's gang. He wasn't just going to walk out with Romy.

And where were they? What if Einar had killed them all and still had Romy? What if Romy had been killed in the crossfire?

He wasn't cut out for this, he realized with a sudden and complete certainty. He was meant to be in his workshop, building tricks and weapons for someone like Crane to use. That was his strength. Officer Makoun had tried to tell him, "do something smart." But he never quite managed to stay on that course for long. He always found a way to convince himself that whatever he thought of was the smart thing.

It definitely hadn't been this time, and he was going to pay for it. Maybe with his life.

"Maybe something went wrong," he said thickly, through his swollen and bloody lips. "On their end. I can try again."

"No, man. Nothing went wrong. It worked before. You're trying to play me."

Manu slowly pressed the tip of the blade against his chest. Georges felt the skin stretch taut beneath the hard steel, then suddenly give way. He gasped in pain.

"How's that?" asked Manu, a sadistic leer on his face. "That okay?"

He drew the blade half an inch across Georges's chest, the skin parting like a zipper.

"You give me my money, or do I keep going?" Manu snarled.

"I told you...I...I can—"

Then there were two quick gunshots. Georges's heart leapt in terror, and he felt the blade move in his skin as Manu tensed.

But then Manu released the knife. He looked down at Georges in surprise, then fell across his lap and didn't move. Gravity slowly pulled the knife down, and the tip of the blade dug a small divot in his flesh as it fell free.

Georges looked up and saw John Crane standing outside the casement window.

Crane stepped through the window, his pistol aimed steadily at the closed door. He crossed the room quickly and grabbed Manu's knife with one hand.

"You all right?" he said as he sliced the cords holding Georges's right arm to the chair.

"I will be."

Crane handed him the knife and returned his attention to the door. Georges started cutting himself free. He heard shouting voices outside, someone banging on the door. Crane raised the pistol and fired three more shots through the top of the door. It was enough to dissuade whoever was out there.

Georges pushed Manu off himself. Manu's body fell to the floor, and he seemed to groan as air was forced from his lungs. Then Georges stood up and gasped in pain as circulation returned to his lower body. He wavered and fell against Crane. Crane put an arm around him to hold him up, and they retreated toward the window, Crane's gun still leveled at the door.

"I'm sorry," Georges said. "I'm sorry."

"You've got courage," said Crane. "I'll give you that." He turned and checked the window, then pushed Georges behind him. "Go. We've still got your sister to deal with."

CHAPTER 53

One of the things Crane had bought on his initial supply run when he arrived was a first aid kit. He got it from the trunk of the car and let Georges work on himself while Crane drove. Georges had taken a couple painkillers from the kit, and now he was applying a large patch bandage to the slash across his chest. He was a bloody mess but that couldn't be helped now.

Hopefully Georges had given him the right location this time. He assumed so. Georges's original plan had gone to hell. Crane figured he was smart enough to see it was time to let him handle the situation.

"What the hell were you thinking?" he finally said as the Yaoundé traffic started to clear, and he could pick up some speed.

"I thought if I told you the truth, you wouldn't let me do it."

Crane scoffed. "You think?"

"I couldn't send you up against that man again," said Georges, "I know what he's capable of."

Crane was quiet for a moment. "I'm a little bit insulted you didn't think I could handle him."

"That's not it!" Georges protested. "I just...this is my problem, not yours. I know I asked you for help, but I shouldn't have."

"Well, that's bullshit."

"All right, all right." Then Georges gasped as he wiped a disinfectant swab on his cut cheek. "I thought I could solve it without putting you in any more danger. I was wrong."

"You figured we've got two enemies now, so why not set them after each other instead of us. Let Einar and Yanis rip each other up."

"Something like that."

Crane shrugged. "It's not the worst idea you've had. But it leaves too much to chance. And it could have gotten you killed, and then how would you help your sister? You ready to let me run this thing now?"

"Yeah. Yeah. I get it."

"All right," said Crane. "I don't know what we're going into, but it's going to be rough. Can you handle the shotgun?"

The paved road gave way to packed red dirt surrounded by tall grass and Moabi trees. Georges remembered valleys like this from his childhood. His parents would take him and his sister out to the country and teach them about the native plants and wildlife. Their mother would collect leaves, seedpods, and feathers as they hiked through the forests. Then they would have a picnic lunch alongside some stream, and their mother would quiz them on what she'd found while their father bargained with the local farmers for produce to take home.

It had been a good life, but it was gone now. He was here for something very different this time.

Georges sat with the Mossberg shotgun in his lap. It was a compact, dangerous looking gun that wasn't like shotguns he'd seen before. There was no shoulder stock, just a short hand grip that ended in a rounded ball. Along with the short barrel, it looked like something that had been sawed down, but apparently it came that way. Crane had checked the tube magazine before he handed it over.

"You've got six shells," he'd said. "This is a twenty gauge gun. It's meant for home defense. And you're not an experienced shooter. So you're not going to have much effective range. Only shoot if somebody's right on you. If they're more than about a hundred feet out, you're better off making yourself hard to hit than standing there shooting at them."

Georges looked down at the gun again. Was he ready to kill someone with this thing? He knew he was capable of killing. He'd done it before. But that was self-defense. He'd killed to save Crane's life and his own. This felt different. They were deliberately going into danger. They would be actively going for Romy, and they would have to fight anyone who got in their way.

Romy. He'd been just as useless to her as he had to his mother. Yanis's goons hadn't viciously attacked her and left her bleeding in the street, but they'd maimed her just the same. Oh yes, he could point the shotgun at one of them and pull the trigger if he had to.

But maybe they would be lucky, he thought as he saw the van parked on the side of the road ahead. Maybe Persson had wiped out the Ibiza Boys, and Yanis had gunned Einar down with his dying breath.

"Here we go," Crane said quietly. He slowed the car and pulled off into the tall grass perhaps fifty yards behind the van. He cut the engine and checked the pistol one more time. As he opened the door, Georges heard distant gunshots, a burst from an automatic rifle, then three single answering shots.

No such luck. That meant Einar was still fighting, along with at least one of Yanis's men.

"Stick close to me," said Crane.

Georges nodded, then hurried after Crane, who had set off into the woods. They moved parallel to the road, but far enough back for the foliage to hide them. As they passed the van, Crane stopped suddenly, then veered toward it. The side door hung open and Georges saw blood on the dirt outside. Then he saw the body hanging out of the door, feet lying still on the ground as the blood pooled around them.

Crane checked the inside of the van, then turned the body over. Georges recognized him from the house. He'd been shot in the belly, not here but somewhere out there among the trees. Now that he was at the van, Georges could see the trail of blood and the marks of hands scratching in the dirt. He'd crawled back here but lacked the strength to climb into the van.

Crane left the body where it lay. He checked the van for keys, but they were gone. Whatever weapon the dead man had carried had been lost somewhere along the way. There was nothing for them here.

But that wasn't quite true, Georges realized suddenly. There was the body and the message it represented. This was where gunfighting brought you, a final crawl through muck and elephant grass while your life oozed away into the thirsty earth. The darkness close behind, overtaking you at the end until all light and life was gone.

Georges knew he could kill if circumstances forced him to. Could he die if he had to?

Crane tapped his shoulder with the back of his hand. "Hey. Let's go."

Georges nodded, and they set out at a steady trot, moving through the grass and rows of trees in the direction of the farmhouse.

Crane had memorized what little detail the online map and satellite view of this place had given him. He kept himself oriented to the house where he assumed Romy was being held but didn't go straight toward it. He led Georges in a ragged arc to approach the house from the side. If Einar was still alive against all of Kamkuma's men—and the sporadic gunshots said that he was—then he wasn't defending a position. He was mobile, striking where he could and moving on.

The shots were coming from different directions, and there was the occasional shout as someone tried to locate a friend. Einar had scattered them. They were crashing around the bush, probably frightened half to death, shooting at any movement. It made the orchard a very dangerous place. But on the other hand, Romy was probably unguarded. He suspected they'd find her tied up somewhere in the house, alone.

They crossed a drainage ditch bridged by a muddy plank and reached a clear area where the one-time farmer had parked his machinery. Crane saw an old sprayer, fresh bullet holes stitched across its rusting tank. There was a toolshed, metal door hanging off its hinges. There was a clutch of aging blue oil drums. And across a few more yards of packed dirt and gravel, there was the house. It was a small, single story building of cream-colored plank siding with a brown metal roof, a doorway at one end, and two square windows cut into the wall. He couldn't make out any movement inside.

He checked Georges one last time, then broke out of the cover of the elephant grass. They crossed quickly to the toolshed. He spotted more blood in the dirt outside the gaping door and stopped. He fell into a crouch against the sunbaked metal wall and saw the remains of a tripwire in the dirt. Einar had expected them to approach this way. He leaned around the corner and searched in the dark until he saw the muzzle of a shotgun positioned in the debris on the floor, aiming up at the door.

It had worked from the look of things. Someone had entered the shed and set it off. There was no body, and less blood than if it had hit its target dead on. But it had winged one of them at least and alerted Einar.

"Watch out for traps," he murmured to Georges.

"This whole place is a trap."

That was true enough, but what else could they do? The best strategy for survival now was to spend as little time in the killing zone as possible.

There was another burst of fire from somewhere and a voice called out, "Help me!" It was far away, in the opposite direction from the house. That was a positive sign. Crane peered around the corner of the shed and saw nothing.

"Come on," he said, then set off for the doorway.

Crane half expected to feel a bullet slam into him as he ran, but there was no shot. They reached the house, and Crane stopped short. Georges was breathing hard behind him. Crane studied the doorway, looking for another tripwire, but saw nothing.

Moment of truth.

Crane took a breath and led with his pistol as he stepped through the door.

He came into what had once been the kitchen. The room was lit only by shafts of sunlight from the windows. Dust danced in the light and the glare made it hard to make things out. There was a door to another room, probably the only other room given the size of the house. Crane saw tracks in the dust.

The floor creaked and groaned as he crossed the kitchen toward the other door. Water dripped from a hand pump onto a metal plate. Crane gestured to Georges to stay out of the line of sight of the doorway.

Then he leveled his pistol and swung around the door frame.

The small room had the other window he'd seen from outside. On the opposite wall was another window and the front door. There were a few sticks of furniture left behind.

"Go away!" shouted a terrified voice. "I swear I'll do it!"

In the gloom of the back corner, tied to a creaking wooden chair, was Romy. Crouched behind her, with a pistol to her head, was Yanis Kamkuma.

CHAPTER 54

Crane gripped his pistol in both hands and stepped forward into the room.

"Be very careful, Yanis. Your life's hanging by a thread."

Yanis thrust the muzzle of his gun against Romy's temple. "I'll kill her! I'll kill her right here!"

Romy was terrified, but she appeared unhurt. Einar had tied her firmly to the chair and covered her mouth with tape. Her nostrils flared as she breathed in fast and hard. Yanis was crouched behind her, his back pressed into the corner. Crane could see the drag marks in the dust where he'd pulled the chair from the middle of the room. He was out of his depth, panicked, just trying to survive. That made him more dangerous than he'd ever been before.

Georges slid around him into the room. "Romy! It's all right," he said. "It's okay. Everything's fine."

Everything was not fine.

"Cover the doors," Crane snapped at him. The shotgun was useless with Romy as Yanis's human shield. But someone might come through the front door at any moment.

"You've got nowhere to go," he said to Yanis. He was stalling, watching how Yanis moved, waiting for the moment when he had the best shot at taking him out without hitting the girl in front of him. "She's all you've got to bargain with, but if you kill her, then it's just you and the two of us. How do you think that ends for you?"

"You're not him," Yanis said. "There's two. Who are you?"

"The other one really tore you up, didn't he? How many of your boys are still standing?"

Crane moved a step to one side, and Yanis scrambled to keep Romy between them.

"None of them here to help you anyway," said Crane. "They've got their own trouble to deal with. You're on your own." As long as he kept Yanis off guard, kept changing up the threat and the situation, sooner or later, Yanis would make a mistake, and then Crane would put a bullet through his skull.

Suddenly Yanis moved the gun down from Romy's head and pressed it hard into the back of her right hand. Her fingers splayed out against the wooden arm of the chair.

"You want her back with that hand, you drop the gun!" he shouted.

Romy gasped behind the tape and looked at Crane in terror.

"I'll do it," said Yanis. "I'll take her apart, and you get her back in pieces. Like you said, man, I got nothing more to lose."

Then Georges was moving fast in the corner of Crane's eye.

"No!"

Georges dropped the shotgun and stepped into Crane's line of fire. He held his hands out to his sides.

"That's enough! No more shooting!"

"Georges, what do you think you're doing?" said Crane.

"Stay cool, John. Lower the gun."

"I'm not putting the gun down."

Crane moved, but Georges moved with him, blocking his aim at Yanis. Crane sighed.

"All right damn it, what's your plan then?"

"I remember the day all this started," Georges said. His eyes were locked on Yanis, but he seemed to be talking to all of them. "When my mother was still in the hospital, someone told me the way to help her wasn't to fight. That was your game, not mine. He told me if I wanted to help, do something smart. I've been trying to do that ever since, but I'm not very good at it. I'm not as smart as people think I am."

Georges stepped forward and gingerly reached out to touch his sister's cheek. Yanis tensed but did nothing. His attention was focused on Georges as much as Crane's and Romy's.

"But I know the smart thing to do now. Look at us! There's a man out there that wants us all dead. Bullets are flying. Your boys are shooting at each other because they're so scared they don't know which way's up. And we're stuck here pointing guns at each other. That's not smart, man. The smart thing is to get the hell out of here."

Crane slowly moved the gun lower and to the side but kept it ready to fire if Yanis did something he didn't like.

"You've had enough, haven't you?" Georges said. "I know I've had enough. This is no place for me. I don't think it's the place for you either. So let's get out. All of us. What do you say, Yanis?"

Yanis looked up at Georges, suspicion struggling against hope that there might actually be a way out of the situation he was in.

"What are you saying?" he said, so quietly Crane could barely hear him.

"We all put down our guns," said Georges. "And we get out of here. That simple. When we get to the cars, we take my sister, we all go our separate ways. And that's it. This...feud is over."

Crane noticed Yanis's gun had drifted from Romy. This would be his moment if Georges wasn't in the line of fire. But

Georges had taken charge of the situation, for better or worse. If this was how he wanted to play it, Crane would let him.

"What about her?" Yanis said. "You speaking for her?"

Georges carefully pulled the tape from Romy's mouth and threw it aside.

"He's got to pay!" Romy spat as soon as the tape was gone.

"He's paying!" said Georges. "He's paying. We're *all* paying. Look around yourself! Enough, Romy! You don't get your life back by throwing it away. Enough. It's over."

Romy said nothing. Outside, Crane heard a burst of fire, closer than previous ones.

"If we're going to do this, we better do it fast," he said.

"All right," said Yanis, "all right." He stood up and looked past Georges at Crane. "He drops his, I'll drop mine."

"Not how it works," said Crane. "The deal is, you drop yours, I don't shoot you with mine. We're not partners here. Take it or leave it."

Georges started to protest, but then realized he wasn't going to win that argument. "You can trust him," he said instead.

Yanis slowly put his gun on the floor.

As they were cutting Romy free, there was more gunfire, sustained this time. A handful of stray bullets slammed into the front of the house. They pierced the wall and the roof, and shafts of sunlight lanced through the dimly lit space. Whatever was happening out there was moving in their direction.

"Out the back," Crane snapped. "Past the shed and run for the treeline."

The approaching gunfire got them moving. Crane scooped up the shotgun as he passed and tossed it to Georges. Then they were out the back door, and the others were running for the trees as Crane brought up the rear to cover them. He scanned the clear area around the house, sweeping the ground with his pistol. Nothing moved. There were no gunshots. But Crane knew someone was nearby.

When they reached the trees, they moved in a tight group as Crane steered them back toward the car. Yanis had completely abandoned his aggressive role. He was acting like another victim in need of rescue. But Crane wasn't taking responsibility for him. He could come with them if he didn't cause any trouble. Having him there might prove helpful if they ran across one of his gang. But once they got back to the car, Yanis was on his own. Maybe he had the keys to the van his gang had arrived in, or maybe he didn't. That wasn't Crane's problem.

They crossed the drainage ditch they'd crossed on the way in. This time Crane turned them along it. He was more interested in finding the shortest route back to the car now. They'd gone about a hundred yards, past long rows of cocoa trees receding into the distance, when Crane spotted movement.

He turned and shouted, "Down!" as a figure emerged from behind a tree on the other side of the ditch. In an instant he took in the bloodstained canvas pants and dark shirt, the rifle, and the close-cropped blond hair of Einar Persson.

"Get down!" he shouted again, but none of the three he was escorting were trained to deal with combat situations. They froze or panicked as Crane spun and aimed his pistol. Einar's rifle cracked as he ran toward them. Another shot. Crane heard Romy scream, and saw the rifle's muzzle pointed at him and the focused rage on Einar's face.

Then Yanis whirled and ran. He passed in front of Crane, blocking his shot. The rifle cracked two more times. Yanis jerked as the first round hit him. The second took him in the throat, and blood sprayed a fan of red mist into the air. Yanis spun and fell to the ground.

On the far side of the ditch, Einar tried to fire again, but he was empty. He dropped the rifle and went for a pistol in his belt.

But he was out of time. Crane steadied his aim and shot him in the chest. Einar's momentum carried him forward, and as Crane fired again, Einar stumbled and fell into the ditch.

Georges had pulled his sister to the ground and now crouched over her, guarding her with the shotgun. Five feet from her, Yanis lay on the ground, his eyes staring blankly at her.

"Is he dead?" she asked Crane.

There was no question about that.

"Yeah, he's dead."

"Good."

Georges was trembling from a huge dump of adrenaline. Crane was glad to see he had his finger alongside the trigger instead of on it. Crane reached down to help Romy up.

"I'm done here," she said. "Let's go home."

Georges put an arm around her. "Yeah," he said, his voice quavering. "Let's go home."

"Car's that way," said Crane as he pointed. "Let's go before we run into someone else."

Crane scanned their perimeter one more time. Nothing was moving. There was no sound from the bottom of the ditch. They turned and ran for the car.

CHAPTER 55

High above the Atlantic in a chartered jet, the world looked very different.

Crane sat in the back nursing a whiskey sour. The pilots had managed to hook up a satellite phone link, so Georges and Romy were up front talking to their parents. There had been a great deal of crying, and Georges stood with his arm around Romy as she held the handset.

The change in Romy was remarkable. She had stepped out of her old life to become a violent executioner driven by vengeance. Then, once that vengeance was complete, it was as if she'd simply stepped back across the line. She'd put down Romy the killer like a tool she was finished with, and now she was the old Romy once more. She told her parents how she missed them and how sorry she was to have made them worry. She was enthusing over all the things they would do to make up for lost time.

But Crane knew the ruthless avenger was still in there, even if Romy had concealed it behind a happy exterior. He'd seen what she was capable of, and how far she would go.

That one would bear watching.

Georges detached himself from his sister's embrace and left her with the phone. He came back and sat beside Crane.

"I think she's going to be all right," he said.

Crane nodded. She was headed back to a more comfortable life now. He hoped it was enough to protect her from the kind of trauma that had set her on her violent path. Time would tell.

"Your parents must be happy," Crane said at last.

"Over the moon." Georges smiled. "I haven't heard my mother sound that happy since…before."

"That's good," said Crane. "Your mother's going to be okay. Romy's coming home. You did it, Georges. Your family was smashed to pieces, but you found a way to save them."

"I'm sorry about before. I ask so much of you, and then I keep getting in your way. I'm sorry I ditched you. I told myself I should have trusted you, but then I did it again. I'm sorry I stepped in front of you. Yanis had a gun. He could have done anything."

Crane put his glass down on the tray beside his seat. He laughed. "You finally did something smart," he said. "Not turning Yanis and Einar against each other. That was clever. Not quite the same thing. And it didn't really work that well. Your parents will freak when they see your face."

Georges laughed as well. "Maybe we'll stay in New York a few days until the bruises fade."

"But I mean when you spared Yanis. You must have hated him as much as your sister did."

Georges looked away, at the screen that showed the icon of their plane over a satellite view of the sea.

"Yes," he murmured. "Oh, yes."

"But you gave up what you wanted to get what you really needed," Crane continued. "That was smart. I would have killed him right there before I trusted him to put his gun down. What you did was better. You wanted revenge, but what you *needed* was to save your sister. That choice restored your family in a way killing Yanis wouldn't have."

"Yeah," Georges said. "I guess it did."

Georges had healed himself as well, Crane realized. The pain and guilt that began when Yanis's gang had destroyed his old life had finally lifted.

"Some advice?" Crane said.

Georges turned to look at him.

"Stay the hell out of the field," Crane said with a grin. "It's not your natural habitat."

Georges laughed. "No, it isn't, is it? You know the first time I ever saw you? It was when Josh showed me the tape of you in Oakland. You saved that man in the shipping container. I needed a hero, and there you were. I was going to arm you with the best equipment I could make and send you out to fight the things I couldn't. That was going to be my smart thing."

"That was smart."

Georges laughed. "Except I keep screwing it up! Whenever something goes wrong, I think I'm to blame and I charge in and make it worse."

"You didn't do so bad. But we do better with you back at Myria. We make a hell of a team that way, Georges."

Georges looked at him and Crane could see he was touched. "Thank you," he said softly.

"Georges! Georges!" Up front, Romy was beckoning him back to the phone.

"You better go," said Crane.

Georges got up from the seat and headed forward. Crane watched him go, then turned and looked out the window as the sun-drenched clouds slid past.

Georges and his family would be all right. But there were still loose ends for him to worry about. He didn't believe Einar Persson had been acting alone. Going to Cameroon had been a spur of the moment decision. Einar couldn't have known beforehand. But he'd followed them there, and within a day he'd been able to locate them as well as setting himself up with weapons and even a safely isolated place to take Romy for his ambush.

There was no way he could have done that on his own. Certainly not as quickly as he had. Someone was helping him. Most likely, someone who was after him and found Einar a useful weapon to attack him with.

He had an enemy out there somewhere. One with widespread resources and excellent intelligence. Crane needed to find out who they were and deal with them before they tried again.

The plane flew on, chasing the sun west toward home. For now, Crane could afford to rest and restore his energy. In a few days, he would take his suspicions to Josh and they would get to work once more.

The police had gone over the orchard, but they weren't trained for this. They'd carted off the bodies, collected the scattered weapons. By twilight, they were gone.

When he'd heard no human sounds for half an hour, Einar rose from the muck, slowly, painfully. He'd been hit twice. One had gone through, puncturing a lung. He was pretty sure the second was still in his shoulder.

He needed medical attention, but he would survive. He would make it out of here. He had unfinished business.

Einar heard the sounds of insects in the gathering darkness. Above him, a root stuck out of the side of the ditch. He grabbed it and pulled. He groaned at the agony in his wounded shoulder, but he made it upright, leaning against the packed dirt. His breathing was shallow, and he could feel the blood bubbling in his chest. He paused until the pain faded enough for his vision to clear. Then he pushed with his legs and grabbed at the dirt at the top of the ditch. Slowly, painfully, he hauled himself up over the lip and fell flat on the ground beside the ditch.

He was visible here. If the police had left anyone to watch the scene, he would be easily spotted. He crawled into the tall grass and collapsed, breathing fast and shallow. He tried to place himself on his mental map of the orchard. His car was hidden in the trees, well off the approach road. He looked around until he was sure of the direction. That way. About a thousand yards through the grass and rows of cocoa trees. There was a first aid kit in the trunk. That would keep him going until he could find a doctor who wouldn't report gunshot wounds to the police.

Einar knew he would make it. He was tough, resilient, a survivor. This wasn't going to kill him. He would make it out. He would recover. He would rebuild his strength and make careful plans.

He would find John Crane and watch him die screaming. That was the purpose that would get him through the agony of the next few hours.

Einar fixed John Crane's face in his mind, gritted his teeth, and began to crawl.

THE END

John Crane will return in

The Vengeful

Coming Soon...

Contact Mark Parragh

Mark Parragh's web site is at markparragh.com. There you can find a complete list of his books and much more. You can also find him on Facebook at facebook.com/MarkParragh, or email him at inbox@markparragh.com.

———

If you enjoyed this book…

…please help someone else enjoy it too. Reviews are hugely important in helping readers find the books they love. Reviews help me keep writing and they make sure the books you enjoy keep coming. Just a few moments to leave a review of this book pays off in so many ways. I'd really appreciate your help.

Thank you!
— Mark Parragh

Made in the USA
Coppell, TX
23 September 2021

62844684R00178